GW01186271

NETWORK APPRENTICE

BEHIND THE SCENES IN TALK TELEVISION

TITLES AND AUTHOR PSEUDONYMS
OF OTHER BOOKS BY GRAYDON "DEE" HUBBARD

Slim to None: A Journey through the Wasteland of Anorexia Treatment
by Gordon Hendricks

Charlie's Pride: A Novel
by Dee Hubbard

At the Altars of Money: A Novel

NETWORK APPRENTICE

BEHIND THE SCENES IN TALK TELEVISION

A NOVEL BY

GRAYDON "DEE" HUBBARD

atmosphere press

© 2024 Graydon "Dee" Hubbard

Published by Atmosphere Press

Cover design by Kevin Stone

No part of this book may be reproduced without permission from the author except in brief quotations and in reviews.

Atmospherepress.com

In loving memory of my daughter Jennie.
Who might've become a Julie.

And for my daughters Laurie and Jill, who are
Julies in their professional careers.

PRINCIPAL PLAYERS

IN ORDER OF APPEARANCE

LOP EAR

A disfigured Grizzly Bear who roams wild and free back of beyond in Yellowstone Park.

THE APPRENTICE

After waiting tables in Boulder, Colorado, to fund her Master's Degree in Broadcast Journalism, Julie Anders vows to maintain independence in thought, words, and actions as she navigates the politicized and male-dominated world of talk television.

THE SCIENTIST

Julie's father and the son of an immigrant steel-worker, Jules Anders, is a career climatologist with NOAA, a genuine expert source for her study of Global Warming and her rock of support in troubled times.

THE NATURALIST

Jason-Jerrold Jennings meets Julie in Yellowstone. Their romance blossoms during a holiday weekend on a historic cattle ranch straddling the upper Colorado River. His career in conservation ends tragically on a trip with Julie to Zion National Park.

THE SCHOLAR

First woman of color to receive a PhD in Political Science from the University of Colorado, Professor Angel Bright is often referred to as Madam Outrageous. Her PolySciFi class grounds Julie in challenging contemporary issues and provides continuing inspiration for her career in a complex profession.

THE PROFESSORS

A triage of faculty members comprising the committee reviewing Julie's thesis for her Master's Degree. "Facultards" their candidates call them.

COLORADO'S LAST REAL COWBOY

Named after John Wesley Powell, JW makes a brief but colorful appearance to immerse Julie in cattle-ranching legacies.

THE SHOWMAN

Mercurial host of the Dan Panders' Show on MRABC and Julie's first boss, Danny is a tormented soul whose vision for his show constantly conflicts with his ratings-driven and rabidly-biased Network Brass.

THE STATION MANAGER

Alan Knight launches Julie's career move to Rocky Mountain PBS, where she becomes a key player nationally in Judy Woodruff's 6:00 PBS News Hour, focusing on numbers-based diagnostics of COVID in its first-year impact.

CONTENTS

PART SIX - FRESH BEGINNINGS?

PART SEVEN - REPORTING THE VIRUS

FOREWORD

That old sorcerer has vanished
And for once has gone away!
Spirits called by him, now banished,
My commands shall soon obey.
Every step and saying
That he used, I know
And with sprites obeying
My arts I will show.

from *The Sorcerer's Apprentice*
a poem by Johann Goethe
1797

PART ONE

BACK OF BEYOND

SEP 2011

CHAPTER 1
LOP EAR'S FEAST

LIKE AN AGING SATYR who indulged too much the night before, he naps all morning sprawled spread-eagle, tongue lolling, drool pooling, flies circling, guts rumbling. Continuous snores and occasional belches spew from his open mouth. Gluttonous dreams dance in his head.

SHARING DRIVING SHIFTS, Jules Anders and his daughter Julie have driven all night from Boulder, Colorado to meet their morning boat charter at Bridge Bay Marina in Yellowstone Park.

"Don't take people up there very often, particularly this time of year," is the skipper's laconic greeting. "Now I'm booked for two lake trips into Yellowstone's wilderness area, and you'll have tent neighbors for your last night there. Another father...with his son. That's as crowded as Beaverdam Creek campground is gonna be this week." Denying wisdom to late-season transport missions, he shakes his head as he eyes his passengers. "Most tourists don't realize how cold it gets here at the end of summer. At least you're dressed for it. You two know how remote your destination is?"

"Remote is why we're going," 17-year-old Julie responds. "Isn't it Dad?" She nudges her father.

Stifling a yawn with a hand, he says, "For sure, Julie. And skip, we've done our homework. This is a father and daughter thing. A trip into Yellowstone's back of beyond is our dream of having a genuine wilderness experience together. Doing it by boat is actually our second choice. We first considered a guided horseback trip into Yellowstone's Thorofare region from the other side."

"Wow," the skipper responds. "So you know about Two Ocean Plateau?"

"Yep, we know it straddles the continental divide and is the only high mountain meadow in America that spawns two major rivers, one flowing west, the other flowing east. We also know it's the most remote region in America's lower 48. But the horseback trip was too expensive. We couldn't afford it. So we downsized...and here we are."

Julie adds, "Hey Dad, remember we want to catch some wild native trout too. Not just do the remote thing and hang out away from the madness of crowds."

"You'll also need to watch out for bears," the skipper mutters. "Lots of them where you're going."

"Yep...for sure we will," is Jules' response.

Julie merely rolls her eyes. *Everyone knows about Yellowstone bears. The ones you see are basically tame*. When you're young, you're cloaked with invincibility and don't take bear cautions too seriously.

Still blurry-eyed and fuzzy-tongued, Jules and his daughter seek cockpit cushions and doze during their long trip across Yellowstone Lake and into its headwaters. They wake up when the skipper cuts the engine and his boat glides into the lake's primitive southeast east arm, a waterfowl preserve where Park regulations prohibit motorized boat travel.

Oaring for the last mile to the lake's Beaverdam Creek inlet improves blood circulation for the oarsman. For his passengers, excitement rises at finding a secluded sanctuary away from hordes of Bermuda-shorted tourists. Julie does a vision 360 spin. Nothing there but water, waterfowl, hints of islands, and empty shores with forests behind. And above? Nothing but open space. No sounds either, other than a rhythmic whooshing of the skipper's oars. *Hooray for remote.*

From the beached boat bow, father and daughter, together with the skipper, manage the step to shore fully loaded with food cartons plus camping, cooking, and fishing gear. After his second load-haul to shore, the skipper confirms pickup arrangements. "Okay, I'll be back for you in four days. That's Wednesday. Same time, same place...and don't be late. I don't wait. However, I will help you take down your camp. And, oh, almost forgot. I should remind you. If you don't have a sat phone, you can't contact me or anyone else unless you walk out. Cell phones and iPhones don't work here, and it's 21 miles around the lake back to civilization."

"We're okay with that," Jules frowns and grumbles. "We both need time off away from excesses of the electronic age... and its over-connectivity. Right, Julie?"

She grimaces and manages a, "Sure, I guess."

A broad grin replaces his frown and spreads across his face as he embraces her in a father/daughter hug. Then they each free an arm and wave a smiling goodbye, as their only connection to civilization oars away from the beach.

WAKENED BY TWO MAGPIES SCREECHING, he scowls at the noisy intrusion and grunts his displeasure. Feeling stiff, he stretches each limb. Then he shakes. Starting with his massive neck, twin tremors ripple along each side of his powerful body and exit his stubby tail. He's thirsty, and his back itches in places he can't reach. Nearest water is a mile away, just a pleasant afternoon amble. Plenty of time to find a good scratching tree along the way.

Although he rises ponderously, his great bulk moves gracefully through a forest of enigmatic lodge-pole pines. The trees stand ageless, characterless, ramrod straight, motionless, and silent...like file after file of olive-drab soldiers at attention, each indistinguishable from the other. Inside the pine forest, a solitary grove of old aspen trees beckons, each tree a distinctive, time-honored patriarch defying mortality. Pummeled and twisted by a hundred years of wind and drifting snow, most are misshapen, as if arthritic. They offer seasonal scratching service to any creature. From lower trunks, winter-blackened as if scorched by fire, scarred and scaly elliptical remains of lost branches peer into the surrounding forest...like unsleeping, searching eyes. Long strands of animal hair trail from the eyes...like lashes. From surviving higher branches, leaves of gold announce the end of summer and chatter into an afternoon breeze...like old men arguing, all talking at the same time, not listening to each other.

His itch satisfied by a favorite aspen, he leaves the forest and enters a small, shrub-choked glen carved into multiple gullies by spring freshets, dry now and waterless for 30 moons. He avoids twisting, towering deadfalls savaged into boulder-like formations by surging snow avalanches. He pushes aside smaller brush piles that block his passage. Because no living thing challenges his supremacy, silence and stealth are foreign to him. They're unnecessary traits he's never learned, despite his naturally cautious nature. Caution, that primitive instinct common to all wild creatures regardless of their ferocity, moderates but rarely guides him.

In a few weeks he'll move the other way...up the glen to timberline. Heavy snow spattering against his muzzle and coating his sleek silver-tipped pelt will activate his need to seek sanctuary interred in the high country. A last burst of energy will temporarily overcome his lethargy and fuel his efforts to grub out a cave-like winter den.

But now, in late summer, he likes to travel down the glen and drink each day where Beaverdam Creek meanders through a wide flood plain and surges into Yellowstone Lake. He can sit in the creek shallows, guzzle until his gullet sloshes and remember spring, just a few months and two hundred pounds ago, when schools of scarlet-throated trout migrated up the creek to spawn. Their backs rose above the surface, so thick in the riffles that they formed living bridges across the creek. He feasted well then, using his giant paws and long, razor sharp claws to slap a dozen fish onto shore. Helpless there, they tried without success to make tails and pectoral fins do what evolution denied them: travel on land and return safely to their watery home.

Closing in on his destination, he rises to his hind legs and sniffs. He strains to decipher everything his uncanny sense of smell can tell him about what lies ahead. There it is again. He first noticed it when he began his descent. Man smell. Only mildly unpleasant. Not threatening. Not even unusual. Just there. It angers him, but he can't reason why. Even when food smells intervene, which is almost always the case, man smell still irritates him, his instinctive reaction to something that doesn't belong. Driven a few years before from closed garbage dumps, he now roams Yellowstone's wild places, where he forages as his mother taught him. A territorial dispute with an older rival has disfigured him and left him with slashing parallel scars traveling from his right eye up to his temple. There they circle his right ear, which lies shriveled and useless against his neck. Then they finally disappear into a thick curl of hunchback fur and muscle. Lop Ear, the rangers call him.

From his scavenging days, Lop Ear knows about two-legged creatures, knows they're all puny and helpless, noisy and stupid, ugly and hairless. They occasionally appear in this corner of his feeding province in summer, but never in spring and seldom after elk begin their autumn bugle. It's by preference, not fear, that he avoids humans and places where they gather. Occasionally, as now, curiosity coaxes him into closer proximity where he might find that a careless camper has left food unprotected against an opportunistic bear.

Continuing down the widest gully, Lop Ear stops before it exits into Beaverdam Creek valley. Flocks of migrating Canada geese rest in the lake just beyond the stream's estuary. Like surfers waiting for a wave, the geese bob, rise, and fall with long sweeping swells, which undulate like wakes from a boat. He can't see the geese, but he can hear their petty bickering as they maneuver for position.

Tuning out the squabbling geese, Lop Ear listens to plaintive sounds of bugling bull elk drifting across the water from breeding grounds pinched between Yellowstone's two south arms. *I'm here, ready, waiting,* they plead, broadcasting their maleness and their availability, competing openly for female favor. Any female. If he knew how, Lop Ear would smile at the pleasant recollections triggered by the familiar sounds of rut.

Man smell is stronger now. Familiar and unnatural food smells attract him. But he lingers. He's still outside the range where his vision, diminished by fighting wounds, can identify the extent of human intrusion ahead of him. With his instinctive curiosity and caution in conflict, his seasonal hunger prevails, and he begins a long arcing detour that will keep him in timber and bring him to the creek just upstream from human presence.

"WHAT'S THAT?" Jules puts words to the startled reactions of both father and daughter. Lunch behind them, they suspend rigging fly rods and listen to thrashing noises emanating from a copse up the creek valley from their campsite.

"An elk, maybe?" she asks.

"Could be. They're in rut, and we've heard them bugle all afternoon...but not from that direction. I'll have a look." He burrows into the bulging center compartment of a full backpack, retrieves a set of field-glasses, adjusts them, and studies the sound source.

"Could be a female answering the bugles?" she persists.

"Not likely, elk move carefully."

"Even when they're horny?"

"Hey, watch your teenage language. Yep, particularly then."

"Okay. Can I have the binocs for a look? I've seen tame Colorado elk in Estes Park, but never an elk truly in the wild."

"Sure, hon. Here. I'm near-sighted, and you may need to adjust them."

She adjusts the binoculars and focuses on the noisy copse. "Can't see anything except bushes."

"Watch for moving bushes."

"Can't see any movement. Sounds are too far back, in too much of a thicket, but I think they're moving toward us. Whoa...sounds have stopped now."

"The source has probably moved into a meadow, and it might be a moose," he says. "They're in rut now too. Meadows and sloughs provide most of their food, and they're not cautious. Don't have to be. They don't care who hears them. But..." he frowns, "I thought I heard something moving about twenty minutes ago and a lot higher up. Moose won't travel that high if they don't have to, and there's plenty of feed in the creek meadows for them. So...any more guesses? Try the obvious."

"Bear!" she growls, feigning fear. "Grizzly?"

"Hope not. Most grizzlies are well into the back country."

"Where do you think we are, Dad? It's 21 miles by trail to the nearest road."

"Good point. Whatever it is, its sounds are gone now."

"Should we move our camp?

"Where to? If it's a Grizzly Bear and he wants to check us out, he'll find us wherever we go. He can smell us miles away. I don't like the situation, Julie. We're in a back-country campground. Rarely used, but still a logical meal-site for a bear about to go into hibernation. So-o-o, with our first wilderness meal behind us, we need to tree our food now. That bear's uncanny sense of smell will eventually lead him here."

Father and daughter have chosen their campsite well, pitching a roomy sidewall tent on a grassy knoll creek-side and overlooking its last gravelly and shallow run into Yellowstone Lake. A solitary pine provides a nearby safe-haven for sequestering food. While Julie removes sleeping bags from an old Army duffel, unrolls them inside the tent, and then repacks the duffel with groceries, her father takes a 40 foot section of climbing rope from his pack, coils it, and heaves it skyward in random attempts to capture a tree branch. Third toss succeeds. Both father and daughter clap approval.

"How high?" Julie asks.

"Ten feet," he answers.

"Why not snug it up all the way to the limb?"

"Makes it too accessible from the tree."

"I didn't think big bears could climb."

"That's a popular fallacy. Even an adult Grizzly can climb, just not as well as a Black Bear."

After knotting the food bag with the rope and giving it three lusty pulls, Jules achieves the desired height, about half way from ground to tree limb. He stands on his toes under the bag and reaches up. His fingertips are still two feet short. "That should do it," he says. Then he ties off the rope on a lower limb and stands back to admire his handiwork. "Two double bowline ties. No bear will figure out how to untie those."

"Won't have to, Dad. He'll just climb the trunk, scramble out the limb, chew through the bag tie, and let our food-bag fall to the ground. Better yet, he'll chew through the rope above your tree-tie, and voila, this time the bag falls into his outstretched arms."

"H-m-m-m. Hadn't thought about that. Just hope bears aren't as smart as you."

Food security complete...maybe, father and daughter stand and search Beaverdam Creek for signs of rising trout. They see none. "Wrong time of day for fishing," Jules says, rationalizing his lethargy-induced reluctance. "We'll go out later. At dusk. Catch our supper then. Okay?"

"Sure," she says. "And I'm really drowsy right now. We're

both suffering from lack of sleep, and our campsite's fully rigged. We've wolfed down a late lunch and protected our food. So what about an afternoon nap for both of us?"

"Yeah...," He yawns, "let's."

They retreat to their tent. Their immediate world; uncrowded, tranquil, and unhurried, is at peace.

THEIR SUNSET DINNER featuring grilled trout is complete. As is the cleanup. Seated on folding camp chairs, father and daughter linger at a campfire whose ebbing flames jab and parry like combatants. With a smoldering stick, Jules stirs the fire into renewed vigor as their conversation drifts to Julie's plans for college just a year away.

"So, kid, is going to the University of Colorado still okay with you?"

"Sure is. I'm a hometown girl...never considered going anywhere else."

"You know I have a good position at NOAA. But...even though my specialization is needed and much in demand, climate scientists working for the Government aren't paid that well. I've enough savings to get you through an undergraduate program at CU. But it's not enough for post-graduate work. And...we're not going to borrow money for education. You'll have to work too if you want to pursue an advanced degree."

"Whoa. One degree at a time. And yes, CU is perfect."

"You sure? Your high school grades are pushing valedictorian. Definitely high enough to attract enrollment offers from more prestigious institutions. Maybe even with a scholarship attached."

"I'm sure. I'm not looking for prestige college credentials."

"And on a related subject. You want to bunk and dine at home or stay in a college dorm, meet others, make new friends, maybe even have a high-rise room overlooking the Flatirons? Then, come to our no-rise home for an occasional Saturday night dinner and overnight with me. I'll do meals. Breakfast is whenever you get up."

She nods her head. "I'd like to do the college dorm thing. Maybe even attract a boyfriend. Enough in the college fund?"

"Should be. Have you thought about participating in the sorority rush week?"

"Yep, I have, and..." she shakes her head..."I don't fit that profile."

"A final subject then. Curriculum. I'm probably old-fashioned, but I'm okay with your just getting a good education. Study whatever your curious mind takes you into. Don't think you have to prepare for a career at the undergraduate level. Learning is a great goal in itself. In today's academic world, maybe there's too much emphasis on preparing for a work life."

"Good advice." She frowns and shakes her head again. "But I haven't thought much about undergraduate classes. Plenty of time left for that. I know I'd like to study some English Literature, take a Shakespeare class, read some of the best plays ever written. Maybe take a class in statistics. I dig numbers. And I've also thought about going for a Master's Degree to prepare for a career in broadcast journalism. Maybe I could make a difference. It's a profession attracting more and more women with amazing talents in analyzing events of the day and expressing themselves."

He chuckles. "Yep...you do indeed have those talents, as did your mom." Then he stands and separates the few fire remnants into glowing embers. "Okay, this evening we've answered some of our questions and solved none of America's escalating and already mountainous problems." Nodding his head up and down, he continues. "But, maybe you should try. Right now it's mind shutdown time, and," he gestures to the open tent flap, "let's get some sleep. It's been a long day. Our afternoon nap was terrific, just not long enough." Then he looks up and around, opens his arms, and extends his hands, palms up as if embracing the starlit sky. "Look at it, Julie. And try to listen to it. You won't hear anything. We're surrounded by wilderness, the heavens above...and silence. How rare is that! We'll go explore the wilderness tomorrow and let our hearing enjoy sounds only of nature waking up and enjoying the day."

Arm and arm, they enter the tent, where Julie pauses to place a hand on her father's shoulder, gaze into his eyes, and say softly, "I really appreciate our conversation this evening and also our opportunity to spend a bunch of quality days together. Just the two of us...far, far away from the Madding Crowd."

"Me too, darlin'." He bends down slightly to kiss her forehead. "Seems like we seldom have the time...or take the time...to talk enough at home, and I pledge we'll have more father/daughter time in the future. I'll also cherish our next few days together. I'm happy for that, but I'm also sad that the mother you never knew can't be here to..." he sniffles and swipes at tears forming in his eyes, "to be part of these precious moments."

AS LOP EAR MOVES DOWN THE CREEK, light from a three-quarter moon replicates life in an elongated, hunchbacked shadow that stalks its creator. Lop Ear is unaware of the darker, larger, more menacing twin image following in his footsteps.

He can see a tent silhouetted against a clear sky just ahead, and sounds of human voices now join with human smell to renew his irritation. It's a natural instinct. He stops beside a pool where he sometimes shares fishing rights with a family of river otters. Man smells and acrid odors of stale wild-animal urine are strong here. He paws the ground for a moment, urinates to mark his territory, sidesteps, and then sits down, paws folded in his lap. His shadow-twin sits dutifully beside him. He waits patiently, like a giant boxer, calm and stoic in his corner of the ring.

For an hour he remains motionless. Only an occasional flaring of his nostrils distinguishes him from some kind of night statue...one with a carbon copy. When tent sounds stop, he pauses for a few minutes, then rises and, with his rolling gate, gambols up the knoll to the campsite, where he sniffs around the tent. He detects no food smells from his usual snack sources...a food container either inside an empty tent or just outside an occupied tent. Grunting with disappointment, he moves along the tent's sidewall.

GROGGY BUT NOT YET ASLEEP and still in sensory overload from so much new experience, Julie is first to hear their night visitor and pokes her father in the side. "Dad, wake up," she whispers. No response. Then she shakes him and repeats a louder, "Wake up, Dad."

She finally gets a groggy response. "Julie? What's wrong?"

"I think there's a bear in camp. I just heard him grunting. Whatta we do?"

Jules rises from his sleeping bag to a sitting position. "Noise scares them...so we keep talking. Do we have anything metal to bang on?"

"The lantern maybe. All our cooking gear is outside."

"I'll bang on the lantern. Use my boot."

RUSTLING NOISES INSIDE THE TENT, followed by human voices and a noisy banging on metal arouse his curiosity. Raising a massive forepaw, Lop Ear swipes at the offending sounds, catches his claws in canvas and slashes sideways, opening a three-foot rent along the side of the tent.

JULES FLINCHES at the sound of ripping canvas. "Whew. His claws just missed me."

Still thinking clearly, he instructs his daughter. "Julie,

quickly now, out of your sleeping bag. We'll both go to the center of the tent, and you move our sleeping bags between us and the tent walls. I'll keep banging."

SHIFTING HIS POSITION, Lop Ear's left hind-foot tangles in a tent rope. Mildly irritated, he grunts and swipes at the rope, shredding it and pulling its stake from the ground in the same motion. Moving slowly around the tent, he methodically repeats his grunting, de-staking maneuver on each supporting rope until the tent collapses inward. He stops for a moment, cocks his head to one side and watches with curiosity as the canvas rolls and squeals like bear cubs wrestling in long grass. He waits for instinct to take control of his actions.

JULES DROPS THE LANTERN and gropes for the collapsed center-pole.

"Dad," Julie hisses, "you said make noise to scare him off. All we've done is piss him off."

"He's angered by tripping on the tent ropes. Noise should work. At least on a Black Bear. As long as there's no food in here."

"So it's a Grizzly?" she shudders. "So we should whisper?

"Probably, and yes," he whispers. "Did you bring that chocolate power bar in here last night?"

"Well, yeah."

"Goddamit. Get rid of it."

"I already did. I ate it." She forces a chuckle.

"That's not funny, Julie."

"Sor-r-y. So, what do we do now? Invite him in for a bedtime story."

"That's not funny either."

"We could go outside, dance with him...by the light of the moon."

"Julie, you're delirious. This is a bad situation. I can't believe my own daughter is trying to be funny."

"You said keep talking, er whispering."

"Not now. We should DO something."

"DAD, he's in control. There's nothing we can do."

"You're right. I'll get us some breathing room. Then, if we remain quiet, and the bear realizes we have no food in here, he'll probably wander off." Jules grasps the center-pole and raises it, lifting the center of the tent a few feet and creating enough space for them to huddle together, trying to prevent body contact with sagging tent walls.

PREPARING THE TENT for further inspection, Lop Ear picks his spot next to its weaving apex, rises on his hind-legs, and swipes again at the canvas in front of him. Turning his claws, he opens a large v-shaped rent. He squats, and with teeth bared, nostrils flared and breathing heavily, he thrusts his head and neck into the gaping hole. His hump catches on the sheared canvas lip.

"He's coming in here with us," Julie whispers.

Jules struggles to maintain the center-pole in a fixed position, his head and right hand inches from the bear's fangs.

"Wh-h-honk," the bear snorts.

Jules flinches.

"Outta here, bear," Julie whispers with forced bravado.

"Wh-h-honk," the bear snorts again and shakes his head.

Jules flinches again but maintains his resolve to hold up the tent.

"So, what now, Dad?"

"Pray he's only sniffing for food."

"We are food."

"Well then, pray he's not that hungry."

SATISFIED THE TENT IS FOODLESS and sickened by its concentrated human smell, Lop Ear shakes his head again as if to clear it of human contamination, removes himself from the rent, backs away on all fours, and then rises again, turns and sniffs a light breeze from the opposite direction. He trots over to the security tree, where food smell is unmistakable and looks up at the duffel bag above his head.

Julie nudges her father and whispers, "I think he's gone."

"Not all gone. I can still hear him grunting. I think he's going for our food bag."

Jules cautiously widens the torn tent-opening just exited by the bear, and both look out.

Eyeing the intervening space up to the duffel bag, Lop Ear rises on his hind legs and pirouettes on his toes, not quite like a ballet dancer. Then he stretches both paws upward to maximum extension, grabs the duffel bag a few inches up from the bottom, pierces the canvas with his claws, and lets his weight sag back down. With a sickening, rending sound, the bag's bottom separates. Food and bear spill to the ground in one thrashing heap. "U-m-fff," he grunts in anticipatory delight.

"Dad," she scolds. "Why didn't you hoist the bag higher?"

"Didn't know there were 10-foot bears."

"So...say goodbye to our food."

"Better than saying goodbye to us," he says as he burrows back into what's left of the tent. "I'll get the sleeping bags. And now, let's you and I say goodbye to here."

"Sure, but where do we go?"

"To the beach. There's plenty of driftwood. We'll build a fire wall between us and the bear and then sleep next to the lake. I'll do the first fire watch."

Still shivering, the two grab their boots, a handful of clothes and jackets, matches, and sleeping bags, then crawl around the side of the collapsed tent away from the bear.

"Why are we crawling?" she whispers.

"Seems the safest thing to do."

"Couldn't we get away faster by running?"

"Okay, let's."

Father and daughter are a blur of Patagonia underwear in motion as they sprint a flanking maneuver around their campsite toward Yellowstone Lake, glimmering peacefully in the moonlight.

Conscious of motion outside his field of vision, Lop Ear is too preoccupied to investigate. He's already licked the insides from a dozen eggs, and his yellow-stained muzzle searches next for the source of a tantalizing meaty smell. His incisors easily peel the side from a six-pound canned ham.

In a few minutes, father and daughter have a massive semi-circular bonfire raging. Inside the half ring and savoring the heat, they lie in their sleeping bags on their stomachs, propped on elbows and listening to gentle waves lap behind them. Through jumping flames, they watch a fat, well-fed bear get fatter as he and his shadowy mimic dine happily on a four-day supply of people food. They watch...and digest reality. Sleep is impossible.

Julie finally breaks the silence. "Did you see his eyes?"

"Well, you're supposed to avoid eye contact, and I was trying not to look at him. But that was impossible. We were literally nose-to-nose?"

"Couldn't you close your eyes?"

"I just couldn't, Julie. He has this scarred, disfigured face and hypnotic, red eyes. He kept staring at me, accusing me, like a living wall mount. I couldn't look away. I felt like I looked straight into his soul and saw some kind of awful pain." He shakes his head to dispel the image. "And his breath! Whew!"

"You smelled his breath!"

"Couldn't avoid that either. He actually breath-gassed me. Like the worst garbage I've ever smelled. No, more like death breath. Didn't you smell it too?"

"You know I have a poor sense of smell. Do you think we're safe now?"

He frowns as he ponders her question and their position, then shakes his head in realization and responds with a rueful,

"Only if we can swim."

"Swim?"

"Yep, if he comes back for us."

"He'd come through the fire?"

"He might come around it."

"So maybe we shouldn't have backed ourselves up to the lake?"

"We didn't have a lot of options, Julie, unless you wanted to wade the creek in your underwear at 30 degrees."

Litter from Lop Ear's feast now spreads over most of the campsite. Satisfied everything edible has been consumed, he waddles a few steps toward lake-shore, turns, defecates to mark his territory...or show his contempt...and lumbers away from a full moon now descending.

"Aw-w-w, no...here he comes," Jules grumbles. "Whew, it's okay, he stopped and turned around."

Julie breaks the tension and expels the first laugh of the long night. "Look, he's mooning us."

"Wrong. He's taking a dump."

"Gross! And look, he's got a shadow-twin behind him."

"Okay, so we'll call those two dip-shit and doo-doo."

"DAD, that's really gross."

"Yep, but it's accurate."

CHAPTER 2
SURVIVAL MODE

POSTPONING A DAMAGE SURVEY, father and daughter enjoy a quiet, bear-less September sunrise dozing on the beach. Later they walk among the ruins, tired and hungry. Nothing unconsumed appears untouched.

"Look," Julie says as she picks up a two-pound tube of cured bacon, which seems unmolested. "May have breakfast after all...whoops...wrong...two fang holes in the back side. Guess we're not that hungry?"

"Bacon? Amazing he didn't rip the container open and finish off everything inside."

"Maybe he was already stuffed."

"With only a cardboard container, bacon should have been first to go. Looks salvageable. Save it, Julie. We may need it. Yeah, we'll have some of the unbitten contents for breakfast."

The two pick through the rest of the refuse. He looks mournfully at a mangled coffee can, grounds spilling through another two puncture wounds. "Hell, I drink too much of this stuff anyway," he grumbles.

"Here's something," Julie calls. "Look," she holds up a huge unbroken jar, "we've got at least a three-day supply of Peter Pan peanut butter to eat."

"Maybe the bear knows something we don't," he says dryly. "Guess his gourmet taste doesn't run to peanut butter."

"Sure looks like he ate or destroyed everything else. What are we gonna do?"

He grimaces and shakes his head. "Honey, I just don't know. For now, let's first see what tent contents are salvageable. We know we have enough food...for at least today under the worst of circumstances. Worst case scenario is we don't get out of here until the skipper brings the father-son combo back in here. But we won't starve...as long as we catch fish. And there should be some ripe berries to eat...if the bears haven't already harvested them."

"So. there aren't any good circumstances...are there?"

"Probably not. But first, let's at least see if we can catch enough food to take care of today. Maybe other campers will show up."

"Wishful thinking?"

"Of course. It helps to stay positive. Now, let's tackle-up and work the early morning bug hatches. Hopefully, we'll then have some fresh fish with bear-sampled bacon for breakfast."

WITH THREE GUTTED AND CLEANED CUTTHROAT TROUT, they soon return to their embattled campsite.

Jules raises a fist of triumph to celebrate their success. "Should be enough to get us through today and maybe most of tomorrow."

"And I've got a secret additional ingredient," Julie says as she holds up a large packet of slivered almonds. "Surprise. I found them in my backpack. So it's trout almandine for lunch and dinner today and again tomorrow...and ah shit...guess that's all we have to eat." With realization, her smile of triumph fades to disgust.

Unrelenting sunshine plus a high protein fish and fat bacon breakfast keep situational depression in check. But father and daughter have decisions to make. Jules summarizes, "We can stay here for two more nights, three at the worst, or take our backpacks, walk out to a road and hitchhike back to Bridge Bay."

"Hike 21 miles with minimal sleep," she says. "No thanks."

"Well, I don't think we should stay here, even though Death Breath has eaten everything in sight and isn't likely to return."

"So what do we do?"

"We could hike up the Yellowstone River," he offers weakly. "The map shows an island two or three miles up, and it looks like an easy hike with a trail all the way. We'll be safe there for two nights. Then come back here, hoping the skipper will make his new delivery as scheduled."

She's skeptical. "And then we'll be...what, 20-plus miles from a road? Is that smart...to go farther away?"

He grimaces and shrugs his shoulders.

"Okay, Dad, let's do it. Can't stay here. Too depressing. So, what should we do about the campsite mess?"

"Leave it," he says. "It's a nice monument to incompatibility. Maybe it'll persuade other foolish campers to turn back."

"Yeah, like our potential rescuers next Tuesday."

An hour later, they remove their hiking boots and wade a shallow river channel to their island sanctuary, which appears benignly bear-less. They prepare a sparse, makeshift campsite consisting of sleeping bags unrolled underneath spreading lower branches of a convenient pine tree.

Julie suggests, "Let's save our trout for dinner tonight and meals tomorrow. Peanut butter okay for lunch today? I'll dig it out of my backpack."

He shrugs his shoulders and mumbles, "Sure. Go for it."

They take turns spooning tasteless, gooey brown blobs into their mouths.

Lunch complete, Jules licks his lips in simulated satisfaction, then frowns. "Ug-g-g-h, no wonder Death Breath ignored this," he says.

"Um-m-mh," she says, closing her eyes. "Just close your eyes like this and imagine it's a juicy Big Mac."

"I don't have that much imagination."

"That's because you have too much attitude."

"And I'm blessed to have...what? A smart-ass daughter?"

"Of course."

Laughter is a welcome companion to finishing a meager meal, after which they decide to nap in the sun. Once again their world is at peace. Julie licks her lips, takes a deep breath and exhales. *Yep, for sure, people can still live happily without fruits and vegetables.*

A stroll around the island is the evening's mission. Arm in arm, sharing camaraderie as they almost share first names in common, they enjoy a peaceful circumference beach stroll made possible by late summer's low water levels. Until... "Look," Julie exclaims, pointing at depressions in the sand. "Are those what I think they are?"

He kneels down to take a closer look at one of the paw prints. Unmistakably beary, they track from water's edge toward the island's interior. The print dwarfs his hand and outstretched fingers. "Awfully big," he says. "Gotta be a grizzly."

"Can you tell for sure?"

"Yep, I can. Grizzlies have very long claws, more like overgrown nails."

"So...you were wrong about grizzlies and islands."

"Maybe it's an old track," he says.

"Wishful thinking," she says. "Should we follow it?"

"Hell no, we might be successful and find its maker." Jules bravely kicks sand over the paw-prints. "I'll improve my attitude, develop my imagination, and pretend the bear was actually backing down to the water to leave."

EMOTIONS THAT NIGHT range from mild apprehension to stark terror as visions of toothy, red-eyed bears with bad breath invade their thoughts. Although they divide an uneventful night into two watches, father and daughter get little sleep. Their following island day and night are uneventful replicas of the first, except nightfall finally grants them both a long, deep sleep of exhaustion.

RETURNING EARLY to their Beaverdam Creek campsite, they again poke about the litter but find no additional signs of depredation. "Only the scat pile," Jules says. "So he didn't come back."

"Not much consolation," she says. "Why should he come back? He ate everything the first time."

CHAPTER 3
RESCUED

SILENT, THOUGHTFUL, AND WEARY, but at least relaxing on the beach, they find huge flat rocks to sit on while they watch threatening clouds...first of the week...sweep across Yellowstone Lake. They wait. And wait. Both are fretful. The boat carrying expected new arrivals in and hopefully providing them with departure out a day earlier than planned is late. A half hour passes. It grows into an hour. Clouds darken, and light rain begins. They pull ponchos from their back packs and don them.

Julie stands and looks into the gathering gloom. "What if they don't come today, and..."

He cuts her off, "Don't even think that."

"But, we're just sitting here in the rain."

"Be thankful it's not snow."

"Just wait. It probably will be."

"Attitude?"

"Sorry. I think I'm finally really scared...for the first time. Aren't you?"

Jules frowns. He says, "I hate to acknowledge it, but I am too. We're already an impressive survival story. Now both of us need to remain confident. Stay here, Julie. I'll walk up to the peninsula where there's a better view of the entry into this arm of the lake."

Half way up, he turns, waves to Julie and then trots back, a broad smile on his face. "They're coming. Already well into the arm. The skipper is rowing now. And look...storm clouds are breaking up, and we're gonna have some more sunshine. A brighter day for us, both emotionally and physically."

Julie wipes tears from her eyes and rushes into his open arms. "I've tried to hide it, Dad. But I've been really scared."

Their embrace lingers, and he whispers in her ear, "Me too darlin'."

"MR. ANDERS, MISS JULIE, meet Mark Jennings and his son Jason-Jerrold."

Brief introductions concluded, a scowling skipper surveys the campsite devastation and grumbles, "What the hell happened here? No, don't tell me. I can guess. Bear?"

"Yep," Jules replies.

"Did you get a good look at him?"

"Too good."

"Was he disfigured in any way?"

"Yep." Jules nods his head. "Something was wrong with an ear, and it seemed like he also had a damaged eye."

"Goddam. It's Lop Ear again. Hasn't been a problem most of the summer...until recently. Rangers need to do something about him before he goes bad."

"He's already bad. We call him Death Breath."

"You and your daughter okay?"

"Yep."

"Must be a helluva survival story?"

"Yep, but can Julie and I spare everyone the details right now? Just know that we're okay...and so grateful you're here."

"You gotta be starving."

"Nope, just tired of peanut butter and trout. Our gourmet dining has included baked trout almandine, pan-fried trout, and even raw trout sushi for appetizers. We never want to eat trout or peanut butter again."

Mark Jennings steps in to commandeer the conversation. "Okay everyone. Have lunch with Jason-Jerrold and me. No trout. We'll celebrate the Anders' survival and the likely brief return of our late summer sun. We've got way more than enough food for all of us. Let's eat and then get the hell out of here. No way Jason-Jerrold and I are staying overnight. Not with this in sight." He gestures to the scene of destruction. "And with the overhanging threat of further bear predation. Plus, the last weather forecast we were able to get at the marina was for the first big snow of late summer moving in tomorrow. Not a good idea to complete our planned holiday here. We'll do our father/son wilderness adventure another time, maybe another place."

LUNCH AND CLEANUP CONCLUDED, they board the boat for a return to civilization. The skipper scowls and looks back. "Uh-oh, we forgot your tent. Don't you want it, Mr. Anders?"

"What for? Even if I could patch it, we'll never sleep in it again."

"Evidence," Mark Jennings suggests. "Combat skepticism when you tell the story to others. You can show the tent as evidence."

"Good point. I'll get it."

As they finally pole off shore, Jules stands and watches a retreating shoreline. Then he raises his sight to the hillside above and speaks softly, "I understand. We trespassed in your personal space. All you really wanted was for us to leave."

LOP EAR STANDS BESIDE HIS FAVORITE NAPPING ROCK. He's remained alert for more than an hour since he again smelled human presence. He knows they're leaving. If he knew how, he would smile with satisfaction. He's become impatient with unwanted intrusion into his domain, and he knows he's getting old. He can feel it when his bones ache before first snow, when sight in his damaged right eye diminishes further each spring, and when his silver-tipped hackles rise more quickly at summer's first distant smell of man.

SHARING THE BOAT'S BOW-SEAT SIDE BY SIDE, Julie and Jason-Jerrold get better acquainted. Julie glances sideways. *Tall and really handsome. But a hyphenated two-name first name? That's weird.* "We were kinda excluded from all the adult conversation at lunch," she says. "So, how do I address you? Two names or one?"

He laughs. "Well, Mom likes Jerrold. My grandparents like Jason. My classmates call me JJ. Dad doubles up a lot. Guess it sounds more impressive for him to have a son with a hyphenated name. Please just call me Jase. I like that best. It's short and sweet."

I think he's tall and sweet. Has a really warm smile and an engagingly natural way about him. And those sea-blue eyes. Wow! "Okay, Jase it is. So...you and your dad like wilderness fishing adventures?"

"Well, we've never tried anything this wild. Ever hear of Silver Creek in Idaho?"

"No, Dad and I mostly do day or weekend trips in Colorado, and I'm not really a connoisseur of the sport. What's Silver Creek?"

"It's a nature preserve, owned and managed by The Nature Conservancy. It was their first wild and major riparian spring-creek acquisition. We've been there a few times."

"And you're now here from where?"

"Suburban Denver. Greenwood Village actually. In the only home I've ever known. But it's no longer a village. It's business district is bigger than downtown Denver. Dad offices there in a high rise. For a supplemental energy source over 30 years ago, he and Mom installed roof solar panels on our home there. First in the neighborhood to do that. Sad part of that story is no one else followed their lead for years. Best part is my curiosity about that installation as a youngster triggered my environmental concerns, then influenced my choice in college curriculum, which eventually led to a conservation career decision. And you, Julie. You're here from where?"

"Small home in the older northwest residential area of Boulder. Too close to the foothills for any high-mountain views. Hey, I think we might be about the same age."

"Which for you is?"

"Sweet 17."

"You look older."

"Thanks, Jase, I think. And you?"

"I'm 20."

"You look younger."

"Thanks, I think."

They both burst into laughter.

Julie's yawn betrays her fatigue level, but she continues the background check. "So Jase, you must be about what? A college Junior?"

"Correct. Starting back next week actually."

"Where?"

"Yale. Dad always wanted me to go Ivy League. I think it's a prestige thing for him, and Yale has a great Environmental Science program. He's a Harvard MBA in finance, but no way I'm going to follow his footsteps into managing other peoples' money. My aspirations are about 180 degrees opposite from his. Ever since I saw what they can accomplish...first-hand at Silver Creek, I've wanted to work for The Nature Conservancy. Their Colorado office is in Boulder. Low pay but high in sense of accomplishment. You picked a college yet?"

"Yep, I'm probably staying in Boulder for my college education. Don't know in what yet. Maybe our paths will cross again?"

"I'd like that. Hey, look the marina's in sight. We're almost outta here. Let's stand and applaud the skipper."

AS THEY'RE LEAVING YELLOWSTONE that afternoon, Jules and Julie stop at Lake Village Ranger Station. A tired and obviously overworked Park Ranger looks up from a mountain of paperwork on his desk.

Jules says, "We want to report an...er...an incident."

The ranger looks up and shakes his head. "I think I can guess. A bear?"

"That's right. A really big one. With a scarred and disfigured head."

"Where were you?"

"Beaverdam Creek."

The ranger nods his head. "Lop Ear again. Anyone hurt?"

"No. Should we fill out a report or something?"

"If no one was hurt, an official report from you two won't be necessary. But tell me what happened. I may have to report it higher up."

"Lop Ear tore up our tent and ate or contaminated all our food, except for a big jar of peanut butter and a package of cured bacon. Probably my fault. Although we suspended our food bag from a tree limb, I didn't tie it off high enough."

With a grim face, the Ranger responds. "Lop Ear is an older bear, and he's lately become a nuisance. Despite the remoteness of his territory, our Park Rangers are getting too many reports similar to yours. There's concern he'll have a more physical confrontation with a Park guest. The Park Superintendent may have a tough decision to make."

Jules frowns. "Euthanasia?"

The Ranger frowns also. "I'm afraid so."

Julie tugs on her father's hand and shakes her head. "I don't like the sound of that. We were in his territory. He was only curious and hungry. Yeah, we were scared. But looking back, we were never threatened physically. He grunted and snorted a lot, but I don't think he ever even growled at us."

"I agree, Julie. And, even though he tripped on one of our tent ropes and reacted aggressively, I never felt he was a threat to us personally."

The Ranger responds. "I understand, and I sympathize with the generosity of your feelings toward one of the Park's most prominent Grizzlies. Because of his immense size and disfigurement, Lop Ear is also the most recognizable bear in the Park. However, I do have to report the incident up through the Park's channels. It'll be the Super's call. Glad it's not mine."

As they leave, Julie tugs again on her father's hand. "It makes me really sad. I wish we hadn't come in here to talk about it."

"Me too, Julie. Welcome to one of the harsh realities involved in the mix of humans with our planet's wildest noble creatures. Humans first. Always. Although slight, the risk that Lop Ear might eventually hurt someone is unacceptable to the authorities."

PART TWO

THE THESIS

CHAPTER 4
POLY SCI FI
JAN 2018

FIDGETING IN THE SECOND ROW, Julie Anders fumes as she waits for her professor to arrive. She has to endure the distraction of a class she would not have taken had it not been a required course for her Master's Degree in Broadcast Journalism.

Political Science Five? Really? At least I don't have to take PoliSci One, Two, Three, and Four. Thank goodness. The class title is an oxymoron. There's no science to politics. Is modern journalism that obsessed with politics?

Anyway, I'll pay close attention. My graduate student advisor said Professor Bright's a rare delight. The advisor also said the Professor's PhD dissertation was a provocative masterpiece. Sheeze, what's the title? Julie frowns as she extracts a note tablet from her briefcase and reads from the first page. "*Purposeful? Misuse of Information by Politicians and the Media...Are They That Stupid, or Do They Really Believe Most Americans Are That Stupid?" Longest title I've ever read but sounds intriguing. Will Dr. Bright require students to read it? Hope she'll at least talk about the codependency that exists between the two professions. Seems an unhealthy relationship. Is politics even a profession? Or has it evolved to just a playground for power-seekers?*

Bet I'm the only student here with a degree in accounting and classwork in actuarial science. Should be an interesting year ahead.

PROFESSOR ANGEL BRIGHT opens with, "Welcome everyone to PoliSci 5, the only class at this campus ending in the number five. Also known as Political Sci Fi...short for Political Science Fiction. May be aptly nick-named. Hopefully my class will be as advanced as its number implies, and my students will take it all...well, at least most of it...as serious stuff. I won't try to make it simple. I don't do simple. And that's not what you're here for either. I realize many of you out there are in this post-graduate class because you have to be, not necessarily because you want to be. So...I'll try to be entertaining as well as informative, challenging to the extent of borderline offending, and maybe even outrageous. You should also know I've sworn a vow of intellectual political chastity. I won't let either side fuck with how I think or what I say. And...I'm tenured. Also the University's first recipient of a PhD in Political Science who's both a person of color and feminine gendered. So, CU can't get rid of me, even if it wanted to. Yeah, intellectual freedom is still alive and well on this college campus." She pauses again to look around her audience. Then, with an open smile and a head nod, she acknowledges the beaming faces she expected and continues.

"Hopefully all of you will learn something here that will serve you well in your afterlife. Except of course for parenting, which no university anywhere has the audacity to weave into its curriculum, even for post-graduate courses. My purpose in this class is to advance your education, not to prepare you for an afterlife in any practical sense. Nor am I here to indoctrinate you to any cause of consequence other than learning. For Master's Degrees we faculty members don't do indoctrinations. Indoctrinations are reserved for that mystical realm of PhD, should any of you be so intimidated by the thought of seeking a real job in the real world that you might choose instead to advance your college education one degree further."

Again her comments draw class smiles and an audible

chuckle from Julie. *Check signals. Believe I'm going to enjoy this.*

"So," Professor Bright continues, "on to a brief introduction to the class you're about to take, assuming you have the stamina and the persistence to endure it.

"First, a comment about our small class size...only 14 students enrolled. I like it small. I have faculty seniority among those few of us teaching Political Science at higher levels, and I always opt for the smallest class. So I can get to know you better.

"Particularly for students soldiering on for a Master's Degree in Broadcast Journalism, I'll focus my lectures on the contemporary scene rather than the past. So I'll begin today with a listing of ten important issues I'll be discussing in class. All are current hot topics. Or in my opinion soon will become so. All are likely to dominate political scenes. All are sure to attract press coverage too often modeled after scavengers circling around, hovering over, or actually feeding on a wounded or already dead food-creature. Yes, I do get cynical sometimes. But I don't apologize for it.

"We'll try to ignore the past, focus on today and what might become tomorrow. No tedious history lessons in this class. From my list, you may find a topic of interest for your Master's Thesis, an endeavor that hopefully provides your ticket out of academics and into the harsh realities of after-college life. You should also know that I'm an advisor to the three-member faculty committee that reviews Master's Theses. Please take advantage of your opportunities to impress me." Again she pauses with a smile at her audience before she continues. "So...here's the list, not necessarily in order of importance:

Deficit spending and excessive Government debt, a gigantic shell game.

Legislative excesses featuring The Affordable Care Act and The Dodd Frank Act.

Congressional oversight committees' overreach.
Student loans.
Abortion.
Climate change.
Racial bias of law enforcement.
Russia, Russia, Russia.
Income tax fraud by non-profits and the media.
Trials by Congress as it charges, investigates, prosecutes, and acts as judge and jury.

"Before I run out of lecture gas...and before you run out of lecture tolerance, we may also explore a broader, more esoteric subject. I call it the Absence of Reason in our Excess Information Age. There's both a scholarly purpose and a practical modern reality that cry out for this subject to receive substantive attention in university classrooms. I suspect very few college curriculums venture into its controversial and provocative waters.

"Now, I'll digress for a minute to present one of the most profound statements ever made by an American President since Lincoln. It relates to what I perceive as the greatest threat facing America today, and I cannot think of a topic more important to cover in an advanced PoliSci class. It's what I call the Cruel Myth of a Riskless Society. Too many Americans, too many politicians, and way too many Government leaders seem to be devoted to a fallacious concept...that Americans are entitled to live in an affordable riskless society and that our country should, can, and will provide that. I'd like to see more adherences to John F. Kennedy's famous and inspirational statement, 'Ask not what your country can do for you. Ask what you can do for your country.' Unfortunately it seems like the morality pendulum here has done a 180. For most politicians, and much of their support base, it's all about what our Government can do for its citizens...and more recently for its illegal immigrants.

"Here's a fetid consequence of our politically abused and hyper-regulated lives in America. America has 1.3 million practicing lawyers. 325,000, or 25% of them, are in two states, New York and California. Country-wide that's 333 lawyers per 100,000 population. By comparison Japan has 18,800 lawyers total or only 15.4 lawyers per 100,000 population. So why is our lawyer population density 22 times that of Japan's? No, I don't want a show of hands for an answer. It's just something I'd like my students to keep in mind as we power and ponder our way through this course together.

"Okay, now let's move on to important class protocols. We won't use textbooks. I don't grade on a curve. Grades are 50% class participation and 50% a final exam. I'm not a glutton for punishment, so I don't do homework assignments or concurrent testing. You won't be submitted to those debilitating undergraduate conventions." Again she pauses to deliver a broad grin to her class and survey their reaction...row-by-row.

As the Professor's gaze moves slowly down row two, Julie detects a wink in her right eye and winks back. *Wow! She's a case. Sure sounds refreshing. I think we students should applaud...now. Yeah...let's do it.* Beginning to clap, her impulse spreads like a virus to the rest of the class. Soon the classroom resonates with sounds of collective student approval of their teacher's opening remarks.

The Professor bows to acknowledge her favorable reception and then continues. "Finally, there will be no long lecture today. Just my relatively short introduction, and then we'll have an informal meet and greet. You can call me 'Angie.' All my students do. Or, 'Emo'...for Madame Outrageous. That works too.

"Now, are there any questions before we adjourn? First, you should know my style with student questions. You raise your hand and ask me a question. When I acknowledge you, I'm going to ask you why you asked it. Makes you think on your feet or, more appropriately, on your student butt. Unless YOU elect to stand."

CHAPTER 5
SELECTION
AUG 2018

JULIE SITS AT HER SMALL DESK in her father's small home squeezed between two large homes on the fringes of an old residential neighborhood on the fringe of the northwestern boundary of Boulder, Colorado...and ponders her future.

Have I bitten off more than I can chew? Okay, so I'm done with eight months of my Master's Degree program. Only a year to go. Whew! Thanks to Professor Bright for helping me select a thesis subject. And my selection. Yeah, right...the March 2010 Affordable Care Act. Really? All of it? Over a thousand pages I'm gonna read, try to understand and analyze as I go. Maybe I'll take another big visual bite and look at the balance sheet of an ACA healthcare insurance provider. Then, somehow reduce my observations to a 40-50 page document. And then, finally, micro-present my thesis in a real time simulation before the camera to a three-person faculty review committee. Facultards the students call them.

Am I really this anal? This into mental self-abuse. What a crazy post-undergraduate present I've given myself. Will a graduate degree be worth all this brain damage? Plus the two years of my life I've already spent working the Boulder restaurant scene and saving money to invest in preparation for a hopefully exciting professional career?

At least I'll begin my career debt free. No student loans for this kid. Graduating college with a huge debt burden is insanity squared. And the borrowing program itself is a putrid example of Federal Government recklessness squared.

And...my dad. He'll be so proud. I'll have a gilt-edged credential.

Well, maybe only a silver lining. A master's degree from the University of Colorado's College of Media, Communications, and Information sure sounds impressive. But I'm told competition for entry-level jobs in Broadcast Journalism is fierce. My credentials may not muster up to those of students graduating from prominent Ivy League or California schools.

As she ponders her future, she must also backup, remember, and acknowledge her past...her heritage, what little she knows about it.

Immigrants from Denmark, with him in tow, her father's parents shortened the family name from Andersen to Anders and settled in Pueblo, Colorado, where Grampa Anders worked 25 grueling years in Pueblo's historic steel mill, continuing a second-generation family tradition begun in 1940 when his father and two uncles worked side-by-side at Kontivaerket, Denmark's world-renowned "Glorious Steel Plant."

After the acquisition of the Pueblo steel mill by Russian interests, Grampa Anders complained about intermittent press stories hyping the speculation that the Pueblo mill was used as a front for Russian spying activities...with most of that effort focused on the top-secret US Military operations buried in the bowels of Cheyenne Mountain adjacent to Colorado Springs. "Never even saw a Russian," he always said.

Grampa Anders insisted on a college education for his two children: Julie's father, Jules, and her Aunt Winnie. With his CU degree in Atmospheric and Ocean Sciences, Jules is a career scientist at an iconic Federal institution, NOAA in Boulder. With her degree from CU's College of Nursing, ranked fourth in the nation, Aunt Winnie is a much admired Physician's Assistant working the emergency rooms of Denver General Hospital.

Death from an aneurysm shortly after Julie's birth left her motherless, with no memories of her mom. Her legacies: a few photographs and a few sketches and original oil paintings to validate an artistic talent as well as a family life cut off far too early; and her father's stories, often told tearfully, of a whirlwind college courtship, a day-after-graduation wedding, and then a brief honeymoon at the historic Broadmoor Hotel in Colorado Springs. Her father has never remarried. "Yet," Julie occasionally reminds him.

CHAPTER 6
PRESENTATION REHEARSAL
AUG 2019

WELL, I MADE IT! Only one more hurdle. Then I'm outta here with my Master's Degree. And with my sanity intact...mostly. Guess I should practice for tomorrow.

My brilliant career now depends on three professors and their reactions to my presentation. Plus Q&A. Yeah, right. Hundreds of hours of research jammed into a 50 page document maybe read by half-a-dozen people. All collapsed further into a five minute monologue. Like openers from a prime-time television talk show host or a human-experience story for TV or radio.

Think I'm ready. Time to rehearse here in my tiny bedroom. In front of the mirror. Which only reflects my upper half above my tiny study-desk. Please, Dad, don't eavesdrop.

Five pages of double-spaced text printed in boldface with 14 pt. font rest on a makeshift podium of four textbooks stacked on Julie's desk. Staring into the mirror, she sticks out her tongue at an inviting smile staring back. It's a striking and unblemished image of a confident young woman. Then she turns her head sideways and corners her eyes back so she can self-admire her long and flowing auburn hair, un-styled in a bold challenge to modern fashion designs. She nods her head in approval. *Yeah, right. No bobs, short shags, or mullets for this kid. Also, no styled cuts, angles, inverts, asymmetricals, choppys, face-framers, featheries, pixies, super-stacks, or wolf cuts. I'll stay natural and simple for as long as I can.*

Resting on the floor beside her is the family's pet Golden Retriever, Shane. Although dozing, Shane provides what a beloved pet provides best...a huge bounty of unconditional love and emotional support. Delivered in silence most of the time...but also with enthusiastic tail-wags, what appears to be a smile, and a slobbering muzzle. Sometimes he barks approval. Or maybe his barks announce HE needs more attention.

Julie reaches down to stroke her pet. "For good luck," she murmurs. "Don't worry, old friend, you don't have to listen. Often I wish you could talk too."

As she stands, Shane rises to sit beside her. Then she smiles at herself, clears her throat and begins.

"Tonight I'd like to talk about our nation's healthcare insurance systems. Mostly from a numbers perspective. I'll begin with some consequences of the Affordable Care Act, which I'll refer to as the ACA.

"When it was enacted nine years ago, the 2010 ACA was about 1,000 pages long and comprised the longest piece of legislation ever enacted by Congress. Before it reached the Supreme Court in 2012, it spawned generations of rules and regulations and swelled to 2,700 pages of Federal Government mandate. Because of its length, Justice Scalia refused to read or permit his Supreme Court clerks to read the entire regulatory package. I couldn't read and digest the whole package either, without doubling the time I'd need to compose a thesis.

"As I settled into an attempt to read and understand at least some of the ACA, here was my first observation. It's a huge question that settled into my mind and never left. How can a regulatory behemoth with such extraordinary dimensions not create more problems than it solves? It has to be mentally constipating to any mind attempting to digest its entire contents.

"Then, after scatter-gun bouts of reading portions of the ACA, I developed an overriding second question that continues to haunt me. Did any member of Congress with a functional mind actually read the ACA? I doubt it. At least I tried to. Here's some of MY story. Hang on. It's mind blowing."

First I need some water. Julie pauses to chug from the mug on her desk-top. Then she reaches down to stroke Shane again and continues.

"So-o-o, on to the first significant ACA finding I address in my thesis. It was an egregious bill-drafting error that nobody...I repeat that NOBODY...detected until after the ACA was passed by Congress and entered into the Congressional record. Actually, to call it a drafting error is being charitable. It was probably an immense collective brain fart from drafters of the bill...probably staffers...that didn't smell bad enough for defective legislative brains to detect." *Whoops, that's gross. Thought I took it out of my final thesis draft. But then, maybe I should leave it in. Let my readers know how I really feel.*

"Anyway, I won't burden you with the details, but this section of the ACA simply wasn't workable. It would have created hundreds of billions of dollars in unnecessary and inappropriate costs to taxpayers.

"No way Congress could pass this thing, I thought at first. But Congress did. Still skeptical, I did some more digging and found that I was indeed reading the exact words passed by Congress. However...thank God for howevers...through some process I don't understand, a functional mind reread the flawed section, recognized its absurdity, and corrected the wording. That's right. The ACA was actually changed post-passage. I could be charitable again and say the post-passage change merely corrected a lengthy typo. I'm skeptical about that. Whether a typo or a conceptual flaw, it was outrageous legislative negligence that such an egregious and obvious mistake of that magnitude was not discovered and corrected pre-passage.

"The ACA soon exhausted my appetite for its contents, but I did continue reading some of the corrected act and soon had another 'OH MY GOD, I can't believe this' moment. So, on to finding number two.

"Here's my conclusion. The ACA provisions intending to limit and control premiums charged by participating insurance companies actually enable exactly the opposite. The ACA incentivizes insurance companies to maximize Direct Healthcare Costs...which I'll hereafter refer to as DHC. It's obviously in insurers' best interests to maximize DHC rather than to help control them. Here's how it works. The ACA REQUIRES insurers to rebate premiums to the extent they result in recoveries of overhead and profit in excess of specified percentages of DHC. Worded a different way but with the same result: in setting premiums, insurers are PERMITTED to add to premiums specified percentages of DHC to cover overhead and profit. This creates a cost plus a percentage-of-cost contract, obviously encouraging insurance companies to maximize DHC in order to enhance their profits. A friend of my dad's who spent a few years of his life auditing government contracts tells me that cost plus a percentage-of-cost contracts with the US Government are ILLEGAL...for obvious reasons.

"So, our Congress actually enacted a law establishing a massive system of illegal contracts with insurers. The ACA is an example of Government excess in full bloom. How many members of Congress didn't bother to read the ACA...ie how many were negligent? And how many did read it, or rely on their staff to read it...ie how many were too incompetent to comprehend what they read or had incompetent staff do the reading? There's another possibility: I'm wrong. I'm just a young person who cares and is trying to finish my college education and get on with my afterlife.

"So, here's a sort of anti-climactic and not unexpected ACA finding number three...an EXPLOSION in annual administrative costs of healthcare insurers and providers. It's the first major adverse impact of ACA I saw that was studied by others. These costs doubled from what they were in 2010 to $496 billion in 2016, broken down as follows: Healthcare

Providers – $282 billion, Private Insurers – $158 billion, Public Insurers...like Medicare and Medicaid – $56 billion.

"Based on studies of admin costs in other high-income countries, experts have concluded that half of America's healthcare admin costs are excessive. Sounds like inefficiency squared. And, I've heard physicians complain that their admin costs more than doubled. annually just to comply with ACA provisions."

Julie pauses to take a deep breath and expel it with a loud "Whew." Then she continues with, "Realizing I needed to move on from the ACA, I wanted to know more about America's healthcare insurance companies. So I also studied recent financial reports of ANTHEM, America's second-largest healthcare insurance provider and the holding company for most, maybe all, Blue Cross/Blue Shield insurance plans. Here's what I found.

"Anthem is technically INSOLVENT. That's because its debts exceed its tangible assets by $2.8 billion. And how did that happen?

"1. From years of very costly acquisition activity, using borrowed money to buy up the competition, Anthem overloaded its balance sheet with $27 billion in intangible assets, consisting mostly of an ephemeral number called Goodwill that can't be seen, touched, heard, smelled, tasted, or verified by an expert. Nor can it be measured, except hopefully as a rational balance between the flim-flam skills of a seller and the avarice appetites of a buyer. It's what's left over from an entity purchase price after all the tangible stuff is valued, and it's appropriately excluded from assets in a solvency test. You might also just call Goodwill a speculation, both reasoned and reckless, on good things...like lots of profits...that MIGHT happen in the future.

"2. During the same period, ANTHEM profits were $25 billion; however the company pissed away $27 billion buying back its own stock in order to buoy up its stock price, a gigantic textbook case of corporate mismanagement.

"After suppressing my own disbelief that this could happen, I asked myself 'How the hell did Anthem strip out ALL its accumulated earnings and effectively eliminate ALL equity risk capital in the enterprise?'

"Like other insurers, ANTHEM is regulated by state insurance commissions. So I read the Colorado insurance regulations and saw that insurance company subsidiaries have to maintain a certain level of tangible assets over and above debt before they can pay dividends to their parent company. Dividend distributions from state subsidiaries to ANTHEM's parent company were the source of money used to repurchase its stock.

"It made no sense. How could an insolvent enterprise with debts in excess of its tangible assets be in compliance with state regulations?

"So I asked Colorado's Insurance Division to send me the ANTHEM financial statement filings permitting the company to take cash out of Colorado. My request was denied. Something phony going on, I thought.

"I think I figured it out. ANTHEM gamed the system. By keeping its goodwill accounts and huge acquisitions indebtedness on its parent company balance sheet, it concealed its excessive debt burden and its insolvency from Colorado regulators, and presumably from other state regulators. That enabled ANTHEM to file subsidiary financial statements with regulators that reflected only tangible assets and relatively insignificant normal debt from operations. The filings presented a clever illusion of solvency.

"I cite the ANTHEM deception to illustrate how easy it was to maneuver around Government regulatory controls. And to show how imprudent actions of a major insurer gutted its tangible equity base, placing its insurance policy holders and its debt holders at significant risk of suffering severe debt default consequences. To my surprise, ANTHEM is still around.

"I haven't studied United Healthcare, America's largest healthcare insurance provider. I'm fearful of what I might find.

"A final comment on our healthcare insurance industry. Unlike life insurance companies, health insurance companies don't establish substantive actuarial reserves for future costs. So, there's no normalization of premium costs over an insured's lifetime. That creates a built-in model for ever-increasing annual premium costs, moderated only by attracting more new and younger Americans into the customer base each year. It's a recipe for huge inflation in healthcare insurance costs.

"So, one of the biggest segments of our American economy is actually blazing the trail to runaway inflation. All parents should prepare their children for this inevitability."

Julie turns over the final page of her text, pauses, sighs in relief, then gazes intently at her mirror and says, "My thanks to the Review Committee for listening to me this afternoon. I'll take your questions now."

She sits down and pushes a whooshing sigh of relief through her mouth. *Okay, so I lied about intending to take out my crude remarks about ACA bill drafters and their brain disorders. Let's see if the Review Committee reacts tomorrow.*

Then she reaches down to stroke Shane, now dozing again and undisturbed by Julie's rehearsal. "So, old guy, what do you think? Should I leave the crude comments about our Congressional brain damage in? You fart all the time." When she leaves her chair, kneels down, leans in closer and then gives her pet a big hug, Shane's response is to wake up and lick her face.

CHAPTER 7

THESIS CRITIQUE

THE NEXT DAY

DRESSED CASUALLY, more like students than faculty, Professors Darwin, Gudinov, and D'Angelo sit at a small table in a small conference room adjacent to the University's simulated telecast studio...away from the confusing jumble of lights, cameras, microphones, chairs, and a seemingly endless mass of cables wound around each other like serpents in a pit.

"So, who's next?" asks Brian Darwin, Thesis Review Committee Chair.

"Julie Anders," responds Boris Gudinov, known affectionately to his students as Boris Bad Enough or Boris the Bad. "She's our last interview and evaluation of the day. Also one of the brightest post-graduate candidates we've had in a while and the lead scholar among all our Master's candidates this semester. Straight A's for her undergraduate work. Except for a stray D in American Literature, where she pissed off an intolerant young English professor. Twice actually. First, Miss Anders boldly scolded him in class for some inappropriate gender and racially biased remarks. Then, those two later had a big classroom dispute about the contemporary relevance of author Ayn Rand, particularly the 60-page manifesto in her dynamic novel, *Atlas Shrugged.* The class agreed with Julie's contention that Ayn Rand was still relevant."

"Yeah," Mario D'Angelo adds. "In my debate class, Julie was always the best debater. Because she had a more compelling point of view, particularly if the debate involved numbers of any kind. Her back-grounding preparation was impeccable. Stuck to facts and sound reasoning. Kept irrational emotionalism and extrapolation out of her arguments. To the extent she actually lost two debates. Sometimes ardent but misguided passion overcomes sound reasoning. Even though it shouldn't."

"Okay then, Committee," Darwin signals the meeting's end by rising from his chair. "Graduate PhD students who helped us with Master's thesis reviews also liked what they read. This is our last review of the day. Seems we have an easy evaluation and a shoo-in winner. Let's go give it a listen. End our day and hers on a positive note. Maybe we'll also learn something."

FIVE MINUTES LATER, Julie completes her presentation, nervously shuffles her papers together on a real podium, and then steps aside. The Committee members rise and applaud. To Julie the applause sounds genuine as well as enthusiastic, not just an automated programmed response. Three smiling faces add to the moment's sense of authenticity.

As he reseats, Darwin says, "Impressive, Miss Anders. Complex but persuasive. Also, maybe very important and very timely. Also relatively short. Thank you. And now for the Q and A. No worries. We'll also keep that brief. Will you please first tell us why you've chosen to go into Broadcast Journalism.

Feeling at ease, Julie smiles as she responds. "Well, I've been told repeatedly that Actuarial Science is the World's most boring profession, and I suspect Accounting is right up there in second place. But I also believe the combination of these two disciplines, plus my own dedication to independent thought and voice, make me uniquely qualified to insert an academically prepared and unbiased voice of reason into the profession. I'm concerned that broadcast journalism suffers from an absence of rational thought. It's also befouled by accommodators for agenda-driven activists and politicians all grandstanding for press attention."

"Not very complimentary of those whose ranks you propose to join, are you?"

"No, I'm not. Should I be?"

"Not necessarily. Your complaints about modern-day journalism's codependency with politics of all flavors are shared by many of our faculty members. But not all. Seems like there's competition in academia...as well as in the media...for which squeaky wheel for or against any cause can attract the most grease. Now, let's move on to our second and final question for you. Why did you select the Affordable Care Act and Healthcare Insurance as subjects for your thesis?"

Another question I expected. Good thing I asked myself the same thing when I selected my thesis topic. Her confidence building, she casts a broad grin to her interrogators. "Well, making a selection decision wasn't easy, but it was carefully considered. When I left my PolySciFi class, I had a list of ten potential subjects to pursue in greater depth. I picked the Affordable Care Act and Healthcare Insurance for several reasons.

"First. These two subjects affect most everyone in America.

"Second. At the time of passage, the ACA was the longest act ever passed by Congress. Wow, what a challenge.

"Third and most important was my feeling of gratitude for what the ACA might do to help others. Not necessarily for me or my family. Until retirement brought or brings them under the Medicare umbrella, my immigrant grandfather, his brothers, my father and his sister all had...or have... jobs with Government or organizations large enough to provide group health insurance coverage to their employees. But then I thought of the millions of small business owners and their employees who don't have access to a group plan until they qualify for Medicare. And I also thought about others who have pre-existing conditions that might jeopardize their access to health insurance. What a great opportunity for a systemic improvement to insuring the delivery of healthcare. Yeah, was I naive or what?

"And finally, Fourth. The ACA was on Professor Bright's hit list as one of the most unnecessarily bloated products of excessive regulatory zeal she'd ever seen. She mentioned that one of the ACA economist architects cynically claimed the American people were 'too stupid' to understand the need for this legislation. Maybe that economist was too stupid to understand the adverse cost consequences of this legislation.

"And now...if I may, I'd like to ask the Committee a question, actually two questions. Have the three of you read the entire content of all the student Master's Degree theses whose candidacy you're empowered to evaluate? Or, have student assistants...like the PhD candidates assigned to you...done most of the reading and reported back to you? Please understand I'm not being provocative. I like the idea of student involvement in these evaluations. Adds a youthful and not overly-cynicalized perspective to the post-graduate scene."

Chuckles from Julie's audience are audible. "Fair enough," Darwin responds. "And the answers to your questions are for the first...no, and for the second...yes. Now, if you'll take a chair, better yet a more relaxing seat on the studio couch, the Committee will adjourn to the conference room and discuss your candidacy. We'll return shortly, and you'll have our decision. And...oh yes. Leave your crude comments about Congressional ACA bill drafters in your thesis. Student reviewers and the three of us all agree with you."

DARWIN SWIPES HIS BROW as he addresses his committee. "Whew, she sure picked two helluva complex subjects for her thesis. So...what's your reaction?"

D'Angelo responds first. "Well, I think we heard something very special today from a very special student. Here are my three takeaways:

"One. Our Julie has exposed a Federal legislative bill-drafting mistake of unprecedented dimension. A mistake that went unrecognized all the way through Congress. I wonder if our President actually signed the bill before it was corrected.

"Two. Our Congress passed a bill creating illegal Federal Government contracts with healthcare insurance providers that also have enormous built-in inflation consequences.

"Three. Our own Colorado state government has concealed and probably enabled improper cash distributions out of state to a major healthcare insurer that's hiding its debt from state regulators. I suspect lawyers could spend years arguing about the legality of that scheme."

Darwin nods his head in agreement, then turns toward Gudinov. "So, Boris, what you got?"

"Not a lot. Mario summed up Julie's thesis quite nicely. I think her work is not only scholarly and impressive but also of enough contemporary significance that her ACA insights should be sent to our Colorado Congressional delegation."

D'Angelo frowns his skepticism, "Yeah, right. Any chance they'll pay some attention to it?"

"Not much," Darwin responds.

"Or even understand it?" D'Angelo continues,

"Not much." Darwin again responds.

"Dammit," Gudinov chimes in. "Can't you see what's happening? It's like our own Federal Government has incentivized a huge segment of American business to commit treason. Any chance Congress might revise the ACA to prevent healthcare insurance companies from maximizing direct healthcare costs?"

Darwin's expression remains glum. "No chance," he says.

D'Angelo's turn again. "And what about the apparent duplicity of our own state regulatory commission? It's helped continue a thinly-concealed scheme of fraudulent extractions of cash from Colorado by an insolvent insurance company in order to make payouts to stockholders in support of its stock price? Shouldn't we pursue that?"

"What?" Darwin shakes his head thoughtfully. "Embroil and maybe jeopardize higher education at CU in a likely dispute originating with a student's thesis? No way."

"Hell," Gudinov adds. "Maybe Julie's just plain wrong."

"Well, dammit, maybe she's right," D'Angelo continues. "She convinced me, and I have a PhD in skepticism."

"Okay, troops." Darwin holds up his hand, palm outstretched. "Check signals on these important, but still peripheral, issues. Let's get back to our mission here today. In order to finalize her Master's Degree, does Julie have our endorsement of her thesis?"

"Absolutely," D'Angelo responds. "I want to be among the first to congratulate her on a brilliant as well as successful effort. Her thesis showcases her talent and tenacity, not just for research but also for a deeper probing into something that doesn't look or smell right. Her eventual calling may be in investigative journalism. I hope so."

"Boris, you agree?"

"Uh-h-h, of course." Gudinov's unenthusiastic response and squinty eyes show some hesitation.

"Okay. Done deal." Darwin stands up. "Let's get back to the presentation room and..."

"Whoa...wait," Gudinov interrupts. He still has a quizzical expression on his face and waves his hand at Darwin. "Hang on a minute. Maybe there's something else we should consider. Have either of you in the last...what...five years since the ACA went through Congress...seen or heard any media commentary that might further validate what our Master's Degree candidate claims she found in her scrutiny of the ACA and one of its healthcare insurance providers?"

Two head shakes are followed by, "Nope."

"So," Gudinov continues, "the three complaints Miss Anders just emphasized are huge deficiencies inherent in the original legislation and in its application. Shouldn't those have come to light and been exposed before? Not all our media are agenda driven into an absence of reason. What if Julie is just flat wrong?"

"C'mon, Boris," D'Angelo responds. "Who cares? Her insights are brilliant and are in a document hardly anyone is ever gonna read."

"Well, I care." Gudinov is still frowning. "It's hard to accept her insights when it seems no one in America's hyper-aggressive broadcast or telecast news scenes has ever commented on either of these two legislative blunders or on the improper financial manipulations by a leading healthcare insurer. Why didn't anyone else focus on them?"

"Try this explanation," Darwin responds with a broad smile. "It's because Miss Anders has unique qualifications. Either of you know of any high-profile big mouth news commentator from any network who is a genuine numbers expert?"

D'Angelo and Gudinov look at each other and shake their heads. D'Angelo adds, "And now I have a final comment. It's on some of her thesis content that she did not include in her presentation today. Again, she showed with examples how far medical costs, particularly for surgeries and hospitalizations, have inflated the last few years, a reality that's masked by the paper write-offs healthcare providers represent they have to take in order to accept the amounts Medicare and other insurers are willing to reimburse. Like the billed amounts are two to five, some even ten times the amounts providers eventually accept from insurers. It's mind-boggling."

"Beyond our ken," Darwin shakes his head. "And also far outside the boundaries of human reasoning. We shouldn't waste our time on that irrational aspect of the demented dollar dimensions of America's healthcare environment." He shakes his head again and continues, "So...okay then. We have an outstanding Master's Degree candidate waiting. Even Angel Bright gives her a top prospect ranking, an evaluation she seldom awards to anybody. Who knows?" Darwin pauses and, with an enigmatic smile, adds, "Our Miss Anders just might be a great match-up with Dan Panders, that new boy-genius who has his own primetime show on MRABC...at age 29. Or maybe they'd clash. He's an Ivy Leaguer. Most say he's brilliant, charming, and dynamic. Some say he's also an over-educated, narcissistic, womanizing, ego-maniacal jerk. I think his critics are mostly jealous of his early success. Remind me to mention his show to her...and include both the positive and negative comments."

"Anyway," Darwin shrugs his shoulders and continues, "anything else about our candidate we need to consider?"

Gudinov scowls and responds. "Her attitude maybe? Sometimes she comes across as harshly judgmental and contemptuous."

D'Angelo replies. "Again...c'mon Boris. She's just self-confident, and not really overly so. Network news is about to gain a great...what should we say? A great apprentice?"

With a chuckle, Darwin expands, "And so what if she's got some attitude? Aren't we all that way sometimes? Hidden or obvious, don't we professors often try to protect our social intercourse flaws, our pomposity, and our own selfish sense of intellectual superiority behind a cloak of academic self-righteousness? We're not here to judge Julie's character or her personality. Let's go give our Julie a green light. Even Angel Bright gives her a top prospect rating, an evaluation she seldom awards to anybody. Also, our acknowledging the excellence of her thesis is an endorsement of her scholarly effort, not necessarily of her conclusions."

THREE SMILING FACES reveal the committee's decision before Darwin speaks.

"Miss Anders, we're unanimous. Congratulations. You've got your Master's Degree. Well earned. Use it well. You've been a model student. You've been diligent in following whatever path your obviously natural curiosity led you to. May your keen intellect and incisive insights enrich the lives of all those you connect with as you pursue an exciting career in Broadcast Journalism. We're confident of your success and will follow it with pride that you've had your basic training right here in Boulder, Colorado.

"To add an employment opportunity tip to our session here today, you might consider applying for a position with The Dan Panders' Show. It's a relatively new network news commentary on MRABC. You may have watched it. Be careful. The show's host has a mixed reputation, which we can discuss later after I close out this formal wrap-up to our session.

"And also...a reminder. Go Buffs. If your success in your chosen profession is substantial, which I'm confident it will be, and the occasion and opportunity both arise, please remember your Alma Mater with any financial beneficence that you may wish to bestow on the University.

"Now...to close...I think it's time for a round of well deserved hugs. Those of us who work these evaluation gigs are a sentimental bunch."

CHAPTER 8
DEBRIEFING
THAT EVENING

"SO, HOW'D IT GO, JULIE?" Her father rises to greet her with a hug and then answers his own question. "Whoa, maybe I don't need an answer from you. I can guess. You're wearing that wonderful smile that lights up your entire face, even highlights your freckles."

She laughs. "You know I inherited freckles from you. You don't need to comment on them all the time."

"Can't help it. On me, freckles are distracting. On you, they're alluring. Anyway, I'm guessing you passed the review with flying colors...as I expected. But you're home later than I expected. I know you were well-rehearsed. I could hear you talking to Shane and practicing before your mirror downstairs last night. But I was off to work early this morning before you got up. Didn't even have a chance to say good luck. So...was it a tough review?"

"Well, it's been quite a day. And, yes, bottom line...I now have a Master's Degree. All I have to do is decide what to do with it. I actually enjoyed my thesis review with the faculty committee, and I appreciated their complimentary remarks. But that's not all the highlights of today's events. I know tomorrow is Saturday and you'll be off work at least some of the day. But I won't be here for lunch tomorrow." A flush of embarrassment crosses her features. "I actually have a lunch date. Guess who with? No, don't guess. I'll tell you. Tomorrow

I'm having lunch with Jason-Jerrold Jennings. Jase, he asked me to call him when we first met. Do you remember that? Jase and his father Mark from...what was it, eight years ago at Beaverdam Creek Campground in Yellowstone. They were our rescuers...sort of."

"Of course I remember. Those two were an important part of our rescue."

"Anyway, it looks like my world may continue to be crowded with the letter J. Like it's some kind of common branding. I literally ran into Jase on the Boulder Mall late this afternoon. I was walking off my jitters and emotional highs from today's faculty review. And no, neither of us was cruising for a connection. The Mall was horribly crowded like it always is late Friday afternoon after campus classes are over. Then, all of a sudden, there we were, side-by-side and staring through the window of Patagonia's retail clothing store. I was prospecting for a gift you might want to give me in celebration of my second college degree, and he was shopping for some outdoor clothing for the Labor Day weekend holiday he and his father are planning. More about that later. But now, I gotta shower-off my stage sweat. Be right back for dinner. By-e-e-e. Love you."

"GREAT MEAL, PAPA. And thanks for the briefing on your work week. I've been so self-absorbed lately. I need to pay more attention to what's going on in your life. By the way, aren't we about out of freezered successes from our trout fishing? Is your Friday night grilling in jeopardy?"

"Are you leading up to something?"

"Sort of. You've suggested I slow down and take some time off. I need that now. The last 18 months have been intense, bordering on insane. Anyway, it looks like I was in the right place at the right time. We're both invited to join Jase and his dad for their Labor Day weekend holiday. Like it's a private reunion for the four of us at a ranch his dad purchased ten years ago on the Colorado River in Middle Park near Kremmling. 'A fisherman's private dream mile of the Colorado River,' Jase says. Has a sprawling log home for the owners and four ancient guest fishing cabins dating back to the 1890s. It's one of the last operating cattle ranches in Middle Park. Lots of early pioneer history. I said yes already. Can you come? I'll drive."

He shakes his head. "I really can't. Sorry hon. Too much going on at NOAA. After your heavy dose of advanced education, *you* need the extended holiday. Enjoy the break, and give my regards and regrets to Jase and his father."

"I will. Sorry you can't join us. Labor Day weekend will be a great start to rediscovering that luxury called leisure time. Maybe we can still have a father/daughter holiday after Labor Day?"

He frowns. "I'd really like that...it's been too long. But I can't. Too intense at work. Too much controversy swirling about climate change and Global Warming, and I'm buried in efforts to complete our annual studies. The Government's fiscal year ends September 30, and updates have to be completed by then. But now...back to your future. What's next for you?"

She shrugs her shoulders. "I don't know. I know what I want to do, which is to find an entry-level position into Broadcast Journalism...Network News, whatever the proper term is. But I'm not sure where I want to do it. My opportunities may be limited, because my search timing for employment is off. Most corporate recruiting for college graduates occurs during spring months, and I wanted to wait until I completed my thesis. So, here I am...a late entry into the job market.

"I did prepare a resume yesterday. But now it's pleasure first for me. Copies will go out to CBS, CNN, MSNBC and MRABC after I'm back from the holiday weekend. I also included an online link to my thesis. A long shot it'll get read, but a sure indication of serious interest if a recruiter does read it. MRABC is the newbie network among the four, and it wasn't on my original list. The Chairman of my thesis review committee suggested it, said that network has a new host for its prime-time news commentary. Dan Panders' Show it's called. I haven't watched it...not yet. Maybe I should. Like tonight. Wanna join me?"

"No way," Jules snorts. "You know how I feel about watching talk television. What I'd really like to do is read your thesis. Maybe I'll learn something."

"No need to read it all. Just know that the Affordable Care Act's title is an oxymoron. Healthcare styled USA is outrageously expensive, and that law is only going to make it worse."

"Now, you've really piqued my curiosity. I'll read it tonight. Save myself from the banality of Friday night television."

She shrugs her shoulders. "Sure Dad. Enjoy. Your comments are welcome. But my thesis is a done deal. An official document. No changes allowed."

PART THREE

INTERLUDE

CHAPTER 9

TRIPLE J RANCH

LABOR DAY WEEKEND, SEP 2019

FINALLY...WHAT A RELIEF, Julie sighs, as she exits old Highway 40 onto a dirt road and drives under a massive wooden sign styled High Chaparral and lettered JJJ! RANCH Shaking her head, she stops her vintage 2010 Subaru Outback, a high school graduation present from her father, and ponders her Saturday morning driving ordeal. *Whew, should've stayed on Highway 40 and gone over Berthold Pass. Traffic out of Denver heading west was a nightmare. Always is on a weekend. Eisenhower Tunnel needs re-boring for at least four lanes, maybe six. A road-building masterpiece when completed, it was then the highest vehicular tunnel in the world. The builders never figured a Denver area growth explosion would make it one of America's worst weekend traffic bottlenecks.*

Eastern-slopers need escapes from the realities of a congested urban life. Visual scenes to the west taunt us daily with the allure of our own Colorado Rockies. Maybe I'll land a job where I can work from home. Dad and I are truly blessed to live in Colorado. But, what if I earn screen time at a network? Will I have to move? Don't think about it. One step at a time. Gotta turn off the job-search side of my brain, start enjoying a genuine holiday weekend with a new friend. Actually not so new.

When she steps from her car, she's greeted with ranch and pastoral river valley scenes she's never paused to study and appreciate before. She's at a T junction. To the right is a classic pioneer settler's clapboard ranch house...painted white. Stretching roadside right for a full 100 ft. to the north-side of the ranch house is a towering bank of hay-bales stacked ten feet high, fresh from a late August harvest. Enough winter feed for the ranch's...*what did Jase tell me...a herd of 200 classic Hereford cattle.*

In front of her is a fenced, rodeo-styled arena, with a deep-sand surface topping pockmarked with hoof-prints. To the right and occupying most of the roadside space leading to the south side of the ranch home is a huge, two story, traditional-styled clapboard barn. It's painted gray, not red. Parked in a massive lot on the barn's western edge is ranch working equipment that's not out for Saturday service. In view are a tractor, a front-end loader, a hay bailer, a horse trailer with a Triple J brand on the side, a pick-up truck also Triple J branded, and three other pieces of mobile equipment that are beyond Julie's meager knowledge of what is needed to keep a working ranch working. She nods her head at the scene. *Jase says managing a cattle ranch in summer is a 60 to 70 hour weekly gig for its manager.*

Noticeably absent from this modernized pioneer homestead setting are ghostlike relics from the past. The scene is pleasing, unlike that of many other rural homes, where ancient machinery, vehicles, equipment, and appliances memorialize local history as they haunt the present and litter the roadside...discarded, permanently abandoned, and left to rust quietly in the isolation of uselessness.

The ranch road extending to the left soon bends right around a corner of the arena. Now bordered on both sides by a classic post and four-rail fence painted white, the road is an invitation down to the river's riparian corridor beyond. As Julie resumes driving slowly, she lowers the car windows so she can enjoy the subtle scents of a looming autumn and a lingering aroma of fresh-cut hay fields. Beyond the fence to the left, eight horses graze in an uncut pasture. *So, does the Triple J have real cowboys who work the cattle operations on horseback? Like, do any modern cowboys still ride horses? Really?*

To the right, there's first a brushy swale, then an open view of freshly-cut hayfields where cattle with calves beside them graze on the harvest's leftover stubble. Straight ahead is another massive vintage barn, also painted gray. A branding chute and corral with a wooden post and siding fence extends beside. There the ranch road makes another right turn and heads between two massive cottonwood trees.

Burnished bronze by impending seasonal change and given motion by a midday breeze, the tree-twins' few fallen leaves scatter-carpet the ground. They rise, weave, and dance about, defying the conclusion of life. Similarly, sibling leaves resist the inevitable autumn separations from host branches as they breathe and chatter together in celebration of continuing life.

Beyond, a wooden bridge invites guest passage across. Julie again slows her car to a crawl. *Of course. Jase mentioned a river-diversion. A man-made spring creek, he said. Named it JW's Creek after its creator, the Triple J Ranch foreman. Waxed eloquent about it. Of course...it carries water diverted from somewhere upriver, and it's not part of the irrigation system. Just crossed that. Irrigation water is ditched to the ranch road, piped underneath there behind me, and then ditched through the swale and into the hayfields beyond. This creek is bigger, and it's gin clear. What a romantic setting!*

She pauses on the bridge to look into the small pool below. There the water ripples, deepens, and then gathers before it flows over a rocky dyke and into a small lake beyond. She gasps. Sure enough, she can see two large trout holding at the edge of the surge-flow into the pool. Although she can't see it yet, she can hear the rush and babble of the Colorado River ahead, just beyond a third huge roadside cottonwood tree. *Like three patriarchs they are. Standing as natural sentinels guarding mixed vintage fishing cabins and a more modern log home. The compound must cluster among the groves of those smaller cottonwood trees I can see ahead. Of course...the spring creek I just crossed has to re-enter the river somewhere below the compound. So...I'm actually going to spend three days on a private island in Colorado's namesake river. WOW. How cool is that?*

As she approaches the river and the last bend in the road, she notices she has river-side company already. Two bald eagles stare at her from perches on parallel branches of the third patriarchal cottonwood tree. Their coloring is identical. One is slightly smaller. *Unmistakable. One of the few feathered species where a mature male and his mate are colored the same. Guess the American Bald Eagle is so dominant that the female doesn't need camouflage feathering. A neat visual welcome to the Triple J. Prophetic maybe? Jase didn't mention I'd be greeted by official living symbols of the USA.*

On the seat beside her are Jason's instructions e-mailed to her and printed out yesterday. Mostly still fresh in her mind, she decides to re-read them and stops her car again. They're thoughtful, lengthy, and composed using complete and grammatically unimpaired full sentences. *Seems he shares my aversion to quickie written intercourse.*

> Julie, I want to give you a preliminary introduction to the Triple J Ranch and its accommodations. So you feel welcomed into familiar territory from the minute you arrive. I don't like to refer to the Triple J as ours. The river and land here belong in perpetuity only to nature. We merely use them. Nature graciously tolerates our presence. Our compound isn't fancy. It is functional, at least when foul weather doesn't knock out our power. When you reach our island compound, the river bank is on your left. Pass the first cabin on your right. It's numbered 5. Cabin 4 is behind it and beside a bathhouse. Also pass the next cabin, which is numbered 3. Yours is the next cabin, numbered 2. With only one main room, it has a huge, L-shaped screened-in porch...and, yes, the mosquitoes are terrible in August, but mostly they're all gone now. Your cabin has its own recent bathroom addition, with a shower and hot water available...most of the time. It also has its own sink, another amenity our other turn-of-the-century cabins are missing. As in the

other cabins don't have running water. In springtime, your cabin hosts a roof-nesting pair of geese, a door-side hummingbird nest, and occasional skunk intrusions into the crawl space beneath the cabin floorboards. With Dad's approval, our ranch manager traps the skunks. For some extra money, he also used to trap and skin beavers, then sell their pelts. Because beavers kill so many trees, the prior ranch owners encouraged their thinning. There's no market for beaver pelts now so beavers again flourish here. But the trees suffer. It's a naturalist's quandary, a paradoxical problem without a really good solution. But, perhaps it's also a natural way of culling an overly-dense riparian forest.

A few years ago, The Nature Channel spent a week here filming a TV special on the life of beavers. When the camera unit crawled into its first beaver den, the stench nearly asphyxiated them.

There's another wildlife preservation here that's very special, perhaps unique. As a relatively new, but dedicated staffer at the Nature Conservancy of Colorado, I'm really intrigued with this nature accommodation by the Triple J. Makes me feel like the Ranch is making a valuable contribution to the preservation of an endangered species, a preservation that could never be accomplished on public land unrestricted and available for public use.

Our preservation effort beneficiary is a family of river otters.

We applaud their presence here. When constructing their dens, they begin excavating under water, then burrow up into high banks of the lake behind cabin 2. They also use high banks along the spring creek for the same purpose. They're reclusive, and we seldom see them, but their paths connecting to and from the river are obvious. So is their scat. When they're after a trout dinner, we occasionally see them porpoising in the river pool behind our cabin. This spring, when the lake was partially thawed but rimmed with surface ice, a sizable snow-field still clung like a mini glacier to the sharply- sloping lake-front just across the lake and below the bridge. Mama and papa otter and their two kits adopted the snow-field as their family sledding run. Dad and I stood and watched as they chattered playfully and slid down their private playground on their bellies, then skidded along the rim ice and into the water beyond.

River otters were extinct in Colorado until 20 years ago, when the Colorado Game and Fish Department restored them to the Colorado River here in Middle Park. One of the four transplanted pairs ended up at the Triple J, and their progeny have survived. Otters eat a lot of trout, and we're okay with that. We don't eat our fish. We hook 'em, torture 'em, then release 'em. So, which is the more savage...man or animal?

Although the source of JW's Creek is a river diversion, we credit that man-made mini riparian setting with providing ideal habitat for many river creatures. And it provides natural spawning beds for both our rainbow and brown trout. Sadly, our native Colorado Cutthroat trout are long gone. I think it's 40 years since they've last been seen here. JW's Creek has an intriguing history, and I'll brief you on that tomorrow.

Our compound road dead-ends just beyond your cabin at the more recently constructed log home where Dad and I are staying. We have three bedrooms, two real bathrooms, a real kitchen, an office for Dad when he has to work here, and even a gas grill outside. Also a television, the Triple J's only concession to modern times, which we rarely turn on, mostly for sports events. Dad and I both dislike viewing TV news commentary when we're in seclusion here, away from the hurried, sometimes frantic pace of our modern World. Maybe you can make a difference in that profession now that you're about to plunge into your chosen career.

Our compound still employs old-fashioned wood cookstoves that also serve to heat the other cabins. Those relics of pioneer times are over a hundred years old.

Don't be alarmed at that life-sized wood-carving of a giant Grizzly bear that stands in our front yard guarding our front door. And, yes, it will probably remind you of that Yellowstone adventure with your father way back when we first met...what was it now, eight years ago? And that was two years after Dad and Mom bought this ranch. Mom died a year later and never had a chance to fully appreciate the interludes of sheer joy and peace this small bit of a historic past provides. A genuine back-to-nature escape from the frenzied pace of our modern World.

Your cabin boasts an ancient electrical heat register that actually works. It's along the floor of your room, below a nice big front window. That window captures intense morning sunlight that bathes the cabin interior when the sun finally crests the cottonwood groves bankside across the river. The scene is a naturally pleasing mood-setter when you wake up. Cabin 2 also features an ancient radio, but it only picks up a few stations, and then the static is so bad most of the time you can't really listen to it. And you actually have a closet. It's overloaded with discarded stuff: ancient retired fishing tackle, related gear, and accompanying abused, abandoned, and maybe unwashed clothing...from decades of service to ranch fishing guests, some of whom weren't very tidy.

Cabin 2 sits only 30 feet from the river. There's a lone major tree in front, a gnarly old river-bank cottonwood bending 45 degrees toward the river with its roots exposed three feet in low water. It bows in perpetuity to honor the river flowing beside it.

Unfiltered by nasty consequences of human activity, our star-filled night sky will offer you untrammeled delight-viewing from two wooden sitting chairs in front of your cabin. Beside them, a massive wooden dining table with bench seating for six is perfect for outdoor lunches. Our ranch manager hand-crafted all three pieces years ago. They provide a functional and visually pleasing blend of nature's material gifts with an unusual man's extraordinary artisan skills.

So, welcome to el rancho primitivo, Julie. Hope it doesn't disappoint. We'll save Saturday lunch for you. And serve it on our huge west-facing deck, which overlooks our spring creek's return to the river and regularly treats us to magnificent mountain sunsets. Unfortunately our riverside setting does not give us a view of Colorado's iconic Gore Range of mountains, which comprise the west boundary of the Blue River drainage from the outlet of Dillon Reservoir all the way to Kremmling. There the Colorado River finally captures the Blue River just before our state's namesake river begins its white-water cataract run down Gore Canyon. That mountain range, the canyon that rims it, and a creek that runs west from Vail Pass through the Vail ski area are all named after an Englishman, Lord Gore. Not Al Gore. Don't think they're related. Not a great legacy. Lord Gore loved to shoot and kill wild animals, and that's what he came to Colorado for.

Bye for now. Can hardly wait to see you,

Jase

ps. In case you meet-up with our ranch manager before you reach the compound, his name is John Wesley. We call him JW, and yeah, he's named after John Wesley Powell. He's also referred to in this valley as Colorado's last real cowboy. More about him later after you've settled in. He'll likely join us this evening.

pps. Oh, yes, the Triple J Ranch is named not for me but after the first Jason Jerrold Jennings, a Colonial ancestor. Lightened during many generations, you can't see my heritage in my or Dad's skin color. However, like many Americans, my father and I are directly descended from a liaison between JJJ the first and one of his plantation slaves two centuries ago. I'm the first descendent to inherit his name. Thanks for that, Dad. More about our full heritage later...if you're interested.

Triple J Ranch described perfectly, and yes, I am interested in his heritage. Julie restarts her car and looks ahead. Smiling broadly, Jason stands in front of cabin 2 waiting for her. He waves a hand in greeting. When she stops, he strides around the car and opens the door for her. She exits the car. Then, with matching broad grins they share a long welcoming embrace. "Thanks, Jase," she says, "I'm enchanted already. More like blown away."

THAT ATERNOON, they tour the ranch riverside. "We'll bother the trout tomorrow morning," Jason says. "Afternoon fishing is dodgy, and we almost always get strong river-valley winds later in the day."

A small footbridge provides a crossing of JW's Creek just above its reunion with the river. Then, hand in hand, they straddle a wide and rutted riverside ranch path, which also carries overflow water from irrigated hayfields back to the river in summer. A four-wire barbed fence borders the hayfields. Where the fence turns 90 degrees to the left and runs on to the river, they open and pass through a gate and then enter higher hummocky and choppy ground strewn with dried cattle droppings and sparsely populated with cottonwood trees.

"Our calving grounds," Jason explains. "Pregnant cows are

cut from the herd in spring and sequestered here for calving. Except for JW's insistence on continuing a ranch-bred string of horses for cowboying, our cow/calf operation is modernized. All prospective moms are artificially impregnated. AI they call the breeding process. Bulls lose a passionate experience, but it's less uncomfortable for the cows.

"Come here in late spring and view the next major ranch event. Castration and branding in the corral you passed on the way in. We changed the cattle brand to Triple J, and now we've added an exclamation point to zest up the brand appearance. No way to modernize that operation. It's quite a scene."

Julie wrinkles her nose. "Ug-g-g. Wel-l-l, thanks for the invite back, Jase. But I think I'll give the late spring scene a pass. Not sure I want to witness emasculations of any creature. Now I'm seeing another Triple J fence ahead with what looks like a sign on it. Goes down to the river, where there's a cable stretched across just a few feet above the surface. It's an obvious barrier, but also one that seems easily circumvented. Just float underneath it or walk around it. So, what's the cable for?"

"It marks the Triple J's downstream property boundary and discourages river trespassers from floating through and walking or wading up. On both sides the sign carries a 'PRIVATE PROPERTY – NO TRESPASSING' warning. It's a duplicate of the cable/sign combination we have upstream where our ranch ownership begins. There are similar river bank signs on our ranch fencing that run from the river back to Highway 40 and separate our property from the two ranches upstream and downstream, which are now cattle-free, in public ownership, and available to the public for fishing. Just below us there's a small sliver of land remaining in private ownership around the founding homesteaders' family home. That's where JW was born and raised. His father still lives there. JW will give you more of a briefing this evening. If you're interested."

"Jase, yes. I'm interested. Fascinating stuff. So...the Triple J is basically surrounded by public land. Seems like a recipe for conflict. Is there a lot of fishing traffic on the public water?"

"Upstream yes. Not as much downstream. Although the river is mostly wadeable and crossable after midsummer, road access is still limited. The river is also accessible by an ancient trail down to the river from the other side. Another good story there. This evening JW may brief you on original Native American presence here. Over 10,000 years ago, they settled on a bench above the river and just above the dirt road that now accesses the public property from the river's other side."

"So Jase, I also get a pure American History lesson tonight. A-l-l-right. But, with public road access on both sides, and the inclinations of some Americans to go to places where they're not supposed to go, doesn't the Triple J still get trespassers?"

"Good question. Of course. But JW takes prisoners...when he can and when local law enforcement cooperates. He'll brief you on his technique tonight. We also get poachers here. This is Gold Medal fishing water regulated by the state's Game and Fish Commission. Only two trout 16 inches or bigger can be taken from the river, and only flies or single-hook lures are allowed.

"Unfortunately, violations both of our property rights and of Colorado's fishing regulations occur here. Fortunately they're not overwhelming...yet. A really egregious violation occurred last year. Before he saw us, Dad and I watched a poacher cast a bobber with a weighted and wormed hook into the pool just above the far-side sign. He proceeded to horse a big trout to the bank, scoop it out of the net, bonk it on the head with a rock, and then stuff it into a bulging gunny sack trailing behind him. Then he saw us and vacated the premises in a hurry. No iPhones with us that day. Nothing we could do. Doesn't happen often, but it does happen. I even considered feeling sorry for the bloke. The Kremmling lumber mill recently shut down, creating a mini-recession for the town, and I thought...what if the poor guy is out-of-work and has to catch some of his own meals? But, with the rig he had, even a poor fisherman could catch meals on public water.

"Hey, I see your eyes are starting to roll. We need to move on. We've got a mile to go upstream before we reach Triple J's upper boundary and complete your indoctrination into the ways of rivers...at least this one. At the rate we're going, we'll miss dinner. I'm doing the grilling tonight, and JW is in charge of telling more Triple J stories."

"Jase, I'm enchanted. And I hope I also have the natural curiosity all successful telecast journalists possess...particularly about our natural surroundings."

"Okay. Great. Next on our show and tell this afternoon, you'll see the two natural islands on Triple J property. You saw most of the artificial island created by JW's creek when you drove in.

"Upriver, the ranch river-side trail has twin ruts. That's from four-wheel ATVs used by predecessors and some of our recent ranch guests. Unfortunately, age, infirmity, and disinclination to hazard a difficult walking terrain are three characteristics of many who fish here. ATVs are a concession to modern times I don't approve of. But then, I've got younger legs."

AS THEY MOVE UPRIVER, the twin-rut trail alternates between higher dry ground and lower marshy ground. When they pass between the ranch corral and the river, an island looms ahead, and they approach an obvious river diversion. Jase pauses and points to it. "It's a man-made partial dam," he explains, "where the river cascades over and then dribbles through a jumble of rocks JW placed in the river with our own ranch equipment. That partial dam pushes the river right toward the island and squeezes it into the chute created between the rock placements and the lower end of the island.

"There at river bank left, you can see a circular and adjustable metal gate cemented into a concrete base. It controls the amount of water diverted into our spring creek. JW checks the control gate regularly and adjusts it as necessary to maintain a consistent flow of river water into his creek."

Julie adds a comment, "Sounds like an important part of ranch chores,"

"It is. And not one common to other cattle ranches in the valley. Other ranches may have some diversions for irrigation. But none has attempted to create an actual river diversion and maintain a creek that flows year round. This Triple J diversion is one of JW's many river engineering masterpieces. It also requires a lot of JW's weekly attention."

"So, how does he adjust the control gate? Is it electrically powered?"

Jason chuckles. "No electrical power, just man-power. The control gate is a huge valve actually, with a big screw-top wheel on top that JW rotates manually to raise or lower as river flows dictate. Without adjustable water releases and JW's oversight, the creek could both flood out in spring and dry up in winter. Colorado River flows here in Colorado's Middle Park are regulated by water releases upriver, mostly from Granby Reservoir. That human interference into the natural way of rivers sourced in high mountains also created the biggest lake in Colorado.

"So, that's the origin of our spring creek," Jason continues. "And there at the end of the island is something else I want to show you. It's all natural and untouched by human hands." He points to an island cottonwood tree that sports a massive nest at the juncture of its first major branch that extends horizontally from the trunk.

"It's an ancestral nest, now occupied by I don't know what generation of Great Horned Owls. Biggest owl in North America, and we have two pairs who nest and raise their young here. Each pair has an exclusive on one of the two Triple J islands. The other island is maybe a half-mile up. We'll pass it just before we come to the upriver property boundary."

"Look, Jase, one of your owls is there now, blinking at us. You're the naturalist. Do their eyes blink that much? And I've heard owls can rotate their necks 180 degrees. Is that true?"

"That's two questions, Julie. Answer to number one. Owls are among the fiercest blinkers on the planet. They have three eyelids, one for blinking, one for sleeping, and a third for keeping their eye-tubes clean. And to question number two... owl eyes can rotate 270 degrees, not just 180."

"Okay, so enough owl trivia. What's next?

"How about some Colorado geography trivia?"

"Why not? Go for it. I need to liberate and nourish my curiosity."

"Okay, you asked for it. Colorado is defined by rivers, the mountains that spawned them, and the valleys they've created. Colorado rivers departing from the state follow the compass in all four directions. It's amazing how many of our great American rivers west of the Mississippi depend significantly on water originating in Colorado. Not just our namesake Colorado River and the Gunnison, its biggest Colorado-sourced tributary, but also both the North and South Platte Rivers, the Arkansas River, the Rio Grande, and the San Juan River. Also, one of the thirstiest areas of America relies on Colorado River water...southern California. Not that well known is that southern Cal's larger water source is not the Colorado but the upper basin of the Green River, which has more water flow at its juncture with the Colorado River in Utah than our by-then depleted home-state river can still deliver.

"Fortunately for southern California, the upstream demands on Green River water are far less than upstream demands on the Colorado. Why? No crowds of people in Wyoming or northwest Utah. And, unlike the Colorado River, there are no diversions of naturally western-flowing water into tunnels underneath the Continental Divide to quench the thirst of agricultural and urban development along the eastern slope of the Continental Divide and spreading out into the great plains. So, enough geography?"

"Interesting stuff, Jase. Thanks. I'm a native Coloradan too, and I've never read or heard such a brief but comprehensive summary of our state's home river impact elsewhere. Impressive."

"Yep, and my riverside lectures are pushing dinnertime. Sorry. We'll leave the rest of upriver Triple J for tomorrow. When we fish in the morning, I'll show you the big head-gate at the upper end of the property. It diverts river water into a historic ditch that's delivered irrigation water into all the local hayfields for more than a hundred years."

CHAPTER 10
COLORADO'S LAST REAL COWBOY

THAT EVENING THE LOCAL HISTORY LESSON reconvenes. Using work commitments as his excuse, Mark Jennings departs the dining table after dessert and heads for his corner office, announcing, "Jase, dinner was great. Thank you. And Julie, it was a delight to reconnect and get better acquainted. I'll leave JW as chaperone in charge of the rest of the evening. Breakfast tomorrow is on me. But I'm not much of a chef. We'll go into Kremmling and patronize the Moose Cafe, originally known as the Mangy Moose Cafe. Don't know why it dropped the Mangy prefix. Probably because it was too offensive to the local moose population, and they organized a town protest. It's still the town's only surviving historic diner, and many of the few remaining old-time ranching families congregate there each Sunday for a late breakfast of heavy-duty cowboy food. Lots of local historic photographs on the walls. Also a monster moose-head...of course."

Jason rises also. "Now, if you remaining two will excuse me also, I'll clear the table and do the dinner dishes. Then I have some catch-up work to do. Won't take long. JW, thanks for joining us for dessert. On the evening's agenda is a further briefing on Triple J Ranch history by you, for Julie. So you're in charge of entertaining...er enlightening...er maybe both. Miss Julie is in charge of listening and may excuse herself if you start to pontificate. I've forewarned her of your extensive repertoire of information. She understands you don't have a lot of opportunities during summer months to entertain non-family listeners other than horses, bulls, cows, and calves. Whoops, guess they're all part of YOUR family. And I should warn you. She has a voracious appetite...or maybe tolerance is a better description...for Triple J trivia. Or maybe she's just being polite and accommodating. Be careful, she might even learn something adaptable and suitable for programming by a television news network and featuring Colorado's Last Real Cowboy. Got a really nice ring to it, don't you think, Julie? JW earned it rodeo riding and refusing to modernize cattle management by using motorized vehicles. He still manages from horseback and has the broken bones to prove it.

"And JW, for your first featured appearance on television, you should keep it genuine and appear in all of the following: your cow-drool stained Levis with that hand-tooled leather belt serviced by its huge pure-silver buckle featuring an embossed image of a grand prize-winning, horse-sitting, bronco-busting cowboy in his first rodeo; your torn and sweat-stained red and white checkered flannel shirt; your cow-dung encrusted, socially unacceptable elephant leather-hided cowboy boots; your genuine cowboy-black felt Stetson hat, also badly sweat-stained; that colorful red and yellow polka-dot bandana around your neck; your horn-rimmed spectacles that make you appear deceptively scholarly; and that three-day beard stubble. No chewing tobacco though, and don't let those tobacco-stained teeth show. And, oh yes, under no circumstances are you to disclose who you work for. And..."

Julie finally intervenes. "Whoa Jase, obviously you two have developed a broadly-tuned camaraderie. And I'm sure JW literally would be a colorful personality to introduce to a television audience. But don't put the cart before the horse. I haven't even had an interview yet, let alone a job offer. And I make no promises to showcase a real cowboy if I do. If I do promise a showcase, I have a hunch I'll get a lot less delightful information from JW tonight than if I instead promise NOT to get him featured on television. Right JW?"

About to burst with controlled laughter, JW responds, "Absolutely, Miss Julie. For sure I ain't interested in playin' no phony stereotype dumb-ass, foul-mouthed, dressed-up cowboy for no phony TV show. And now Mr. JJJ the last, before I'm compelled in self defense to reveal your ancestral history to her, which is as colorful as your flawed description of my workday clothing, is it okay if Miss Julie and I adjourn to the couch in the sitting room and not turn on the television?"

"Yes, go. Sorry JW, about my denigration of your appearance. Most unworthy of me. Must have been the wine. And Julie, so you know, but JW won't tell you, he's an honors graduate of Colorado State University, with degrees in both Animal Science and American History."

IN THE SITTING ROOM, JW presages the conversation with a deep draw on a can of Mountain Dew and begins, "As you can tell, Julie, Jason and I joke around a lot. Probably a sign of genuine affection. I have two grown daughters but no sons. So, he may be sort of a surrogate son. Okay if I drop the Miss affectation and just call you Julie?"

"Sure," she says, still chuckling. "I have some knowledge of Colorado's agricultural history east of the Continental Divide, but not of the state's cattle ranching heritage here on the Western Slope. So, if it's okay with you, I'll practice some investigative journalism tonight. I'll mostly listen, and you're free to highlight Triple J Ranch history for me in your own personalized fashion. No need to sanitize anything. Got some unique stuff to start with?"

"Yep, pretty unique. On your tour with Jason this afternoon, you were exposed to some recent history. I'll cover earlier history, then some other recent stuff. And if you're still up for it, I can also take you back 120 centuries."

"Wow. That's got my attention. Go for it. I'm all ears."

"I suspect there's also an unusually keen mind behind the ears. First, I'll highlight a bit of Ranch history circa early 1800s. Among original settlers along the Colorado River here in Middle Park, the first owners of this ranch were Barney Hulse Day and his wife Suphronia. Their only child, also Barney, was the first white person born in Grand County.

"Now, fast forward to more recent times. I'll start with an unusual co-op arrangement between the Ranch and the state of Colorado. It's a program not currently active, but for many years the Ranch allowed Colorado Parks and Wildlife early access to the Triple J mile of the river before spring's snow-melt turned it into a raging torrent. CPW brought in a crew to net our spawning rainbow trout females. Then they stripped the unfertilized eggs for transport back to a state hatchery, where they were fertilized and eventually provided finger-ling trout for stocking in public waters. A neat example of private and public collaboration for mutual benefit. Because this property's been in private hands for so many years with public access denied, we still have what CPW calls CRRs, an abbreviation for native Colorado River Rainbows. That's actu-ally an oxymoron, because rainbow trout were never native to Colorado. Rainbows were introduced into the Colorado River system maybe a hundred years ago, and we still have some of their progeny right here."

"Nice arrangement JW. Was there a quid pro quo?"

"Yep. Of course. Our river mile got planted occasionally with state-hatched youngsters. Also, for many years we've received CPW approval for periodic river improvements to the Triple J mile of the river, at Ranch expense of course. You've seen the rock dikes angling downstream from river's edge into the center of the river. They serve several functions. They push water back away from the banks and prevent them from eroding when the spring runoffs peak. They also prevent adjacent road and roadside cabins from flooding. Pools form behind the dikes, and riffled water extends downriver from the ends of the dikes. Both are ideal trout habitat. We've also deepened other sections of the river and added boulder placements in the river itself, again to create and improve habitat for our fish."

"So, has the trout population improved?"

JW frowns. "In size, yes. But sadly, not in numbers of fish. We do have a few monster trout in the river, and they've had a long, happy life here. Except when they're tortured by fishermen looking for bragging rights about hooking, landing, and releasing a trophy fish. At a time when we also stocked hybrid cutthroat/rainbow crosses, the Ranch actually produced a World record cut-bow cross breed.

"But our trout population is declining, because populations of natural insects the fish feed on have dramatically diminished. Their river habitat is ravaged every year by toxic chemicals used in the Colorado Highway Department's snow removal from Highway 40. For example, the river's natural fecundity used to produce massive hatches of huge salmon flies in June. Every spring our River banks were festooned with their shell casings. It's an interesting metamorphosis. The bugs crawl out of the water and onto riverside vegetation. Then they dry in the sun and shed their casings to liberate their wings so they can fly around, dance, court, mate, return to the water to lay their eggs...and then die a natural death. Now most die an unnatural death long before they reach maturity. Sad.

"But we do still have grasshoppers along the river in summer, and also a few Damsel flies, another important and substantial food for large trout, which the pools we designed into my namesake creek produce."

JW pauses to drain his can of Mountain Dew in just a few gulps, and Julie takes advantage of the lecture pause to ask. "Any prospects for eliminating river contaminations from the chemicals used in snow removal?"

JW shakes his head and frowns. "Not really. There's nothing we can do. Now, about dealing with the frustrations of contemporary cattle ranching and fishing here in Middle Park and what's become the most controversial issue not only for the Triple J but also the few remaining private ranches in this valley. Also many other ranches throughout Colorado, mostly in summer and early autumn. Would you like a briefing?"

"Yep. I've just devoted a big chunk of my education to preparing for a career that's likely to push me into controversies of all kinds. Go for it."

"Okay, and this is also gonna get very personal. Conflicts between riparian ranch private ownership rights and increasing demands for more public river access are very contentious. The conflict mostly affects Colorado west of the Continental Divide. It's not really that complex of an issue, and it was supposedly resolved by a 1979 Colorado Supreme Court decision. It's personal because that court case resulted from a blatant trespass here on this ranch. The Court held that, and I quote, 'The public has no right to the use of waters overlying private lands for recreational purposes without consent of the landowner.' Underpinning the Court's decision is a fundamental Colorado law that land ownership along a river includes the river bed. Although that sounds simple and should be straightforward, it isn't.

"Subsequent media deceptions and an improper legislative intervention have compounded the problem. You sure you're okay with going into all this?"

"More than okay, JW. What you just said about media and Government is about to dominate my work-space, time, and attention. I think. Don't know for sure yet. Keep briefing. And it doesn't have to be brief. I tolerate lengthy. Had to in order to get an advanced college degree."

"Hokay. Stop me if I get too preachy. Several years ago, one of Denver's two prominent sports news columnists seriously misinformed his readers, although not likely with an intention to mislead. Basically, he ignored the Supreme Court's mandate and helped popularize the false notion that landowners have

NO restrictive surface rights. Because of public misconceptions, regular violations of our constitutional Ranch rights occur. Mostly in summer and most of which we can't really do much about. Ignoring the Supreme Court ruling, river floaters regularly come through without asking permission. It's heartbreaking to those few of us remaining who've spent an entire lifetime here...beside, on, and in the river.

"Violations also profane the resting place of many who've gone before. Literally. Their ashes were spread here, a symbolic honoring of the traditional 'may he or she rest in peace' prayer for those who've died. Yep, although the river rages in a runoff fury in spring, in autumn it also gradually works its way down to whisper in peace.

"Some examples. Not far from here, on a bend in the river and embedded riverside on a high south bank, are two bronze plaques memorializing the launch site 50 years ago of the contents from two funeral-ash urns. The deceased were lessee sportsmen who'd fished the river for 40 years before their deaths. That they used the river both in their lifetime and in their death commemorates not only their lives but also their love for the river and its riparian corridor. It's inspiring. They were Denver area physicians, and that stretch of the river is known locally as The Doctors Hole.

"For centuries, cliff swallows have also called The Doctors Hole their river home. Cliff faces on the north side of the river provide nesting outcrops, and the river itself has served them well. Literally. It provides incredible bug hatches for their evening meals. The swallows dart about, swoop, dive, and then glide along just above the river surface as they harvest dinner for themselves and their nestlings. It's an uplifting sight. Sadly, as the river's bug life has diminished, so has the number of swallow families."

JW pauses...deep in thought for a moment, and then continues. "And I think I'd also like to tell you about Bob Craig, a former part-owner of this property. About Bob..."

"Sorry to interrupt," Jason enters the room and intervenes with a hand on Julie's shoulder. "Just passing through. Had a text message I need to talk to Dad about, also to the two of you sometime. Yeah, it's about my work. As you both know, lots of dedicated people also work some on weekends, even on holidays, even a naturalist working for a not-for-profit organization."

Julie's right hand moves up to cover Jason's hand on her shoulder. "Lots of things still going on this evening, Jase. I have something to talk to you about too. Okay? Later?"

Jason excuses himself out with an, "Okay. Later."

"About Bob Craig," JW continues. "From the manor-house library I've brought two books in I want to show you. Both are rare first editions and author inscribed by Bob. They're mountaineering classics and among the Ranch's most prized possessions. They stay here in perpetuity. Not to be removed from the premises. The first book is *Storm and Sorrow in the High Pamirs.* It's the book Bob wrote about the 1974 expedition of women climbers he led into the Russian Himalayas. Bob also contributed to the second book. It's titled *K-2 the Savage Mountain,* and it commemorates the 1953 American expedition to K-2. Yes, that's the same year Everest was first climbed. Had a fierce storm not held them captive for five nights in the death zone at 26,000 feet in elevation, Bob and his companions could have been the first to gain that summit. It's one of the great survival tales in all of mountaineering literature.

"The point I'm making here is that when Bob died in 2015, his ashes also went into the river....in front of Cabin Two actually. Of all the places this man's wanderlust took him, such was his love for the Colorado River and our tight little island that he wanted his remains here in perpetuity.

"The river has also received the ashes of many beloved canine pets, after death took them away from the river banks and ended their harassment of our fish.

"Now, getting personal again. To stand on the bank of this

historic river and watch flotillas of boats, rafts, kayaks, and inner-tubes drift by brings a powerful sense of personal violation. In a conventional perspective, the Colorado River here barely qualifies as a river. It's more like a stream, and in late summer and fall, its deeper pools and runs don't exceed three feet in depth. Not until it picks up the Blue River and Muddy Creek below Kremmling and then enters the gorge farther down does it grow big enough to be navigable in a conventional recreational sense. That's where legitimate business use of the river by commercial outfitters offering guided river trips really begins. It's painful to see the river here, maybe 25 miles above the commercial stretch, used for illegal public entertainment, whether unguided or professionally guided. To me and others who live in the valley this illegal use is also a desecration bringing feelings of deep sadness that are not easy to describe. Some of that sadness is an instinctive fear of extensive environmental abuse that always seems to accompany overuse by humans, a condition that leads to eventual and unavoidable degradation of our natural surroundings."

Julie pauses him with a hand to his forearm. "JW, that's a very perceptive and totally rational reaction. I think many others would sympathize with you. We're living in an age of widespread environmental concern. Support for restricting environmental predation from human activity is extensive. Sorry I interrupted. Please go on."

"Thanks, Julie. Appreciate your sensitivity. And now back to Ranch rights. Confusion deepened later when The Colorado General Assembly enacted a statute declaring that it's not a crime to float through private property, providing the floater doesn't touch the streambed or banks. This legislation has been widely misinterpreted as permitting river access without landowner permission...period. Wrong. Our state legislature cannot override a state Supreme Court constitutional right decision. That requires a constitutional amendment approved by a majority of registered voters.

"Although floating without permission is not a criminal trespass...unless the trespasser does touch river banks or river bottom...it's still a civil trespass which entitles the landowner to pursue a damage action. Yeah, right, good luck with a civil action for damages.

"And criminal trespasses still occur. More frequently every year. That's because this mile of river is un-floatable without touching the bottom or the banks, except in springtime when the runoff pushes river flows to a near flood-stage that makes it unsafe for floating. Being blunt about it, in summer and autumn most all floaters will actually commit a crime. Because they never ever ask for permission.

"To use a crude example. If an unpermitted floater gets out of the boat and stands in the river or squats on the bank... or on one of our islands...to pee or take a dump, he or she has committed a crime. The most common criminal trespass is bouncing and scraping along the river bottom as boaters come through our many rapids. In summer and autumn, it's not possible to float our river mile without this occurring. In many cases boaters have to get out of the boat and wade the rapids in order to guide their boats through safely.

"Then, there's a systemic problem with enforcement of landowner rights. Enforcement officers may consider them petty law violations that don't warrant arrests or even warnings. So, if I report a violation to the Sheriff's office, the response may be, 'Look, I don't have time to come out. Just tell the violator to get the hell out of the river and don't come back.' If an officer does come out, the dialog goes like this. The trespasser says, 'I'm sorry officer, I didn't know I was trespassing.' The officer responds, 'Didn't you see the "No Trespassing sign?"' The answer, 'No sir, I didn't.' Or they get into an argument about needing landowner consent. So the officer just issues a warning. Now, if the trespasser is also fishing, he or she may forfeit a license, and that's a serious penalty. Just the threat of forfeiture should be an effective deterrent to trespass.

But it isn't. Plus Jason's a softy. Last summer he apprehended a mother with a pre-teen son who were trespass fishing above the upper island. "Please be our guest," was his response.

"Now that there's public water both above and below the Ranch, river access is easier. Reality is that the Colorado River through the Ranch becomes more of a public playground every year."

Julie's frowning, and her eyes are squinty. "I understand JW, and I'm getting sympathetic depression just listening. Your concern is contagious."

"So, enough of my complaining. You ready for some genuine ancient history."

"For sure. I'm still in investigative journalist mode. So... turn the time clock back for me."

"Okay. The time clock goes way back. Back 12,800 years to hunter-gatherers who spent long winters on the benches of Barger Gulch just across the river from the Triple J. It's a Folsom site, one of very few sites in America from that ancient time. Archeologist Todd Surovell has spent nine seasons gathering a museum quality collection of artifacts and studying the site, and he has a new book coming out about his research and findings. Should be available in a year or so. My personal contribution to his collection of archeological antiquities was an ancient rhinoceros skull that I retrieved from the Triple J river bed 20 years ago."

Rejoining the conversation, Jason signals another time out. "Okay you two. I've got something I need to tell you. Then, can we all adjourn? It's late, and JW needs his sleep. This time of year he's up before dawn every day to work on a long chore list that never gets short."

JW shrugs his shoulders. "Sure, Boss...er uh, Son of Boss. Good timing. I just finished the brief ancient history lesson."

Jason turns to Julie. "Okay if we conclude your interview of JW?"

"Sure, Jase." She pauses to turn and touch JW on his shoulder. "JW, thanks for the briefing. You've continued my introduction to a very special place with a fascinating history. And it was also great interview practice. Jase told me you've performed in rodeo arenas. Maybe I really should take you into the arena of talk television someday...if I ever have that opportunity. You could become a star...with no risk of being bucked off. Now Jase, what you got for us? Sounds mysterious."

His expression sobers. "I guess it's an official announcement. The Nature Conservancy wants me to tackle a three-month assignment in Chile. To bolster our presence there. Our state director is an Argentine with incredible conservation and legal credentials. He's also a helluva effective leader. And, yeah, although I'm not fluent, I can speak a little Spanish. I needed foreign language credits for my college degree, and I picked what I thought was the easiest. I said yes to the assignment, and now I'm outta here in a week or so for my first trip ever into a foreign country." He pauses and frowns. "I'll miss the Triple J's gorgeous early autumn, a time of genuine serenity here. And Julie, can we talk more after JW leaves?"

"Sure Jase."

As he heads for the door, JW claps Jason on the shoulder. "Congratulations Jason. And good luck with your assignment. Our fish will miss you. Me too."

Julie squirms in her seat. *Like I've just started a relationship with a fascinating guy, and now he's on a foreign assignment already. O-h-h, stop being so self centered.* "Jase, that sounds really exciting. Congratulations from me too."

"Thanks you two."

After JW leaves, Jason and Julie sit side-by-side on the couch. Jason turns toward her, clasps her right hand in his hands and gazes deeply into her eyes. "So, now Julie, enough about my future. It's your turn. What about you? Any surprises in your future?"

She shakes her head. "No surprises...I hope. You know I'm

about to enter the job market. For something other than waitressing, as we've already talked about. And Jase, I am interested in learning more about the Jennings family history, particularly after hearing JW's comments. I'll tell you my history if you tell me yours. So, before we end my briefing, can we switch back to the past? Like most Americans, both you and I are apparently descended from immigrants."

"Okay Julie, time for family history. You first."

"... SO JASE, THAT'S ABOUT IT. Yeah, I don't know much about my family history. Just nothing there back before my paternal grandparents emigrated from Denmark apparently you're the one with colorful ancestors...literally...who go way back into American history. Tell me about them."

"Aw-w-w, JW was just teasing, being literal. Nothing really unique or all that unusual about my ancestry. Like many other descendants of Colonial immigrants that settled in the south and became plantation owners, I'm of mixed blood, but you can't see it in my skin color. Probably because the African side of my heritage has been diluted through a bunch of generations without replenishment.

"Anyway, my grandmother on my father's side became really curious about her husband's family heritage and did the research. Apparently I have a great-great grandfather who died of Civil War wounds. He and a son, my great-grandfather, both fought for the North. The elder was the great-grandson of the liaison of a colonist plantation owner with one of his African slaves. Still a slave at the time, that ancestor accompanied an eldest son half-brother who gave up his property ownership birth rights to flee the south and disavow slave ownership.

"Dad tells me we might qualify for taxpayer funded reparation payments if we lived in California, even though we certainly don't need the money. That's an absurd program.

He's thinking about establishing a specialized foundation privately funded by him and others of both pure and mixed black African bloodlines who have also been really fortunate. His purpose would be to help less fortunate Americans of black African slave descent. Assistance would be based on need. Not based on entitlement, which has become an emotional characterization without a rational foundation and based mostly on heritage. He'd insist that this effort not be politicized, stay in the private hands of philanthropists. No Government participation. He wants to avoid bureaucratic structures and media exploitations that public funding might be subjected to.

"There are many other wealthy Americans of mixed descent, but with darker skin color, who have traceable ancestry back to slave-owners, maybe also to the Mayflower. Hopefully, they would be interested in participating."

Julie removes her hand still clasped in his, rises, and yawns. "Fascinating stuff, Jase. Really. Please excuse the yawn. So...can we call it an evening now? My drive-over in the holiday rush to get out of the Denver-Boulder areas was tiring. Yours too?"

"Yep, mine too." He rises and then clasps both her hands in his. She returns the pressure, and he adds, "Maybe we both need a beauty sleep tonight to be presentable to our highly selective trout tomorrow. And there's no moon tonight. That's good for fishing. Not so good for finding your way back to cabin #2 in the dark. If you'll release me, I'll go grab a flashlight and escort you. And no, like this is not a poorly disguised plan to escalate an escort service to a seduction and sleep over."

Julie smirks, "Okay, smart guy. For your information, even after a long day, maybe I'm really not that tired. So, what if I say I'm actually attracted to the notion of an escalated escort service, exactly as you so aggressively suggested?"

"So, is that an invitation? Now who's being aggressive?"

"I'm not exactly sure Jason-Jerrold Jennings. Maybe we both need to be aggressive with each other. I can't think of a better way to celebrate the end of such a delightful day."

"But, what will my father say?"

"Don't tell him. Or, go ahead and confess to him. He'll probably applaud your great taste in women. I can also kick you out of cabin 2 before sunrise, and he'll never know."

"And what if I admit to you that I'm not very experienced?"

"That's perfect. I'll admit to the same deficit so we can explore more experience together."

"Julie, I...I really never expected this."

"Nor did I, even when I accepted your invitation and came over here solo."

"And to be totally honest with you, I don't think I've ever been so totally attracted to a woman before, both physically and intellectually...and so quickly."

"And I the same...u-h-h-h to a man that is. And Jase, do we call it fate that we met again? Maybe it was destined. And right there in the Boulder Mall...of all places."

"Yeah, how romantic is that?"

"Not," she laughs. "But, I'm so happy that it...well that it just happened. And at an incredibly right time in my life."

"And in mine."

"So, Jase, maybe this can really be the beginning of a truly loving relationship? For both of us? Can we seal that prospect with a kiss? Right now? Please."

They embrace, and she raises her lips first to his, then to his ear and whispers, "Enough of the verbal foreplay. Let's transfer to cabin 2 and go inside."

RESPONDING TO A BRILLIANT MORNING SUNRISE, a heavy mist is rising from the river. It blankets the riparian corridor in a ghostlike gray shroud. As Julie waits for Jason, her eyes are captive to the surreal natural surroundings. Her thoughts remain captive to the realities of the night before...and their implications. *A night of self-realization and unbridled passion? Yes.*

Oh my God yes, beyond my wildest imagination. What have we done? More like, what have we begun? Enough agonizing. No self-reproaches. Let the drama play on. Will it endure through Jason's absence and his service to nature in South America? And also survive my hopefully beginning a career in Broadcast Journalism? So soon, so far apart, and for so long do our paths diverge. Will they reunite?

Like a phantom in the mist, Jason approaches cabin 2 from the family manor-house. An ear-to-ear grin bisects his features. *He's still thinking about last night, too.*

"Maybe a change in plans for today, Julie. Just checked the weather forecast. Bad storm warnings for western Colorado start tomorrow afternoon. I know we were both planning a late-day return to Boulder then. Let's rethink that, get out of here earlier. Then backup tomorrow into today. Plan A was to fish here today, then sneak away tomorrow for a day hike of the Devil's Causeway in the Flattops Wilderness southwest of Steamboat Springs. How about we check out of here now and do the hike today? Then on Monday we'll grab a couple hours of morning fishing on the river and still beat the storm and most rush-hour traffic back to Boulder. What do you think? Your call. I'm just the tour guide."

"Jase, you're a lot more than a tour guide. So sure, let's go to Plan B. And...so, where is it exactly we're going? The Devil's Causeway, you said. So, after a night of delight, we're gonna do something that sounds really sinister?"

"Absolutely, and to balance out today's adventure, I promise to guide you to Angel's Landing on our next outing together. It's Zion National Park's pre-eminent hike."

"So Jase, we go to hell first, and then sometime in our undiagnosed future we get resurrected and seek redemption in a rise to heaven?"

"Of course. Can you really think of a dynamic duo of destinations more romantic, more diverse...or more unusual? Might be a good idea to call your Dad, let him know where we're going."

CHAPTER 11
THE DEVIL'S CAUSEWAY

ABOUT TO PULL AWAY later on Sunday morning, Jason shifts back into park and excuses himself. "Sorry Julie. Forgot something." He returns to the manor house, retrieves a ring binder, and brings it back to the car. "Here's some homework for you to read along the way. It's an unpublished short story by an outdoorsman who's not prominent and unlikely ever to be prominent. He's also a fisherman with a Ranch connection and an occasionally hyper imagination. Although the story is a bit unusual and deals with some nasty problems in an unhappy marital relationship, it also gives you an accurate preview of where we're going today and how we're going to get there. I thought you'd enjoy it. It's obviously fictional, but it's also an appropriate briefing for today's adventure...better than anything I can verbalize for you. Read it now while I'm driving. It's not that long. Although I don't think it will, if the story discourages you from doing the hike...we can always turn back."

"Hokay Jase. Sounds intriguing." Julie retrieves the manuscript from its folder and begins reading as Jason leaves the Ranch and turns West onto Highway 40.

IN THE DEVIL'S FOOTSTEPS

On the highest sunlit ridge, well above the last grove of stunted, wind-disfigured pines at timberline, two figures trudge upward in silhouette against the summer sky.

The taller one leads; the smaller follows closely behind. Shadows trailing, they travel where moccasined feet haven't trod before. Nor does a game trail guide their way. They're first to seek solitude's redemption in a place where the earth and heavens join.

When they reach the ridge-crest, they pause to rest, their chests heaving, their breathing labored. Ahead and expanding fanlike to three horizons is a broad alpine plateau, imaging an immense mountain massif shorn of its peaks by some unimaginable force. Rippling in the wind, lush fields of grass cover a flattened, treeless vista. The pastoral landscape fills with open, sun-drenched spaces...vast, humble and inviting, a transient presence of serenity ever vulnerable to sudden storm.

Clouds advance across the plateau, descend too closely and threaten a forced mating of land with vapor. No rain yet falls, but a peaceful scene abruptly turns hostile and unforgiving. Serenity disappears. Darkness extinguishes the afternoon sun and envelops the sky. Light flees, and earth no longer gilded relinquishes her splendor. Lifeless gray images tarnish a landscape turned barren by lost definition.

As if rendered soulless by their vanished shadows, the two figures shudder at what they see. Directly before them, a natural hazard interrupts passage to the plateau. Now gradually descending, their ascent ridge pinches into a long narrow causeway of canted and jumbled rock rising from sheer cliff faces on both sides.

Instinctively, the man turns around, raises an arm, and shields the boy with his elk-skin cloak, providing fragile protection against a frightening way forward and the mounting fury of a summer storm beyond. Behind and below, their pathless way back widens into a beckoning pass. The man gazes over his shoulder and frowns. His eyes dance along the causeway, searching for a route across.

Dare they attempt it? His headshake is barely perceptible. Then he returns his gaze to the pass and grimaces. Must he turn back, retreat to safety...and to shame? Another headshake. Uncertainty torments him. Reality threatens his aspirations.

An angry gale shrieks across the plateau toward them. Over the causeway it races, loud and fierce like a pack of raging wolves. Lightning streaks the blackened heavens, and giant crooked arrows of fire strike close by, blinding them with unearthly brightness. Scorched air singes their throats and lungs. From rocks beside them an electrical buzzing erupts, like the hiss and rattle of a hundred venomous snakes. Booming thunder deafens them with ominous threats from gods who smite invisible stone mountains in the sky. More punishing than external elements, fear pummels them from within.

The man gathers his son close to him and feels two small arms lock around his waist. In an appeal for mercy, he turns once more to face the storm, frees a hand and raises it, palm toward the sky. But the tempest offers no abatement. A look of despair crosses his lined features. "No my son," he whispers hoarsely. "We dare not cross, and we cannot go around. It's a place for evil spirits, not for us or others like us. We've been warned. No one should climb higher than the trees."

Slowly they retrace their steps, wind snarling around them, sleet spitting in their faces. The man weeps silently, but two tears trickle down his impassive face and reveal his lapse of stoicism. Disillusionment remains unforgotten.

- CENTURIES PASS -

Through leftover night mists a Basque shepherd plods along behind his charges. His cheerful whistling hovers in the unmoving morning air, like a wakening song from the first spring bluebird.

His sheepdog keeps the flock moving steadily forward as she runs back and forth around its flanks, barking commands and nipping at the heels of stragglers. Young lambs mewl, protesting the forced pace. Dams bleat an anxious response. Delivering unheeded warnings, ravens circle above and scold harshly. Relentless camp followers, coyotes yip in the distance, a reminder of the need for constant vigilance. A blended cacophony of all these creatures drifts across a steppe-like plain covered with nutrient-rich alpine grasses and patches of lingering snow.

Following no trail, only his instincts, the shepherd seeks a new, more generous pasture in a higher, untrammeled plateau. Yesterday's horizon is tomorrow's promise.

The ground narrows and loses shape in the mist. The flock slows, then stops, and the dog takes her usual shortcut to investigate. She leaps from sheep-back to sheep-back in a swift but bumpy dash to the front. Through the turmoil of milling, confused animals, the shepherd makes his way more slowly. From a gap in the mist, a narrow span of uneven rock and eroded earth emerges, a ghostly, shattered causeway connecting land, cloud and sky. Cries of terror fill his ears as the shepherd arrives too late. Pushed beyond safety by frightened animals behind, his three leading sheep lose their footing a few feet across the arch and fall. Feet scrabbling at nothing, they disappear into a cloud-filled abyss. Blocking further passage, his dog lies motionless on a rock, panting, silent and remorseful, her head between her forepaws, tongue lolling, eyes downcast.

Cautiously the shepherd lies down beside his dog, peers over an edge and strains to hear sounds from the cloud-clogged void below. Silence confirms his expectation, and he sits up, makes the sign of the cross over his chest, then pets his dog and strokes her ears, offering her needed reassurance. Through the clearing mist, he looks forward and studies the traverse connecting to safer ground too many paces beyond. Searching each rock carefully, he tries to visualize where feet and hands might find a secure passage across. His frown of concentration breaks into a smile as he speaks, "Es possible...eh perra?" Then he laughs and raises his fist in defiance. "Madre de Dios, not even in high passes of the Pyrenees did I travel such a terrible traverse. Sendero del Diablo we will call it...eh perra...footpath of the Devil. None should attempt such a crossing."

- DECADES PASS -

Appearing ageless and indistinguishable from a distance, a couple moves unevenly up the mountain path. Neither carries a pack or rain slicker. Both wear dirty tennis shoes, soiled cotton shorts, and sweat-stained tee shirts. Los Angeles Dodgers baseball caps perch atop their shoulder-length blond hair, and a pint-size plastic water bottle swings from the forefinger of each right hand.

From the left front pocket of the man's shorts, an iPhone protrudes, crowded by an overhanging roll of flesh. With eyes only for the trail in front of him, he strides rapidly ahead at a forced pace. Walking more slowly, his companion pauses and kneels down. She brushes her fingertips over a wildflower's petals and sighs at the dewy freshness of a returned caress. "Harold, look at this patch of Columbine. No wonder it's Colorado's state flower. It's bluer than the sky and its form is perfection, like a motionless ballerina. And there, all those red-blossomed shrubs surrounding it...Indian paintbrush, I think. I've never seen so many intense but different shades of crimson. It's all so...so spectacular."

He glances back and then turns, hands on hips in the universal posture of impatience. "Jesus, Maureen," he shouts. "Our fourth stop already. Are you okay?" A straining voice betrays his effort to suppress anger and express concern.

Rising, she resumes an unhurried pace. As she approaches him she mouths, 'Fuck you, Harold,' in a hoarse whisper, intending for him to hear but believe she didn't want him to hear. With satisfaction, she sees an angry glare flash across his face before he averts his eyes. *Coward*, she thinks. *When he's resentful, he's afraid to look at me.* Then she speaks in loud, insolent bursts, "So...what's your hurry?"

His words are tightly controlled and emotionless. "I'm not in a hurry. Just tired of waiting for you...as usual."

"Then don't wait. Go at your own pace."

"But you can't keep up. You're struggling."

"You don't get it. I'm not struggling. I'm just not in a hurry. Where we're going isn't important; how we get there might be. I want to admire the flowers.

"Where we're going is also spectacular. It's in the wilderness."

"Wilderness. Right. You're the one who's so eager to have a wilderness experience, and then you bring along that stupid iPhone."

"So my office can reach me."

"Your office can manage without you. You're not that important."

"Thanks for your high esteem."

"I have even less esteem for our destination. Why The Devil's Causeway?"

"Because I want to cross it."

Always what he wants. "Why?" she challenges.

"Why not?" he responds.

"Because it sounds evil...a place named for the prince of darkness."

"It's not evil. It's just a name."

"Names always have a reason, a history."

"Maureen, you're being difficult."

"Me difficult? At least I'm not trying to impress anyone with how fast I can go up the mountain."

"You think that's what I'm doing? Trying to impress someone?"

"Certainly not me. You haven't impressed me for ages."

For the first time, his words are animated and full of emotion. "Now it's you who doesn't understand. I want to go fast. It makes me feel alive. It's exhilarating...all that adrenaline going and my heart pumping...the blood pounding in my arteries...and it's like...it's like...you know...making love. Well...almost."

"You mean like we used to make love," she smirks.

His voice turns petulant. "Jesus, Maureen. That's not my fault. It's you. You've become so...distant...and unavailable...and untouchable...like your flesh has turned to stone... hard, cold gray stone...nothing left that's soft and warm."

"Harold, I can't stand it when you sulk like a frustrated, hormone driven teenager."

He now looks and sounds forlorn. "Well, I can't get the feeling with you anymore, and I sure can't get it from hiking if I have to dawdle along the trail."

She knows the forlorn facade is just another of his false personas. "Then, don't dawdle. Go. Go fast if you have to. Leave me. I give you permission to leave me."

"But...you'll lose the trail."

She gestures ahead of them, where thousands of determined feet-filled boots and shoes combined with decades of erosion have worn multiple ruts cutting deeply into the soil between rocks. "Harold, quit faking manly solicitude. No way I'll get lost. You're not trying to help me. You just want to find fault with me. Quit pretending you're so concerned."

"Okay, so I'm not concerned. It's hard to be concerned when I know you're going slow on purpose, just to piss me off."

"Maybe you shouldn't hike so fast. We only arrived from sea level yesterday, and where are we today? Maybe 11,000 ft already. So high in the stratosphere we both have trouble breathing normally. I'm the one who should be concerned. You're not a kid anymore. You're 44. You drink too much, eat too much, and still smoke dope like a college dropout. And you're in terrible physical condition. Look at your belly roll. It's disgusting. That's why you can't make love to me anymore. You've indulged yourself too much, gotten too heavy and awkward. So you've lost your desire...for me...for most everything."

A grim smile of triumph crosses his features, and his voice turns mocking. "No, my love. My desire has merely lost interest in you."

She raises both arms and thrusts her hands forward as if to force him away. "Just go Harold. Go find your precious feeling somewhere else."

Shrugging his shoulders, he turns his back and stalks off, a disapproving frown frozen on his face.

That she claimed the last word brings her no sense of satisfaction. Tears she would not permit him to see finally well in her eyes, and she rubs them with a knuckle. She sniffles and brushes a wrist along her nostrils. When she turns and sits on a lichen-covered rock, a chill dampness penetrates through to her skin. Grimacing, she stands up again, brushing at her backside. *Now I gotta put up with a cold, wet butt as well as an asshole husband.*

As she gazes back along the way just traveled, her mood turns dreamy, and she focuses on a blue lake shimmering in the distance. *Stillwater...like me.* Lowering her gaze, she kneels down and smiles transfixed at a clump of purple flowers next to her where a yellow and black-banded bumblebee busily prospects for nectar. She debates putting a hand in harm's way, deliberately courting an angry sting. *Could an insect's barbs be more painful?*

Wheezing with shortness of breath but determined not to abate his pace, Harold moves rapidly upward, hoping distance will ease the pain of argument. *She always scolds me, and then she accuses me of finding fault with her. Why is she so hostile? Menopause maybe? Already?*

Thirty minutes later, panting painfully, he breaches timberline, pauses and gazes ahead, where the trail switchbacks up a steep mountainside before him. Exercise euphoria deserts him and misgivings assail him. He suppresses feelings of inadequacy. *At least I finally can see where I'm headed. That high ridge arcing up to the left of the pass must be it. One of northwest Colorado's most scenic wonders. Wonder why they call it The Devil's Causeway? Gotta rest now, before I tackle all that steep stuff. My head hurts, and my legs are burning and shaking. Better not sit down, though. Don't want to cramp up. Whoops, gotta pee...bad.*

Urination is stingingly painful, and a sudden gust of wind redirects his stream backward, drenching his left knee. He tries to correct and splatters his right shin. Finished, he grunts to bend over, brushes at his wet places with his fingers, wipes them on his shorts and then massages his bulging, trembling thighs. He backs up to lean against a boulder, gulps water from his bottle and sucks noisily on the last drops. Then he extracts a Hershey bar from his back pocket.

"Damn," he exclaims, "melted already." As he sucks the chocolate from its wrapper, sticky ooze spreads to cover his fingers. He licks them greedily and then wipes them again on his shorts, adding brown accents to the yellow stains already present.

From below, a spare figure approaches. Long silvery hair frames a deeply tanned and sun-wrinkled countenance. Undimmed by age, clear blue eyes gleam with a knowing look of wisdom earned and saved.

"You passed my wife?" Harold asks.

"Yes. Maybe 400 yards back. She asked me to tell you

not to wait for her."

Good. "Was she okay?" he asks.

"Seemed to be. She was climbing well and at a steady pace."

God, the old guy looks fit. "You headed for the Causeway?" Harold asks.

"Yes, and you?"

"If my legs can keep going."

The man smiles and points to Harold's tennis shoes with a walking staff. "The wrong footwear doesn't help. Try taking small steps and then lock your knees briefly with each step. It rests your leg muscles."

"Thanks for the tip." Harold watches enviously as the man strides off with an easy, effortless rhythm. *The old guy devours yardage like a silver-streak tailback. Must be over 70 and isn't even breathing hard.* Determined not to be outpaced and ignoring protests from muscles drenched in lactic acid, Harold struggles onward.

Afternoon clouds are beginning to form as he gains the pass. A cool breeze assails him, and he shivers. The sweat-drenched tee shirt now plastered to his body chills him. His feeling of triumph is premature and short-lived.

"Aw shit," he gasps as he gazes at the trail, now ascending steeply and step-like along the ridge to his left. "It gets worse."

Preoccupied with the ordeal to come, his senses are too battered to enjoy the vistas that stretch for miles on both sides of him. He cranes his head upward and watches the older man scramble nimbly up a final rocky crest and disappear from sight. He turns and looks back down the trail. Maureen is ascending the first switchback. He sees her small figure pause, raise her head and look up at him, and then his vision blurs.

He doesn't see her right hand hesitate, then rise, then hesitate again and finally wave to him. Frowning, he abruptly turns his back. Frustrated by the impairment to his sight, he finds that by squinting he has enough vision to refocus on the trail ahead. His tired mind cannot think about Maureen now. It has but one focus: *I must complete the climb.*

Below, Maureen is encouraged by her steady progress but hurt by the perceived rejection. 'Bastard...Bastard... Bastard,' she mutters between breaths. *But I won't let him win. Not now when I feel so good. I'm not even tired. Harold was right about pushing yourself to hike uphill. Once you get into the rhythm there's a feeling of exultation. Must be all those endorphins racing around inside me, gobbling up negative feelings like little packmen.*

Heart thumping and breathing in wheezy bursts, Harold reaches the final rocky crest. His throat is phlegmy and constricted. Although he shakes his head and coughs, his throat doesn't clear. Before him, he sees a blurred outline of the older man standing motionless nearby, hair streaming in the wind. Harold rubs his eyes, but his vision doesn't clear. "Is it...much further?" he asks. His voice is hoarse and raspy.

"No, not really. It's just there." The older man points with his walking staff. "Maybe only 50 yards – all a gentle downhill on a narrowing ridge."

"And then?"

"Then there's an even narrower, eroding traverse of disorganized, weather-cracked and unstable rock, some of it loose, some of it gravelly, some of it slick, most all of it slanted toward one edge or the other. Sheer drop-offs on both sides, but not far across to safer ground."

"The Devil's Causeway?"

"Yes."

"You've already been over and back?"

"No."

"Why not?"

The older man smiles enigmatically. "I have a fear of heights."

"You? You climb like a mountain goat."

"The fear is in my head, not my feet."

"So...the Causeway is unsafe?"

"Not if you're careful. The crossing isn't difficult, just scary. Each summer hundreds of hikers and climbers come here, like pilgrims seeking a shrine. Many turn back, particularly the inexperienced, but others do cross successfully. A few of those remain upright, but most scramble on all fours. My reason assures me I can cross safely. Unfortunately, fear of heights is impervious to reason and seldom succumbs to courage. Fear hangs in my mind, persistent and defiant, like a hungry vulture feeding on a lifetime accumulation of mental carrion. Even trivia cannot drive it out. Fear is my faithful climbing companion."

"So...why do you climb?"

"Because not climbing is unthinkable. There are pleasures in climbing other than crossing a causeway, just as there are pleasures in life not derived from achievement. And a little fear is not a bad thing. It reminds me of my own human frailty. It helps me maintain a healthy balance between ego and humility."

"You've obviously been here before."

"Ten times I've come, seeking to cross that satanic arch. Ten times I've turned back."

"Whew. And you keep trying?"

"Of course. But nature denies my small gains. Each year I gain advantage over my fear and advance a little farther, but each year erosion also makes the passage more hazardous. Because one side of the Causeway has fractured and is sloughing off, I know that collapse of the entire arch is inevitable, and that contributes to my discomfort, even though I suspect inevitability may be centuries away."

"So...why keep coming? Why keep trying?"

A pause and an enigmatic smile responds. Then... "I'm an old man now with many achievements behind me. Also many failures. I no longer seek answers, and results are no longer important to me. They neither tempt nor intimidate me. There are few challenges left that interest me and no person left for me to accommodate, except myself. I keep trying simply to please myself. It's the effort that matters to me."

"Surely you will succeed some day."

"I'm not sure I want to."

"Why not?"

With a whimsical expression, the older man runs a hand through his white hair. "And after that...what?"

"Ah...yes. I think I understand."

"And you? You who are not young, but also not so old. What is it you seek here? Maybe to rekindle the impetuosity of youth?"

Harold looks forlorn. "Probably something like that."

"Or maybe tangible accomplishments to compensate for a troubled marriage?"

Harold is visibly startled. "Jesus, how'd you know?"

"I arrived in the parking lot and started on the trail before you left. But I saw how you and your wife glared at each other. Be careful. What you seek may not be found here in high mountains and open, limitless spaces. It's not a matter of external geography. It's internal. You must find what you seek within yourself, in your mind and in your heart."

Now pensive, Harold struggles with new, complex thoughts and remains silent. He attempts to refocus on the trail ahead and rubs his eyes again.

"Blurred vision?" the older man asks.

"Yes, it started when I slowed down. I can't seem to shake it."

"Lightheaded?"

"Very. The top side of my head feels like it's about to leave the rest of me and float into space."

"Headache?"

"Worst ever. Rest of my head feels like there's a jackhammer inside trying to blast out."

"Throat?"

"Like cotton...parched and all tightened up."

"Nauseous?"

"Now that you mention it...yes. I thought it was the candy bar."

The older man moves his head slowly up and down. His features show a look of concern, which Harold's faulty vision doesn't detect. "You're altitude sick, and it could be serious."

"How serious?"

"Life threatening. It can advance to pulmonary edema and a risk of blood clotting...or worse, cerebral edema when your brain virtually explodes inside your head."

Harold shudders. "Ugghh. That's serious."

"Did you bring a map?"

"No."

"If you did, you would know we're at almost 12,000 ft. Last year a 20-year-old Air Force cadet died from altitude sickness not far from here...on maneuvers at 10,000 ft. They couldn't save her, even with an experienced medic in camp."

"A woman cadet?" Harold asks. *That figures.*

The old man's enigmatic smile returns. "I know what you're thinking. Disabuse yourself of any weaker-sex notions. Many women rank among the world's best climbers. Women have more patience, more sensitivity to their surroundings, a lower center of gravity that gives them better balance, and they're less inclined to take foolish risks. The only climbing disadvantage women may have is lesser upper body strength, but that's frequently offset by stronger legs. Altitude sickness is gender neutral."

Harold frowns. *Just what I don't need, a lecture on the superiority of women.*

"And you're also badly dehydrated," the older man continues. "You can't produce enough tears to keep your eyes moist, and that aggravates your vision problem." He looks at Harold's water bottle, dangling empty from a forefinger. "Out of water?"

"Finished it long ago."

"Here, take some of mine. I carry plenty." The older man offers Harold one of the two flasks flanking a hip pack. "And here's two aspirin you should also take." From his pocket he removes a small plastic container and shakes two tablets from it.

Harold gulps the tablets, promptly coughs them up, tries again, successfully this time, and greedily drinks from the flask in a series of gurgling swallows. *What I really need is a joint.* "Thanks," he says, "I feel better already."

"Nevertheless, you should descend immediately."

Harold shakes his head stubbornly. "No way. I don't fear heights."

"It might be better if you did. Your fearlessness gives you a false sense of security. What you have is not a mind problem, like mine. It's a body condition unaffected by your mind. Altitude sickness is not a trifling or a sissy thing. There's no shame in turning back."

Harold can't bear the expectation of meeting Maureen on the trail still plodding upward. *What would I say to her?* "I'm not a quitter," he says.

"Your wife will think no less of you if you turn back now than if you foolishly continue."

Like he's reading my thoughts. "But...but, I will."

"Ummh. Preservation of self-image...the ultimate conceit. A last time, I urge you to descend now to a safe elevation."

Again Harold shakes his head but remains silent.

"So, what I say makes no difference." It's a statement, not a question.

"Not now," Harold grunts, eyes downcast.

The older man shrugs his shoulders and speaks softly, "Then...let striving for lost youth be its own folly." He strides away and begins quick-stepping down the ridge with gravity-enhanced vigor.

Paradoxically, Harold loses vigor when uphill steps are no longer required. On unsteady feet, he staggers down toward the Causeway, a grim look of determination stamped on a chalky face. He again squints to help his troubled vision and swats angrily at his trembling thighs.

"Move legs," he mumbles, "Goddammit...move."

Briefed on Harold's condition by the older man on his descent, Maureen anxiously increases her pace. Anger challenges her concern. *Why should I feel any responsibility for him? This stupid climb was his idea, his notion of an extreme adventure. The more I protested, the more he insisted. He doesn't care about what I think or what I feel. Why should I be concerned about him when he doesn't care about himself? Why is he doing this? It's like he's purposely tempting the Devil on the Devil's own playground.*

Panting, she reaches the rocky crest and sees her husband take a first hesitant step across the Causeway. "No, Harold, no," she shrieks. "Turn back. You must turn back."

From across the exposed ridge, wind gusts race toward her and devour her words. She watches in horror as her husband takes two more halting steps forward, then teeters unbalanced, arms flailing in the wind as if desperately searching for a handhold in space. His baseball cap sails from his head and dances back along the pathway toward her.

Abruptly, he drops to all fours and stabilizes his position. He rises again, but his feet slip on gravel-covered rocks. He falls forward, and his legs skid sideways to a sharply sloping ledge of slick granite. His lower body begins a slow slide over the edge. His hands grasp at a rock. It pulls free, and he inches farther toward a freefall in space. Finally he grips a well-anchored rock and pulls himself to safety.

Sobbing, Maureen forces her pace to a trot. "Stop, Harold, stop," she screams. Again, the wind swallows her cry.

Appearing unable to rise, Harold scrabbles crablike up and over a stubby tower of rock. He's nearly halfway across when Maureen pauses where the narrowed ridge becomes a fully exposed arch.

As if commanded by some unseen force, Maureen's eyes stray from her husband to the sheer drop-offs on both sides of her. Dizziness overcomes her, and a new anxiety pierces her mind like a stiletto. Fear renders her powerless and she sinks to the ground. Her heart pounds and her body trembles. She can progress no further. Harold's plight becomes subordinate to hers. *I have to get away from here...NOW.* Staring at her feet to avoid the terror on both sides of her, she sits down, leans back, and begins a reverse crawl on her haunches, using her heels and palms to propel her body backwards. She doesn't see her husband stop and pivot, levering his legs over the abyss in an unsuccessful attempt to turn around. His body begins another slide toward the edge, and, digging his fingertips into loose soil, he arrests his slide, pulls himself back to safety and finally resumes a slow forward progress.

When empty space no longer flanks her, Maureen's trembling eases and her heart rate slows. Then she stands and looks up. Harold is nearly across. She watches him crawl the last few yards on his belly, using his hands and arms to pull himself along. His legs stretch behind him, appearing useless as if paralyzed. He rolls to his back and struggles to a sitting position. His face is ashen and expressionless. Blood streams from a gash on his forehead. Vomit streaks his chin. He makes no effort to crawl back across the arch.

"HAR...OLD," she screams between wind gusts. Although she can see his eyes staring vacantly at her, he shows no sign of comprehension, no acknowledgment of her presence. Then his eyes close and his body slumps. The wind torments her with faint sounds of his labored breathing, a wheezing inhale followed by a raspy coughing exhale.

Why is he just sitting there? "HAR...OLD," she screams again. This time, no wind blocks her cry. She waves her arms and hands in front of her. "COME BACK HAROLD." There's no answering response, no movement, no sound of any kind. He remains slumped, head sunken, chin to his chest, arms crossed in his lap as if meditating.

Maureen shakes her head side to side. 'No...no,' she moans.

She feels an ice-cold squeezing deep inside her, a powerful surge of loneliness that punishes her already battered senses. Kneeling down, she plucks Harold's baseball cap from a rock crevice beside her. For a moment she feels an urge to cry. Instinctively, she brushes her other hand across her eyes, but there are no tears.

She rises again, very slowly. Turning her back to the Causeway and her husband, she retraces her steps back to the rocky crest and then pauses. *But what if he's badly hurt and needs help? Of course...he can use his new iPhone.* Then, as she begins the steep descent below, she smiles. *If it works up here.*

...END...

Julie replaces the manuscript in its folder and turns to touch Jason on the shoulder. "Jeeze, Jase. We're taking on an arduous and perhaps dangerous climb with quite a history, not just a hike. What'd I sign up for?"

"Just an exciting day with me. The Devil's Causeway hike is not really difficult, and not as hazardous as what you've just read implies. What'd you think of the story?"

"Mixed reviews. Strong characterizations. Particularly the older man. Not a nice couple though. Their marital conflicts seemed a bit extreme...but maybe authentic in contemporary reality. Nice author touches on imagining that Satanic arch's history. Gripping details of the climb. Seemed realistic. Genuinely scary rendition of that final crossing of the causeway. Weird ending though. Oh-oh-oh, JAY-SON, you wrote it, didn't you!"

"Yeah, I did. Dad has a sister married to a guy like that. They live in Los Angeles, and we don't see them very often, thank goodness. No kids, also thank goodness. Amazing how reality can be woven into fiction."

PART FOUR

DAN PANDERS' SHOW

OCT - DEC, 2019

Come, old broomstick, you are needed,
Long my orders you have heeded. By my wishes
now I've bound you.
Have two legs and stand,
And a head for you.

from *The Sorcerer's Apprentice*

CHAPTER 12
THE INTERVIEW

THE MORNING AFTER HER RETURN from the Triple J Ranch, Julie's computer delivers four e-mail responses to her job applications. Three are standard-form rejections. The fourth is from MRABC. It's not a rejection. "Whoopee," Julie shouts to Shane, still dozing beside her.

She dresses in a blur of motion, then races upstairs to join her father for breakfast. "Good news, Dad. There's a positive response to one of my job applications. MRABC is interested, and they want to interview me. More information to come, they say."

"Congratulations, Julie. Does that mean I'm about to lose my star boarder and you're about to move out and become a fully-fledged fledgling? I'll have mixed emotions about that."

"Slow down. I don't have a job offer yet. The interview may not be until October. The new position opens then, but they don't say where the new position is located, and I have no idea where I might end up. Their main studio and center of action is in Los Angeles...Hollywood actually."

MORE INFORMATION greets Julie when she returns to her workspace. It reads:

> Dan Panders will do the interview. You're under consideration for a new Apprentice position, recently created

for someone to do research and provide data support for our prime-time talk show programs. Danny's our lead host. No need to come to Hollywood for the interview. We have a new satellite studio and offices in Denver. He'll interview you there and will text you directions as to date, time, and location.

DAN PANDERS' TEXT MESSAGE is on her iPhone when Julie wakes up on Wednesday.

Hi Julie. Excited to meet you. Come to our new Denver LODO studio at 16th and Larimer after rush hour on Mon Oct 14. Say 10:00 AM. Timing OK? Let me know. Read your thesis last night. Impressive. Time for network news to revisit the Affordable Care Act and its awful fiscal consequences? Dan Panders

Wow! He actually read my thesis. Impressive. And he likes brevity. I'll respond in kind. But not until I get dressed. Doesn't seem appropriate to correspond about a job in pajamas. No, that's silly. This isn't face time. I'll text back right now, save what-to-wear anxiety for my interview next month.

Hi Dan. I'll be there. Timing is perfect. Thanks for sparing me from rush hour traffic. And I really appreciate your interest in me. Julie Anders

ps. Yes, it's time network news revisited the ACA and its fiscal disaster. I've also accumulated info on other important subjects.

ON INTERVIEW MONDAY MORNING Julie rises early. *Now, what clothes do I wear today?* She quickly decides. *Might as well go two-fors. Keep it simple. Wear the same new outfit I bought for my thesis review. It's the only garment in my closet styled for the Modern Professional Woman...whoever that is. Clothing selection straight from an internet website of the same name. Modern technology's gift to an unsophisticated college graduate...feminine gendered and facing her first job interview. Should be perfect for the modern professional workplace... whatever that is. So what if the website clothes highlight my freckles. My long auburn hair naturally accentuates freckles. Nothing I can do about it.*

Next decision. What shoes to wear? I've studied photos of Dan Panders on the internet. He's not tall. Probably about my height... 5 ft 8 inches. So...won't wear my only pair of high heels today. Don't want to intimidate him... if it's even possible to intimidate a prime-time media hot-shot.

Although her interview timing will keep her out of a congested commuting rush from Boulder to Denver, she also acknowledges she's in a rare situation she's not accustomed to. She actually has surplus morning-time available. Enough time to obsess about the new Apprentice position.

So, what will I do? 'Research and data support,' they said. Sounds like a perfect match. Only one Apprentice position? How many shows will I support? Where will I be located? Hope it's not Hollywood. Maybe it'll be Washington or New York. Intimidating, but might be good for me to get out of my comfort zone, face the realities of living totally independently. Gotta do that someday...unless I find an acceptable male crazy enough to propose marriage to my father's only child. He's spoiled me.

Will I office in an MRABC studio complex? Stay connected to where all the real on-screen action is?

Or will I end up in a conventional administrative support office in a conventional downtown big-city high-rise? Sounds like really uninspiring space. BORING. But, do I need inspiring space? Do I even want it? Is that part of my aspirations? Isn't what I do more important than where I do it? Is inspiring space available to an Apprentice? Does it even exist? How the hell would I know?

Or, in this modern age, maybe I'll office here in the only home I've known for almost 26 years? Here I can decor furnish and accessorize to suit my own taste...if Dad will let me relocate upstairs and convert our unused bedroom to work-space. Wow, I'd even have a great view of Boulder's Flatirons from that room's big bay window. But, would that view be too distracting? I'd avoid the banality of conventional office buildings and retain a Rocky Mountains flavor in my own private office... if Dad will continue to put up with my living at home. Should I offer to pay him rent?

But, if I office from home I'll miss the collegiality of a formal office environment. No opportunity to make new friends other than electronically. Couldn't participate in break-time and lunch-time chatter and gossip. I'd be saddled with a self-imposed isolation from others...except by using electronic devices. Would I feel like a prisoner in my own home, experiencing an interment like one forced on me by a catastrophic event or illness overwhelming the country?

Whoa, Julie. Enough. Quit obsessing. Quit being so negative. What will be will be. You don't even have a job offer yet.

HE LEADS HER TO A SEAT at a table for four in a small office. Then he takes the seat opposite. A huge grin dominates his features as he begins the interview. "Hi Julie. Please call me Danny. My mom always called me that, and I've never aged out of it.

"Welcome to our new studio here in Denver. Our Network Brass tells me you're the prime candidate for our new Apprentice position. MRABC is looking for a fresh face straight out of a post-graduate level college education, someone unsullied by working previously at another network. We've already ruled out two other candidates from this recruiting region. Both male, actually. And no, unlike some of our competitors, MRABC doesn't have a gender quota system for new hires. Rest assured we hire based solely on merit, and your credentials already blow away the competition.

"Interesting job title, isn't it? Apprentice kind of implies you'll work with a Master and eventually take over his or her job. Or someday maybe you and I will just partner up, call ourselves...in alphabetical order...The Anders and Panders Show. A&P for short. Sort of like that chain of grocery stores maybe? Just kidding. This new position supports all our network news shows. I don't get an exclusive.

"And, as you may have already guessed about me, I'm affectionately referred to by my colleagues as the 'resident smart ass.' The competition calls me 'Dan the Showman.' Not sure that's a compliment. So...enough about me. Our session here is mostly about you, and then any questions you may have about MRABC and about me. I'll start the Q and A with... why did you decide to go into broadcast journalism?"

If he can open our interview the way he did, maybe I can too. "Well, my Dad calls me the 'resident smart ass' also. So maybe that's why I decided to go into broadcast journalism...so I could work with others similarly afflicted. But, isn't that term generally reserved for exclusive use in describing the male of our species?"

Their laughter is spontaneous and unaffected.

"So...looks like we already have a couple of things in common," he continues. "Like a weird sense of humor and brazen cockiness. What else motivates you?"

"Well, my credentials might make me a uniquely qualified candidate. With an undergraduate degree in accounting and some accreditation in actuarial science bundled with a Master's in Broadcast Journalism, I'm confident I can bring to the profession an academic preparation that's special and especially needed. I know that a focus on numbers can be difficult to convey. Particularly to a viewing public in an on-camera but still verbally dominated environment. I think I'm up to that challenge."

"Okay, I get it. Your credentials are indeed unique. And, more importantly, I agree with you that they're sorely needed. Now tell me more about you, the person." With that, Danny leans back, crosses his arms over his chest, and adopts the pose of an experienced listener.

Uncomfortable talking about herself, Julie briefs him on what little she knows of her family history. Then she progresses to her undergraduate college classes, her waitressing work experience stemming from a determination not to borrow money for an advanced degree, and the intense classroom and related studies to conclude her college education. She finishes with, "I think I could make a difference in this profession, and I would really like to try."

"Okay then Julie. No decision deferral on this side of the table. Although there are a few other candidates being interviewed in other recruiting districts, I'm the decision-maker for this new position, and I've decided. I want you on our team. Bottom line here today is....you're hired. Whoops," he grimaces and shakes his head, "I neglected to ask. Any other job interviews or prospects pending for you? Do I have any competition?"

She purses her lips and shakes her head side to side. "Nope."

"Okay then. Can you start Friday?"

She grins and shakes her head up and down. "Yep."

He's grinning also. "Great, I actually have a first assignment for you. It's related to prime-time programming for my show, which begins in a new format just a week from now. But...we'll get into that later, probably Friday. Now it's your turn to ask questions. What do you have for me?"

She laughs. "For openers, where do I start work?" *Please God, don't let it be Hollywood.*

With his head bent and a hand now covering his eyes, he chuckles. "Sorry Julie. Guess I neglected that part. You'll start here in our Denver satellite studio. We have a really nice work-space. Big windows overlooking a multi-block complex of modern office buildings, street-side gourmet dining establishments, and hi-rise living compounds that have replaced Denver's skid-row tenements. Not many homeless street people here in this classy, urban-modern setting. And...the Colorado Rockies baseball stadium is also within walking distance. I suspect you already know all this downtown Denver LODO stuff.

"Or, there's an alternative. You can opt to work at home, use FaceTime when appropriate, use e-mail to convey your work results, come in here when necessary.

"Whoops, guess I also forgot to mention salary. Network Brass haven't decided yet. I'll push for top dollar. This new position is really important."

"No problem, Danny." She shrugs her shoulders. "The salary is what it is. I'm not in this for the money. I live rent-free with Dad in Boulder. And I've always been a cheap date. My bottom line is I'd like to join your team."

"Great Julie." He rises from the table, circles it as she rises also, and they shake hands. "Congratulations and welcome aboard. Now, I'd like you to see our studio and offices here, and also meet the rest of our staff. Then, if your schedule permits, can you have lunch with me at the Brown Palace Club? I'm staying at the Brown Palace Hotel...in the unrenovated section of downtown Denver. Lots of history and tradition there too. The Boettchers, one of Denver's most prominent founding and also philanthropic families, used to live there in the hotel's penthouse suite."

"Of course, Danny. I'd love to have lunch at the Brown Palace. Does dining at the palace make me a Princess?"

He laughs. "Of course. But then, does it make me a Prince... or a rogue? I'll leave that question for you to ponder. Now let's go on tour."

As she rises from her seat, her mind spins a few qualms. *What's with the name-dropping? I don't need to be impressed that way. Hope he's not setting me up for something else at the Brown Palace. Something other than just getting better acquainted. Oh, stop it Julie. Don't get paranoid. Danny seems like a genuinely nice guy. It does feel a bit weird though...calling him Danny. Seems juvenile. Too affected?*

THAT EVENING, DAUGHTER and father relax on the porch and celebrate her new employment with a pre-dinner celebratory glass of wine, for which he abandons his usual bottle of Coors beer. Shane relaxes supine at his feet. He raises his glass first. "Here's to you, my daughter and your new job. Or should I fancy it up a bit? Call it a position?"

"Yep, let's call it a position. Apprentice also implies expectations, both for me to move up...and of me to deliver. And now about dinner. It's my treat this evening. I know you do most of the cooking. But it's payback time. I brought home some fresh salmon. Will I be invading your territory if I do the grilling tonight?"

"No. Have at it. So, where do you start work Friday? You haven't said yet. I assume not Hollywood?"

"Definitely not Hollywood. Although I have the option of working from home, I'm going to the MRABC Denver studio and offices again on Friday. I'd like to work my first full day there to get better acquainted with the people and the surroundings. I was impressed with both in the brief time I was there today."

"And your network boss? Likes to be called Danny you said?"

"Yep, and I like him. I know his competition calls him Dan the Showman, and I wonder if he'll be ego-driven...and maybe difficult to work with...as that nickname implies. Hope not. And I really don't think so. But he does have a tainted reputation, based on comments from a college professor. However, my interview impression of Danny was positive. I think there's a lot more substance and depth to him than his nickname implies. He doesn't like what others call him. He's aggressive, yes. And, despite the last name his parents branded him with, I don't think Danny panders to anyone. Guess I'll find out."

"All that's good to hear, Julie. Do you have an initial assignment yet?"

"Not yet. That comes on Friday. Danny will be back in

Hollywood then, but he and I have a FaceTime scheduled on Friday morning. And sometime in the next few weeks I need to organize better home-office work space. Shane and I are tired of hunkering down in my garden-level bedroom below. That was okay when I was just a crazy college kid doing my homework. Now I need somewhere for adult work from home rather than student homework. Something more creative. How about I move upstairs into our unused master bedroom, treat myself to better above-ground views? I'll pop for any new furnishings needed. I know you have mixed feelings about that space...your and Mom's bedroom. Too painful for you to sleep there after she died. Too many memories. I get that. But, is it okay if I move up?"

"Absolutely. I'd like that. We should have done it years ago. That unused room haunts me. My memories fade. But they'll never leave me. That room should not be just a sanctuary for memories in a secluded space. Time that room serves to make new memories for you. Time I removed those photos of your mom and me together in the happy times. I'll transfer them to my bedroom. Please do move upstairs into the master bedroom. We'll call it the mistress bedroom. Shane should sleep upstairs too. I need the company.

"And now Julie...on another subject. About your love life. I know that you and Jason-Jerrold Jennings are maintaining a pretty heavy long-distance courtship via e-mails. How's that going?"

A big grin bisects her blush. "Really well so far. We're for sure compatible. Early every Sunday he e-mails in a really thorough...u-h-h, I don't really know how best to describe it. Love letter? Work description? Travelogue? Natural history lesson?" She shrugs her shoulders. "Combination of all four I guess. There's a three hour time difference between here and Chile, so his composition always greets me when I open new e-mails on Sunday morning. A really nice way to end the week. We don't do FaceTime very often. Jason says he's too tongue-tied and doesn't do well telling me spontaneously how he feels or what and how he's doing. He literally has to compose his thoughts first. He's a good writer. Most of the time. And I love his letters. He's also ventured into some serious fiction. Back in September, he let me read his first and only short story. Very creative. However, creative writing is not a career aspiration for him, at least not at this early stage of his adult life.

"Anyway, yesterday was our fifth long-distance date by e-mail. And he also included some photos. Not many. He avoids crowded tourist scenes where groups walk, gawk, and then take a zillion photographs to share with folks back home or on the internet. He says group visitors into southern Chile seem to trivialize their travel experiences by over-imaging what they see and assuming a vicarious enjoyment by others. He thinks many recipients of those photo-travelogues are reluctant to acknowledge any boredom, so they avoid criticizing the visual overload for fear of offending the sender. What photos Jason does send me always show an artistic touch in composition. They're never effusive or redundant. He prefers and really enjoys traveling on his own, more intimately and away from the rush and babble of crowds. He likes the feeling of being personally and directly imbedded in the Chilean culture, its people, and its natural surroundings. That way he avoids the diversions, delays, unrelenting background chatter, and other complications involved in group travel. Tell you what. Jason is visiting Laguna San Rafael in southern Chile this coming weekend, and I'll share his comments and photos with you next Sunday.

"I also try to respond to Jason in the same spirit he shows and the same format he follows. Although I sure don't have any travel experiences to share with him, I try to maintain an intense focus on the relevant that avoids the commonplace. Probably better than I'm doing right now with you in conversation. Actually, I'm saving all our correspondence for our children and grandchildren to read someday. For you too if you'd like. None of it's x-rated...yet. Whoops. I'm getting ahead of ourselves. No marriage proposals yet. Neither of us has proposed marriage to the other...yet. His out-of-country assignment has for sure interfered with any kind of conventional in-person courtship ritual we might otherwise be enjoying, particularly the physical part.

"And, oh yes. Now he's growing a beard but says he won't do another FaceTime or send me a selfie until he graduates from ruggedly and raggedly unshaven to moderately presentable."

CHAPTER 13
USA IS BANKRUPT

DANNY'S EBULLIENT MOOD is evident as he opens their Friday morning briefing session with a broad, playful smile. "Good morning to my show's new Data Demon," he addresses her. "Thanks for checking in on FaceTime."

Not sure she likes her new Network nickname, Julie suppresses the urge to frown, forces a smile back at the screen image in front of her, and responds, "Sure, Danny, I really appreciate being able to work from home or in Denver. I'm not ready for a move to Hollywood...not just yet."

"No problem," he continues. "There may be times when I'll ask you to be in our Denver studio before a live show or even during a show being taped for later viewing. Just be sure you always bring your work computer and iPhone with you, as well as that super-charged mind of yours. No booze allowed."

"Got it, chief."

"So, here's what you do need to know now, and it may occupy a bunch of your time today and tomorrow. Yeah, Saturdays are generally big plan and prepare days, so on most Saturday mornings stay alert for an early morning text message from me to begin our back and forths. As I mentioned Monday, next week my show's going to a different program format. I recommended it, and the Network Brass finally approved it. Beginning now, and for each week starting on Monday, Dan Panders' Show will try to devote at least one evening to feature an important subject not currently receiving much attention in other network news commentary, and I may need supporting weekend data work from you for each of these specials. Okay?"

"Danny, of course it's okay. I know I didn't sign on for a conventional work week." *Hope he starts with something I studied in PoliSciFi.*

"Good. And now, before we dive into your first week on the job, I need to brief you on some of the programming realities in this business." His playful smile departs. A grim visage and pursed lips replace his screen image. "It's something I need to do face-to-face. That's why I asked you to link-in on FaceTime. Bear with me. It may take a while. Think of it as a quick post-post-graduate course on the insanity imbedded in a lot of prime-time network news commentary.

"Like most other network talk shows, evening programming at MRABC frequently centers around what's perceived as current events, particularly late-breaking and attention-grabbing events. Dramatic and disturbing events are the Kings of Commentary. With adroit presentation, they can be elevated in the minds of viewers to systemic national problems or disastrous crisis situations. Those events always take precedence over pre-planning and may dominate my show for a string of evenings. What's important to our Network Brass is to seduce our audience into Oh-My-God reactions and keep them glued to the screen. Aberrant behaviors in our society are highlighted even though most of them can't be rationally extrapolated to endemic societal problems worthy of broad public concern. They should not be given so much prime-time focus, but, unfortunately, they generally are.

"Actually, even our Kings of commentary are also preempted regularly by the absolute Monarch of all prime-time television news shows...the Queen of commentary. And she is of course, in one simple word, 'politics.' She's very seductive to many viewers and, as in the ancient game of Chess, she's also more powerful than all the Kings.

Mostly, Queen Politico lives forever, never leaves the public scene, and is more adept than any other subject in dispensing divisiveness, agitating the insecure, promoting paranoia, and excessively influencing impressionable minds of others. When it comes to programming for the public stage, the national hyper-focus on politics has engulfed and infected talk television like a highly contagious and insidious disease. There's very little unbiased political commentary left in nightly news programming. Too much of it lacks in-depth substance and overly focuses on four defining de's of political news commentary: namely defame, debase, demonize and destroy a targeted political figure. Political scene commentaries dispense never-ending streams of fear and loathing. It concerns me that, like most of our competition, my Network Brass seem overly committed to political bias, and political neutrality is a difficult concept for them to accept. I try to maintain neutrality in my own commentary and also try to bias balance the guests on my show, something our competition rarely does these days. But I do have regular conflicts with my Network Brass about this approach.

"So, welcome to the harsh realities of prime-time talk television. Manipulating the minds of others is the name of the game. And...whoops...guess I'm obviously guilty of pontifications also. Sorry about that. Mostly I try to limit my criticism of the Queen to occasional venting in private conversations...like right now...and avoid it religiously when I'm blabber-mouthing something that political devotees consider essential on the TV screen.

"Now, back to Dan Panders' Show business. For our first week trying to develop a new format and challenge the drama seekers with more substantive programming, our go-to subject is actually a triage of three interwoven subjects for you to research. That is if we can work them into what I have to confess is still mostly a current-events drama show patterned after our more established prime-time competition. And, yes, our quest for more substantive material and subjects is an ambitious programming effort. Here's where you come in.

"Next week, if not preempted by the Queen, my show will tackle dollar-dominated subjects: federal spending, budget deficits, and America's debt. Right down your numbers alley. That's really important stuff, but never seems to get the substantive media attention it should. Probably because in-depth coverage gets complicated, can be difficult to present, and might be tough for a viewing audience to fully understand. Those concerns always torment thoughtful efforts not to become irrelevant by over-focusing on relatively trivial matters masquerading as important or critical. That's a modern generic condition that threatens the survival of genuine journalism in our excess information age. Call it too much prototype tabloid journalism transferred to the television screen. It's a verbalization by aggressive mouths, which are dramatized and enforced by a highly-selective camera focused on talking heads committed to sensationalism. Absent are thoughtful journalized considerations by sensitive and intelligent pens committed to carefully written presentations of all relevant information.

"So, enough of my ranting. What do you think of the three topics that comprise your first assignment?"

Bingo, Angie Bright sure called this one. "Great, Danny," Julie says. "I've already done some research and accumulated data on America's budget deficits and our national debt. Deficit spending and excessive debt were featured in a Political Science class I was required to take for my Master's Degree. Number one on the topics list actually. Plus," she chuckles, "here at home there's a resident outspoken critic both of Government overspending and of inappropriate Government interventions into the daily lives of Americans. He's called my dad, and he works for a Federal Government agency he's justifiably proud of."

"Ah, yes," Danny responds. "Fathers know best. Good luck

with your research today. I'll touch base with you tomorrow. Probably early. Probably by text. That it for today?"

"Yep. And thanks Danny...for your honest but disconcerting intro to the profession we've both chosen. And most of all for an actual assignment I'm interested in. I'll get on it and report back tomorrow. Probably by extensive e-mails. Over and out."

Whew, she sighs as she clicks off, *what have I signed-up for?*

"SO, HOW WAS DAY ONE on the job?" Jules asks his daughter that evening as they embrace at the doorstep.

"Well, in a single word, hectic. Other appropriate words would be interesting, enlightening, in a way discouraging, and for sure challenging."

"Julie, you beat me home this evening, and I didn't work overtime. Couldn't have been too hectic plus all those other words."

"Let's just call it an intense day. I'm tired, and I don't say that very often."

"Okay, so dinner tonight is on me. First, let's sit here on the porch and you tell me more about day one with MRABC."

"Thanks. I'd like that. Actually I just got home too. Like all Friday evenings, rush hour car traffic back to Boulder from Denver was intense and early. I'll get Shane. He needs some outdoor time. Maybe he'd like to hear too. Want a beer?"

"Yes, please."

He's seated and watching the sunset when she returns to the porch with Shane. First, handing him an uncapped bottle of Coors Light, she pats him on the shoulder and then sits down. "Yeah, today was really intense. Everything moves at warp speed in this business, particularly when there's a nightly show to program. Danny tries to stay a week ahead with pre-program preparations. But, there are always last minute changes. So he can jump into late-breaking events or that obscene scene that never ends...politics styled USA. My work primarily supports his show, and I already have information on the first subject I've been assigned. It was part of my classwork in PolySciFi.

"I'll provide more about the details of my first assignment at dinner. But here's an overview. It involves a major issue that never goes away, always warms up as the Government nears the end of its September 30 Fiscal Year, but doesn't seem to get much in-depth news coverage. Yeah, it's about money and how our Federal Government can best spend America to death.

"Politicians are battling over the size of next year's Federal Budget deficit. After only a few years' respite, America's deficit spending may again reach a trillion dollars. That should be newsworthy enough to dedicate a bunch of TV news time to the subject. Danny doesn't think that's happening." She pauses to frown and shake her head. "For many in the media and their viewing audience, is this just another 'been there done that'? Doesn't anyone care?"

"Whoa, Julie. I, for sure don't want to try and answer your enigmatic questions. So, like you said, let's just enjoy the sunset."

Julie sighs and her smile returns, "Perfect. Sor-r-ry. Guess I just can't disconnect that quickly. And it's also time I asked you more often about you. Now that I'm a bonafide, fully-educated, fully-fledged adult child who finally has a real job, we need more two-way show and tells. I want to be more attentive and show my concern for you. And also for your workday life, as it is now. Finally beyond its long dedication to the support and education of your only child. For that I'll be forever grateful. So, you take some stage time at dinner too. For now, will you please stand?"

As he rises, she opens her arms to embrace him. "Before we sit back down and really enjoy the views, let's have a big father and daughter hug. We both need it. I love you Dad. And now let's just relax. You have your evening beer, and we'll both watch the sun set. I need to unwind."

A TEXT MESSAGE ALERT greets Julie when she rises on Saturday morning and begins her day checking her iPhone. *Yeah, as I expected. Texting replaces e-mail as the quick communication vehicle for my new professional life. Much as I dislike texting. Too insipid. Can't be nuanced properly. Discourages thoughtful discourse. And what about old-fashioned phone conversations? Those out too? Looks like working weekends and rising before dawn are necessary. But, start a workday in pajamas? Gotta get dressed first, then read Danny's text and respond. Then have breakfast. Then get going on a longer e-mail. Prime Danny with what I think he's looking for.*

FEELING MORE PROFESSIONALLY DRESSED and now seated at her desk, she punches up Danny's message.

> Morning Julie. I'm sure you had an intense day in Denver yesterday. Appreciate your attentiveness. Government over-spending still concerns me and many others. What you got so far? I'll present it sometime next week. DP

She laughs at the message. *Sometime means when the planned focus isn't preempted by more pressing and dramatic daily events. Or by Queen Politico, that omnipresent adversary of rational thought.*

She texts back.

> Danny, I'll e-mail in a response. May take a while. Lots of research material to condense and decide how best to present. You always up and charging before dawn? JA

His response is immediate.

> Yep, always. The east coast is three hours ahead of me. Go have breakfast. I'll look for your comments later. DP

RETURNING TO HER WORK COMPUTER after a breakfast without her sleeping-in father, Julie sorts through her research notes and spreadsheets. *I'll start with numbers...as usual. Danny should call me the data donkey. Is that any better than the data demon? Should my workup be simple? No, dammit. Complexity isn't a proper reason to deny what's important. Dollar dominated topics need visuals in addition to text. Like tables and charts. Gotta use Excel spreadsheets. Try to keep them simple? No, damned if I'll dumb them down.*

'Danny,' she begins.

> I've developed information on America's annual budget deficits and our Federal Government's total debt position. I've also measured the relationship between those amounts and our GDP. That's Gross Domestic Product. America's debt-to-GDP ratio is an important tool used by most economists to evaluate America's ability to carry its Federal debt load. But economists don't calculate our national debt properly. What they present for public consumption is a gross understatement of America's debt to others. Bottom line is that by any rational evaluation America is bankrupt and probably has been for a long time. Yep, that's my opinion.
>
> 'Federal Government fiscal irresponsibility is frightening. For ease in copying and having a template for screen presentation, what follows is an Excel chart. I'm sending it on a separate page. I present only 26 numbers. Won't overcrowd viewers' minds unless their interest in the subject is minimal. Which it shouldn't be. To restrain myself, I've vowed never to exceed 30 numbers on any chart I prepare for presentation on a television screen. For this screen, I've highlighted and will discuss eight numbers.

FEDERAL DEFICITS, DEBT, AND GDP

Amounts in Billions

Fiscal		Annual Deficit		Total US Treasury Debt	
YE 9/30	GDP	Amount	% of GDP	Amount	% of GDP
2008	14,743	459	4.6%	10,025	**68%**
2009	14,418	1,413	9.8%	11,910	83%
2014	17,321	485	2.8%	17,824	103%
2019 –					
As expected	21,391	**984**	4.6%	**22,719**	**106%**
Adjustment by economists to reduce debt by that held by Federal Agencies, mostly by Social Security				(5,860)	
As analyzed (improperly) by economists				16,859	**83%**
Adjustment to add back the present value (1) of Federal Agencies' Indebtedness, mostly of Social Security, to third parties				13,900	
Proper relationship of Federal debt to GDP				30,759	148%

(1) As calculated and reported by Agency actuaries.

DISCUSSION:

- After apparently peaking in the recession year 2009, the Federal budget deficit again approaches the trillion dollar level.
- Total US Treasury debt has more than doubled since 2008. To $22.7 trillion. As a percent of GDP (in an improper calculation by economists) it's presented as an increase from 68% to 106%. Those percentages seriously understate actual Federal indebtedness. 106% should be 148%.
- To downplay the explosion in US Treasury debt, a prominent economist whose work I reviewed employed a fallacious downward adjustment to eliminate the amount of Treasury debt held by Federal Agencies, mostly by Social Security, improperly adjusting net Federal debt down to 83% of GDP.

- This adjustment promulgates a false sense of security about our massive Federal indebtedness. Because it doesn't recognize underlying indebtedness of Federal Agencies to third parties, again primarily Social Security obligations to its retirees. When those amounts enter the equation, as they should, Federal debt jumps by $13.9 trillion to over $30 trillion. Whether the economist purposely distorted his calculation to deceive or is simply guilty of a monstrous conceptual flaw, I don't know.

I haven't researched how other economists evaluate our debt-carrying capability. I suspect many of them use the same flawed metric. Otherwise, the consequences of America's escalating debt would attract more private and public concern. Our debt growth is unsustainable. Looming at some point on the horizon are enormous increases in income or other taxes and a clawback of entitlement promises to pay or to subsidize, of which the Affordable Care Act subsidies are a big component.

The specter of a disastrous default on Treasury Bond indebtedness stalks America's deteriorating financial condition. Rating agencies will soon be compelled to downgrade Government debt. Maybe they'll finally confess to the absence of any credible evaluation techniques in their rating process. It's like they just shrug their shoulders and say, "Hell, it's our own Federal Government, they'll never default, so we gotta rate all their paper trash AAA. What a hoax." End of rant.

For your show, you may want to bring in other economists and a CPA (or an actuary) and have them comment on the State of the Union's debt burden and its future implications. I suspect MRABC likes to have recognized experts guest on your show, and I haven't surveyed the field to see how other prominent economists view the debt-to-GDP relationship. You might try for Paul Krugman at the New York Times. He's one of the most recognized economists in America, certainly the most prolific. You might also consider Jeanna Smialek, another and younger economist at the New York Times. She's a specialist in the Federal Reserve. I don't know if either of those two is also a devotee of the flawed debt-to-GDP metric.

Or, go for a previous Secretary of the Treasury or Chair of the Federal Reserve. Lots of prominent names related to those positions. Alan Greenspan maybe. I think he's still around. Ben Bernanke and Janet Yellen also come to mind. See if any of those big names might acknowledge the flawed metric and provide an expert opinion about the likelihood of an imminent decline and fall of the mighty US dollar.

My consolidating add-back of underlying Federal Agency third party debt into our total Federal indebtedness is not rocket science. Any student who's done class-work in consolidations would probably suffice. Like a college sophomore maybe? Although rules shouldn't be necessary to apply to this situation...where it's simply a matter of sound reasoning, there may be some official accounting rules out there that apply. So you could try to get someone from the FASB...that's the Financial Accounting Standards Board...or perhaps the Chief Accountant of the SEC, or maybe even America's Comptroller General. Or maybe you'd prefer not to address a controversy initiated by your rookie Apprentice or Data Demon...whatever you want to call me. It's like...who really cares?

A final comment on USA debt. I saw one expert's financial model, which projected the ratio of Federal debt to GDP to rise to over 400% before the end of this century if current trends of excessive and irresponsible Government spending aren't reversed. So... is America on a down-spiral to economic death by overspending? Or does inflation also escalate to drive GDP to meteoric heights and keep the ratio in balance? Like with gasoline going to $20 per gallon? And the same price for a Big Mac? It's too much for my mind to wrap around.

So, those are my comments on the fascinating and confusing subject of America's looming bankruptcy. I have three more topics to send you...all relative shorties... about subjects related to America's debt. I'm still working on them. The first will summarize holdings of those who buy our US Treasury debt. The second will identify major department beneficiaries of the Federal Government's extravagant borrowing. The third gets into a more esoteric but still related subject of what might happen to the solvency of our commercial banking system if...or more likely when...our interest rates trend sharply upward from their present near-historically low levels. As undisciplined inflation continues to rise, so will interest rates. Rising interest rates will destroy the capitalization of many of our nation's banks, which have imprudently invested too much depositors' money in medium or long-term bonds. It's a speculative look into the future, which is a bit complicated, but I think it would be digestible by most of your show's audience. Whoops, change that reassurance. I think it might make them vomit.

Onward,

Julie.

ps. Or, have too many Americans recessed to the point where the size and implications imbedded in these numbers are beyond comprehension? Should everyone just relax, accept complacency as the norm, ignore the consequences of Government over-spending, and adopt the philosophy of what will be will be...nothin' we can do about it? Not me.

Now, I need a short break.

She presses the Send command.

WHEN SHE RETURNS to her workspace, Julie's iPhone is squawking. *Oh my God, has Danny responded already?*

He has. His text message reads:

> To answer your questions. Yes, the numbers and their implications may be beyond comprehension. But no, we can't relax. We have a duty to inform our viewers. Now I'll read the rest of your e-mail. Look forward (I think) to more brain damage coming. DP

Julie shrugs her shoulders and sighs. *Now, back to the computer and e-mail submissions number two, three, and four. Whew! Am I a glutton for punishment or what?*

> Danny, submissions on the three other important features of America's binge borrowing follow.
>
> SUBMISSION #2. Winding down fiscal 2019, holdings of the biggest buyers/owners of US Treasury Debt are...in billions (rounded) of dollars:
>
> 1. $8,000B Our own Federal Reserve (the Fed) system and Federal agencies.
> 2. $6,500B Foreign Governments. Japan and China lead, followed by the UK, Belgium, Luxemburg. Cayman Islands come in 6th place in the Foreign division.
>
> A speculation: how much of Cayman Islands' holdings are from offshore accounts of USA and other countries' citizens seeking income tax avoidance on investment earnings in this notorious tax haven country?
>
> 3. $2,200B mutual funds.
> 4. $800B USA depository institutions, ie banks.

5. $800B states and local government institutions.
6. $800B pension funds.
7. $400B Insurance companies.
8. $150B US savings bonds.
9. About $2,500B all other.

So, what happens if (maybe when) these buyers and holders of USA debt decide to quit buying...or worse, start selling? The Chinese have already stopped adding to their US debt holdings.

Or, God help us, what if our money lenders decide to unload their USA debt, either because they're running out of money or they've lost confidence in the American dollar? I can't wrap my mind around these two possibilities. It's clear that America's financial stability is vulnerable to the whims of others and the questionable validity of their judgments. Here's another aspect of marketability of US debt that news media doesn't cover. America's credit rating agencies lost credibility years ago when investors finally realized that credit ratings couldn't be relied upon for investing in derivatives or in Fannie Mae and Freddie Mac securities. The Gov stepped in then and bailed out a lot of stupid investments. There's no rational way credit rating agencies can continue to defend AAA ratings for Treasury Bond indebtedness. Ability to repay our debt is far too dependent on future conditions and future events, which have enormous imbedded uncertainties (like legislative bungling and the unwillingness of politicians to do sensible things on a timely basis).

Enuf. I need a break. I'm gonna take Shane...that's our Golden Retriever...on a two-hour hike along our foothill trails just up the street. That's where our local Boulder civilization ends...sort of...and the great Colorado Rocky

Mountains begin, only modestly blemished with human intrusions. Maybe Dad will join us. We'll do Mt. Sanitas, an historic foothills peak overlooking the town below. Or should I say city? Boulder is exploding and growing its own suburbs eastward into the Colorado plains.

Looks like I'm already into Dad's habit of working on Saturdays. "Price paid for devotion to duty," he says. I know that for him it's more than duty. He loves his work. Will I develop the same commitment? Also love my work? Hope so. Be patient. I'll conclude soon with my third and fourth e-mails of the day. They'll be short. I promise. I've already done the research. After a post-break burst of productivity, I'll probably be brain dead and call my work-day finished.

Onward, Julie

"DAD, THANKS FOR JOINING SHANE AND ME this afternoon. Great hike. I'll finish my Dan Panders' Show assignment in time for supper. I promise." Still on a high-energy, outdoor-activity boost and its emotional high, Julie separates from her father. She's confident she can return to her work station with restored enthusiasm. *Outdoor activity can refresh and stimulate the mind as well as the body.*

Then she heads back downstairs and frowns at her familiar but poorly lit garden-level space. *And a daughter's thanks also for encouraging me to move upstairs. Soon I'll work in natural light, and sleep beside a window full of stars.* Still panting, Shane follows her and takes his usual resting station on the doggie bed beside her computer desk. Her iPhone shows no text messages. Switching to her work computer, she accesses an e-mail message from Danny. She smiles and nods her head. *Thought he might need to respond with more than a text!*

Good workups so far, Julie. Intense. Maybe too complex for some viewers. But really important stuff. My staff started yesterday working on potential experts to join the show next week. Should we consider prominent politicians? They have the biggest mouths and love to grandstand for the press. I'll try to book a member of the House Budget Committee...or even the Speaker herself, then get Rand Paul to challenge the Committee and her. DP

ps Hope you develop your Dad's work commitment. Weekend work on the following week's shows is unavoidable. Make that up by avoiding weekday talk television, including my show. I won't be offended. Hell, watch Rachel Maddow's show for me. I have to compete with her in the same time slot every weekday night. You can brief me. About Rachel, her $20 million annual salary is tops in the business. Yeah, I know, you're not into the mad money thing. Good. I'm not either. But our Network Brass wants me to un-throne her #1 ranking in viewer poles. Mission impossible?

Julie texts back.

Prominent politicians are a plague on our society. But you've got great guest considerations going for the DPS next week. De-throning Rachel is likely impossible. Good luck. I'm disappointed with her. Don't watch her show anymore. My e-mail submissions 3 and 4 soon to follow. JA

Switching to her computer, Julie's fingers are soon flying again. *Glad I already did the research for 3 and 4.*

'Danny, here's e-mail SUBMISSION #3, discussing some of the Federal Reserve's balance sheet. The following data is as of Dec 31, 2018, in $ billions.

Holdings of US Treasuries	$2,302

Holdings of Government sponsored, mortgage-backed bonds	$1,684
Obligations to member banks for their deposits at the Fed	$(1,556)

Contrary to popular belief, the Fed's expansion of its balance sheet to these unprecedented levels (almost $4 trillion in bond holdings) is not just funded by printing more money. It's also based on increased deposits at the Fed by member banks.

There's a very significant accounting practice difference between the Fed and its member banks. A fundamental cause-and-effect relationship is in play. When interest rates go up, the values of US Treasury bonds and mortgage-backed bonds (like Fannie Mae and Freddy Mac) decline. Because its practice is to hold bonds until they mature, the Fed is not required to write-down its holdings to current market value. Conversely, major member banks holding **direct** investments in similar bonds are required to write them down to current market value. The conundrum here is that banks, **indirectly** through the Fed, are basically investing in US Treasuries and mortgage-backed bonds, which, if held directly, would require write-downs that might, in an environment of rapidly rising interest rates, jeopardize their compliance with regulatory capital requirements.

This is another troubling situation that I've not seen covered by the media, not even those committed to dramatizing major adverse consequences of Government indiscretions.

And, what happens to the Treasury Bond market when the Fed decides to reduce its Balance Sheet and no longer replaces its maturing Treasury Bonds by reinvesting in new Treasuries? That's a monster new and single-source domestic cash demand on the US Treasury, and our Treasury Department will have to flood the rest of its markets with new bond issues. Will other (than the Fed) Treasury markets be hungry enough to escalate their bond purchases sufficiently to fund the Fed's cashing-in a huge stack of US Treasury chips? Better find a Fed/US Treasury expert to address this dilemma, if there is such a debt-obsessed person around with appropriate credentials.

I don't think similar circumstances of this magnitude have ever occurred before. Maybe our current US Treasurer, Steve Mnuchin, would come on your show? He hasn't been defrocked...yet. Ask him where he's gonna get the money to cash out the Fed when they begin redeeming their maturing Treasury bonds. Maybe he'll say, "We'll just print it."

I know this stuff is esoteric. But it's also reality. Call or text if you have questions.

Okay, over and out for #3. Submission #4 follows. Last of the day. Onward,

Goo-goo eyed Julie.

She jabs "Send" and immediately starts a new e-mail.

'Danny, here...finally...is e-mail last. SUBMISSION #4 summarizes and compares Federal Government budget categories and their appropriations in ten-year intervals.

FEDERAL BUDGET EXPENSE DATA

In billions

	1999	2009	2019
Medicare and Medicaid	228	786	1,438
Social Security	390	644	1,000
Defense	275	698	676
Interest	230	260	375
Smaller and fast growing –			
International affairs	15	38	136
Transportation	42	68	94

Veterans	43	45	85
All other	479	561	596
	1,702	3,100	4,400

Note: A study by the Watson Institute at Brown University sifted out 18 years of costs for the War on Terror. Total = $5.9 trillion.

So, maybe $5.9 trillion pissed away. Also a huge diversion of time, talent, and money that cost 900,000 lives. A staggering price to pay for what? Insidious paranoia? Safety from lethal actions against Americans from abroad? Really? Can Government decision-makers be that naive? Is America really any safer than we were 20 years ago? The war in Iraq was before my time. But one of my accounting professors loved to call that conflict the consequence of bad bookkeeping. America went to war because the Iraqis couldn't come up with the paperwork to document the elimination of their weapons of mass destruction. So America sent the troops abroad but they couldn't find any weapons of mass destruction. Is America always failing to recognize its most insidious enemy? As the revered American philosopher Pogo said long ago, when I was still a naive young girl who read the comics, "We have met the enemy, and he is us."

COMMENTARY:

- Interest on Federal debt. Could quickly rise to $1 trillion annually at the rate of deficit spending and when...not if...interest rates go back up, likely in an attempt to curb the inevitable rise in inflation. Not a pleasant scenario.
- 20-year budget % increase percentages by category:

International affairs	807
Medicare and Medicaid	531
Social Security	156

Defense	146
Education	Infinity...education wasn't around 20 years ago. Er, I mean delivery of education wasn't controlled by Government 20 years ago!
Transportation	124
Veteran	98
Interest	63
All other	24

And...what to do about continuing huge budget deficits? Is it too audacious for a rookie Network Apprentice, er Data Demon, to suggest anything? How about politicians first give up their addictions to big deficit spending and focus on balancing the budget? Rand Paul has actually advanced a plan to balance the budget in just five years. Revolutionary concept. How dare he suggest balancing the budget! It's un-American. Could the majority of our politicians ever accept such a ludicrous concept? A huge challenge, considering the built-in momentum of annual deficit spending plus commitments to spend aggressively into the future that are embedded in America's Social Security, Medicare, and Medicaid programs, and in our Affordable Care Act subsidies.

I don't have magical insights into budget balancing. Here are a few suggestions, some of which originated in college classes. Some have been in the public dialog for years. Some may be fanciful ideas that sprouted from the audacious minds of others, including mine.

- Discontinue massive Government subsidies, both direct and indirect...like debt forgiveness for tens of millions of young Americans seduced into borrowing excessively by poorly designed student loan programs.
- Eliminate Federal subsidies imbedded in the unaffordable Affordable Care Act.

- Put the brakes on foreign aid. There's no sensible reason for America to fund big checking accounts for other countries' problems when we can't fund perceived solutions to our own problems without borrowing from other countries.
- Corporate tax rate reductions in 2018 were too generous. Hike them back up.
- Reduce the Federal estate tax exemption back to its prior level.
- Eliminate (or raise) the wage and salary cap on withholdings and employer match for Social Security and Medicare. The 2019 per-employee max of $8,240 (plus a like amount from employers) is insufficient to fund these programs. This should appeal to many who believe high-income Americans should pay more taxes of all kinds.
- I believe most Americans have generous souls. Lots of wealthy Americans put their money where their souls are. It's my impression that too much American philanthropy is diverted to Foreign causes. Enlist and challenge our most generous philanthropists and our biggest philanthropic foundations to help reverse America's rapid descent into irreversible insolvency. As a **starter**, turn Medicaid over to philanthropy. Yeah, I know that's a revolutionary, probably even a crazy idea. Maybe America needs more similar ideas that may also provide practical offsets to politicians' dedication to deficit spending.
- Encourage the most successful entrepreneurial minds emerging in modern America to turn their genius, their initiative, and their resources into solving expensive domestic problems without

depending on Government subsidy. Bezos, Buffet, and Gates have already talked about a new private sector healthcare initiative. Recruit them to run a new program. Add Elon Musk to that list, and call the new program An Entrepreneurial Plan to Rescue America from Financial Ruin...or EPRA from FR for short. The four can decide which one will be CEO.

Okay, Danny. Over and out. Dad, Shane, and I are watching Turner Classic Movies tonight. Gets our minds out of the present and back into a less confusing and less discouraging past. Is that abdicating our citizen responsibility to be continuously offended by watching disturbing current events unfold in exploitive evening news commentaries...talk television intended mostly to spread what you've called fear and loathing among the population? Absolutely!

And, did I supply enough fodder to help with your shows next week?

DANNY'S E-MAIL RESPONSE is waiting for her as Julie steps out of the shower.

Yeah. Enuf fodder already. And thanks a lot, I think... for saddling me with your data deluges. Gotta figure out how to present this stuff to news-weary viewers. Or maybe they're more like news-addicted viewers. Weary ones have already tuned out. Techies will be working on video visuals. Take Sunday off. DP

ps. Didn't realize I'd hired such a pontificator.

Still wrapped in a towel, she replies immediately.

Re pontification. Just want to fit in. This oral disease runs in the family. You should hear my father when he gets going. As he works for the Government, he figures he's entitled. You should take Sunday off also. JA

E-MAIL MESSAGES DOMINATE their interchange during the following show week.

From Danny on Monday morning.

Finished studying your stuff. Brain damaged but still functional. Although not approved by Network Brass (NB) yet, I've made a decision. Absent catastrophic events that need my immediate attention, I'm using material you provided in my opening monologues Tues through Fri. Check signals on what I said Saturday: don't watch Rachel Maddow. Don't want to offend your sense of reason. Please be available evenings in case I need you. At home OK. In Denver if you need access to our evening staff or office facilities. **Miscalculation of USA debt compared to GDP** leads off tomorrow night. DP

Just risen, Julie's a bit goo-goo eyed. *So, I'm still in pajamas again. So what. He can't see me. Here goes.*

Have what I need here, so I'll stay home this first show week. Good luck Danny. Good lead-off choice. Grateful for your confidence in me. JA

Their second interchange is late that afternoon. From Danny,

Working on prospective guest appearances. Not going well. Contacted former Dean of Stanford Graduate School of Business. Was also an accounting professor there. Said you're absolutely right about $13.9 T add-back of Federal

Agency debt to third parties. Said economists got it wrong and they should stay out of consolidated balance sheet constructions. Invited him to Hollywood. Said no thanks. Too old. Then tried to contact Krugman. No response. Then contacted a professor in UCLA's Econ Dep't. He said you're "absolutely fucking wrong and fucking accountants should stick to fucking accounting." Said he "Won't come on your fucking show. Too fucking busy."

I'm still planning to present your chart. Contacted office of chief actuary of OASDI whatever that is. Said they don't do talk TV gigs as a matter of Agency policy. Also said your $13.9 T add-back number was way too low because it was based on PV for only 40 years out. Said you cut off too short. Said you should have used an out-to-infinity calculation of $43.2 T. So, how long is infinity? Which number should I dramatize tomorrow? Do I need to know more details about how Present Value (PV) of Social Security obligations is calculated? DP

And Julie's response.

Answers in inverse order to your three questions. **Quick answer to #3.** You don't need to know precisely how PV is calculated. Too convoluted even for me and would only give jaded viewers a good reason to switch channels. Here's an oversimplified short shot at how I think PV of Social Security obligations is (or should be) calculated. It can get more complicated, but a quicky answer is PV of Social Security's basic obligations is comprised of two parts: (1) PV of retired participants no longer paying in and (2) PV of participants not retired yet and still paying in. For part (1) it's a relatively simple calculation of what will likely be **paid out** annually over remaining lives of participants based on life expectancy tables, then discounted to present value using assumed interest rates.

I don't know what rate is now used...spent over an hour searching and couldn't find rate info. Frustrating. Part (2) is more complex. For participants still paying in, PV is first the same calculation as in part (1), then that amount is reduced for the PV of expected remaining amounts to be **paid-in** before retirement. Yes, as you may have noticed, this creates net benefits to the system from amounts paid in by unmarried participants who die before they reach retirement age.

Quicker answer to #2. Dramatize the smaller number. The larger number is too catastrophic. Beyond comprehension actually.

Quickest answer to #1. Infinity is forever, and I haven't the foggiest idea how to define forever.

Anything else? JA

He replies.

Got it. Thanks. Enuf already. Now I gotta prepare for tonight. I've scheduled Wed night for discussing budget deficits. Will contact you about that tomorrow. DP

TUESDAY MORNING their e-mail interchanges continue. This time Julie is up and dressed, expecting renewal of the dawn back-and-forth. *Weird workday hours. Don't know if I like them.*

As expected, Danny's opening e-mail comes in before sunrise.

To start with. I like our maintaining the work connection either by text or e-mail. That way neither of us has to take extensive notes on a phone conversation and everything's documented. Okay, about tomorrow night, here's where we stand on your workup of USA **Budget Deficits**, the costs of the **War on Terror**, and your ideas for **Balancing the Budget**. For prospective show guests from the political scene, our guest appearance co-ordinator (GAC) handles all attempts to connect with those potential guests, generally through their staff assistants (SA). Did score with Rand Paul who said...through his SA of course...for sure he'd come on the Show. His SA said he was particularly interested in your turnover to Philanthropy concept and your suggestion to call for help from the most successful private sector brains in business. Also said he might be interested in your becoming a staff advisor to his office. Wow, you're getting that kind of compliment already. Please don't go to greener pastures yet...you might find them dung infested. Bad news is we couldn't book any Congressional reps to come on the show with Paul. Tried the Speaker of the House, Her SA said no. My GAC said she thought she could hear someone in the background grumbling, "What does an Ophthalmologist know about money? Fucking conservative congenital idiot." Also tried unsuccessfully to get Dubya...that's George W. Bush...to comment on $5.9 T spent for his declared War on Terror. No luck there either. Tonight I'm going it alone on debt to GDP. DP

WEDNESDAY MORNING the e-mail interchanges continue. This time Julie initiates.

Danny, your monologue on debt to GDP last night was terrific. Dad even watched the show, and he mostly doesn't do talk TV. JA

Danny's response is after breakfast.

Thanks, Julie. Some bad news for the rest of the week. NB says no to Rand Paul. It's a partisan thing with them, and they own the Network. They've bankrolled us from the start. Please don't discuss their partisan bias with anyone. Our owners' vision for MRABC is for them to be to this network as Rupert Murdoch is to Fox News, but with an opposite political bias and without the public knowledge and exposure that Murdoch has. So, I'm sad to say, we work for a bias brand that's in direct competition with MSNBC for dominance of TV political news commentary from the far left. The NB tolerates my political neutrality because I'm considered a rising star. But they don't encourage it and won't directly support it. They're also hypersensitive to TV program ratings. They expect me to deliver top ratings, and I'm trying to do that and still maintain my intellectual integrity. Call it a tough gig for me emotionally. May need therapy some day. For Thursday, I'll cover the big lenders, ie the buyers of US Treasury bonds, who are funding America's deficit spending and challenge the ability of our US Treasury to get enough $$$ from them to retire **maturing US Bonds** held by the Fed. Our GAC will try to loop Mnuchin into this. Shouldn't be a politicized subject. For Friday I'll use your charts to show the rises in Federal spending over the last 20 years by component, emphasizing the meteoric rises in **Medicare**, **Medicaid**, and **Social Security**. They dominate the deficit scene, leaving **Defense** spending way back in the dust. Still looking for a POP (person of prominence) to join the show. DP

ps. Do I need to provide you with our private Network dictionary of approved abbreviations for complicated titles?

Julie immediately responds.

No dictionary, please. I think I've memorized all the abbreviations. I appreciate the confidence you have in me, Danny. Enough that you persevere in showcasing at least some of my work. Another broad observation you might feature. And it's not original. There's a cruel myth reflected in the numbers I developed and you presented last week. It's subtle, but not incomprehensible. I and lots of others in my limited social circle of friends believe it's destroying America. It was first addressed in one of my advanced college classes by a brilliant and highly-credentialed Sociology professor. His assertion, which he well-documented, was that there are widely-held presumptions that Americans are entitled to live in an affordable, riskless society, and our Governments should, can, and will provide that...and will also provide direct financial aid if and when necessary. Those presumptions and their fallacy were also reinforced for me and my classmates in the PolySciFi class we took in graduate school. Yep, our instructor, Professor Angel Bright, was kind of 'out there.' But her class was the most informative, currently relevant, and intellectually challenging classroom experience in my postgraduate study program.

I should pause and acknowledge something you've probably already figured out. I've kept my textbooks and class notes from many of my college courses and the related faculty lectures. So, what you generally see from me is a blend of takeaways from important and relevant college classrooms and my own research and analyses. And, sure, of course, my father. We don't always agree but I respect his views. JA

AFTER THEIR RITUAL Saturday morning breakfast of pancakes, sausage, and fresh berries, Jules asks his daughter. "So, Julie, I know last week was your first full week on duty. Was it okay with you that I didn't watch all of Dan Panders' shows?"

Julie chuckles. "Of course. I get your aversion to talk television and your viewing preference for PBS evening programming."

"Well, with you working evening shifts most of the week, we didn't get to talk very much about anything. Was your first week a good experience?"

"Mixed results. Good part is that Danny and I work well together and have established a foundation of mutual respect. We also have the same weird sense of humor. And Danny's show ratings last week were decent. Most of my work made it to the MSABC television screen and was well-presented. However, the Network Brass or NB, as Danny abbreviates them, vetoed his selection of a key guest for the show. Then Danny and his staff couldn't entice other prominent persons with appropriate credentials to come on his show and discuss or debate my visuals. Danny's NB weren't very supportive of his venture into issues related to excessive and irresponsible Government spending. He said they were also dissatisfied with the numbers focus in his opening monologs.

"The harsh reality of his numbers focus was that much of Danny's audience reaction was sort of 'ho hum, nothing new or exciting about Government overspending.' Guess I sorta expected that. Still disappointing.

"And, here was Danny's network news competition...the eight most reported events that dominated news scenes so far this month. Thought you'd be interested, and I wrote them down." She reaches for a notepad and reads from the scribbling on its top page, "New Governor in Puerto Rico. Two USA mass shootings in 24 hours...only two? String of stabbings in California...of course. Jeffrey Epstein found dead in jail, hanged himself, suicide presumed...really? A shooting in Philadelphia...only one? Protests in Portland heat up...didn't realize they ever cooled off. First vaping death reported...only one? New cases of measles reported...how many?

"And here's the great eight for last month. Two mall shootings in two days...so hurrah for the 29 days that were free of mall shootings. No one killed? Blast in Florida shopping center. More measles cases reported. Illness outbreak in a retirement home ...only one? Power outage in New York City...nowhere else? Federal inmates to be released under new law. Strikes in Puerto Rico...nowhere else? Border wall has been funded... so what's gonna stop those illegals who climb over or tunnel under?

"Can you believe it...there's actually a website that keeps track of this stuff. Seems like the media scene is dominated by stories of human violence, of aberrant behaviors of irrelevant persons, of isolated aberrant events, and of illness outbreaks... plus stories using scare porn. Even some stories of ho-hum events. All seem to be more popular television fodder than news about Government dedicated to spending America into decay, ruin, and death. Here's what bugs me and a lot of my classmates about contemporary network news. Some of our biggest societal concerns are apparently perceived by most viewers and by most media program hosts as just business as usual, not worthy of in depth coverage. Like the Government just closed its books on another fiscal year of runaway spending, but there's no substantive network news coverage of over-borrowing. Or, maybe I'm just too obsessed with numbers and have a low tolerance for what I perceive as over-preoccupation with news stories that don't and really shouldn't define America or Americans. Irrelevant stuff leads to inappropriate extrapolations. Is that what the news presenters intend to happen?"

Her father's eyes glaze over as he shakes his head and wiggles his hand at her. "Whew. Julie, enough about last week. I get your disdain for what dominates the news scene. So, what's coming up for you next week and after?"

"Well. I also support a few shows other than Danny's, and I expect two very busy weeks ahead. I can work from home, but some days I'll be working behind the scenes in Denver. For near-term programming, Danny wants me to help with another really important subject. I'm inclined to characterize it as Excessive Regulatory Zeal. More focus on Government legislative atrocities. Then, longer-term I may suggest he consider future programming on alleged Racial Bias in law enforcement and on Global Warming.

They're both provocative and controversial subjects, hot topics...one literally...that never cool down and don't ever go away. They generate unrelenting media attention and viewer interest. You're sure a genuine expert on the second subject, and I may want to interview you. Off-camera of course.

CHAPTER 14

EXCESSIVE REGULATORY ZEAL

OCT 26, 2019

AS SHE EXPECTED, Danny's Saturday morning e-mail awaits her when she wakens.

> You've probably figured it out. My work weeks and therefore your work weeks begin on Sat. But at least we get Sun. off...most of the time. Next week, If my superiors don't sabotage it, I'd like to showcase notorious examples of excessive Government regulation. Any suggestions? DP

Now fully initiated into beginning Saturday morning work in pajamas before sunrise, then dressing, and then having breakfast while her Dad sleeps in, Julie responds.

> Ah-h, excessive Government regulatory zeal. Danny, let's call it ERZ. Does America have too many laws and too many regulations, most of them of excessive length? Answer to both questions...yes. Is it a disease of democracy? Or maybe just a consequence of having superfluous lawmakers? Answer...the latter. Democracy is pure in concept. Unfortunately it gets carried to the extreme in application. ERZ is one of my favorite subjects (out of several) that most of my friends are tired of hearing me talk about. It should be a separate and required course at

all colleges and universities. Linking to what DPS featured last week, ERZ is likely the root cause of both America's inflation and its insolvency. Consider starting next week with two amazing and deplorable statistics. From my college civics class: 1. Only 26% of American citizens can name all three branches of Federal Government. 2. Public trust in Government has now dropped to only 18% of American citizens. So, something's fundamentally wrong. Obviously. Analyzing Government's ERZ is an ordeal. ERZ is a widespread national disease. Politicians conceive, incubate, and spread it. Too many in the media applaud it. Everyone has to endure it. But maybe more citizens will also try to do something about it. Now I am hungry. Got to fortify myself for the ordeal ahead. More commentary coming after breakfast. Probably by e-mail. I'm too wordy to text message. Also too obsessed with writing in sentences and trying always to spell and punctuate properly. Twin curses imposed on me by college English teachers. JA

SHANE STUMBLES as he follows her back downstairs. Julie reaches down to pat him, then reassures him, "Yeah, I know. Lots of up and down stairs for your elderly and arthritic legs. No worries. We'll be fully moved upstairs by this evening, and I'll be sleeping in a King-size bed. You're officially invited to join me on...not in...the bed if you promise not to snore. Come snooze beside me on your doggy bed downstairs for the last time. We may be there a while."

Her computer is soon chattering back to her in perfect sync with flying fingers.

Danny, I'll start with a few numbers. You'd expect that of me. Here's a simple yet still an OMG listing that will set the stage for what follows. It's the indigestible word-counts of the ten longest laws passed by Congress over a ten year period 2000-2009. Number one, of course, is the Affordable Care Act at 314,900 words, followed by laws of:

314,800
314,600
296,100
276,800
274,600
258,200
250,300
247,000 and
226,500 words.

Congress has enacted four to six million words into new laws in each two-year session since the end of WWII. So, in 36 sessions through 2018, that's about 180 million compulsory words added to the Federal Register by the Legislative branch. Then there are rules and regulations added to the compulsory word count by Federal Agencies who administer the laws. Then there are laws, rules, and regulations dumped on citizens by individual states, counties, and cities. So there are billions of words out there attempting to regulate not just the behaviors and activities of people, but also dogs, cats, other pets, businesses, schools, churches, charitable organizations, trusts, estates, inventions...maybe even ideas someday?... homeowners' associations, sporting events, celebratory public events, other organized public events (like protests), even rivers, streams, paths, and trails, even government agencies themselves.

Coming soon...as speculated by some...are rules, regulations and permitting requirements governing private in-home gatherings of seven people or more for such purposes as celebrating birthdays, anniversaries; individual achievements like graduations; playing neighborhood poker or other fun games for money; and any gatherings involving the consumption of alcohol or use of drugs... including marijuana, hallucinatory mushrooms, etcetera, etcetera, etcetera.

Also, some pundits forecast that by 2035, half of America's work force will have to be employed by Government, be employed by businesses to deal with regulatory compliance, or be employed in law enforcement. It's also forecast that Americans will soon see laws of 3,000+ pages generating one million plus words each, perhaps even 5,000+ pages in one law. It's rumored that there's a $500 annual award funded by Elon Musk to be presented each year to the most ferocious word-generator in Congress. It's called the Augustless Legislator Award. No wonder my PolySciFi instructor calls the law-originating branch of Congress the House of Absurdities. Dad's even worse. He calls it the House of Atrocities.

There are further adverse consequences from the American explosion in laws, rules, and regulations. A paper shortage of irreversible magnitude looms. My economics professor staged the crisis for her students in a scholarly essay she planned to submit for publication in the *American Economic Review*. Ironically, she actually passed around a paper copy of her essay to each of her students. I saved my copy. Here are some excerpts from it.

> "America is running out of trees, and the Chinese have purchased most of America's paper mills. As a consequence, the cost of paper is expected to double every five years if consumption continues at its present pace.
>
> "The biggest **consumer** of paper is of course our Governments. So a Federal Government initiative is necessary. What's needed is a new Federal law that will require all Federal, State, County and City

governments, agencies, commissions, and any other body constituted by Government that:

1. All new laws, rules, regulations, policies and all other actions at all levels be documented digitally only...no paper.

2. All existing laws, rules, regulations, policies and all other actions at all levels that are presently in paper documents be converted to digital, and the millions of tons of waste paper created be recycled.

"The biggest single non-Government direct **use** of paper in America is a consequence of Government. That includes filings and submissions in satisfaction of Government requirements for compliance reporting. For examples, think about (1) annual income tax return filings (both Federal and State) for hundreds of millions of citizens, millions of businesses and another million or so of not-for-profit organizations, and (2) tens of millions of annual and special compliance filings by millions of organizations subject to regulatory control. All new compliance submissions should be digitized. All existing paper records from previous submissions should also be digitized. Again, the resulting millions of tons of wastepaper should be recycled.

"The conversion to digital of existing paper documents probably involves billions of pieces of paper containing trillions of words filed away in Government archives. The recycling of the resulting wastepaper should eliminate the need for paper mills for many years and drive the monopolistic Chinese out of that American enterprise sector.

"Unless robots can be designed and manufactured

> to staff these enormous conversion and recycling efforts, a huge increase in employment of people will be necessary. Perhaps 1,000,000 to 2,000,000 new jobs will be created, excluding training needs of people who will staff the new jobs. America's unemployment rate should decline for at least the estimated five years needed to complete all the conversions and recycling. Unfortunately there will be job attrition in employment for records-keeping and for construction of new facilities to store paper documents."

Okay, that's enough from this professorial essay. But here's a recent related development. A Save our Trees (SOT) activist organization has been established. It's a spinoff from the Save our Planet (SOP) reversal of Global Warming initiative. For starters, SOT, with SOP's endorsement, is advocating a switch to renewables for toilet paper. SOT advocates the use of corncobs, which can be cleaned and recycled after each use.

Sorry, just kidding. I apologize. Couldn't resist lightening it up a bit. All these somber realities and monumental ERZ travesties get to be depressing. It's frightening how even the most bizarre advocacies can appear totally credible and appealing.

So, anyway, back to ERZ. Here's a list of seven potential ERZ topics for your show that I'll address today. No emphasis on lots of numbers or $$$ amounts. No charts. Breathe a sigh of relief. Mostly just my words. Maybe that's worse. Call them a concerned citizen's protest against excessive Government interventions into the lives of its citizens and illegal immigrants.

First, *three suggestions* for curtailment of the present environment in which ERZ flourishes. Hang on. They're simple in concept. Probably too radical in the minds of those who admire and are devoted to big Government.

1. Streamline the structure of all American governmental units – a fantasy.

2. Establish time limits for Congress persons and limit their staff – another fantasy?

3. Cap the length of Congressional bills enacted – beyond fantasy and into absurdity.

'Then some commentary on the foul stench imbedded in the *following three areas* of Federal ERZ. Yeah, only three out of a total universe of what? 100s, maybe 1,000s? Maybe I'm too cynical? Sorry. No, not sorry. Someone has to complain. Loudly enough to be heard.

4. Subsidizing higher education with taxpayer $$$.

5. Dodd Frank Act (DFA) and other Federal bank regulatory requirements.

6. Sarbanes Oxley Act (SOA) and creation of the Public Company Accounting Oversight Board (PCAOB).

And finally, 7. A cornucopia of idiocies proposed by a member of Congress but not acted on yet...thank God.'

THE SELECTED SEVEN FLESHED OUT

1. Streamline the legislative structure. I don't know if you can work this into your program commentary, but here's an intriguing observation by my Civics Professor at CU. He received a round of applause from every member of the class when he introduced it. Actually, it was a standing ovation. I was the first to stand. Streamlining is for sure a revolutionary concept. Probably too outrageous ever to be seriously considered. Maybe even too

far-fetched to be even discussed. But it's also totally rational, and part of it merely patterns after our neighbors to the north. "Government finally waving goodbye to the Horse and Buggy Era," the prof called it. He maintained that America should and could eliminate all State governments and consolidate them into 12 Provinces (Canada has 10 Provinces) of three each for the four geographical areas that comprise our time zones. He would then eliminate all city governments and consolidate them into the county governments in which the cities are located. All this downsizing makes too much good sense to be seriously considered. Right? It sure addresses rationally a big part of America's fundamental ERZ problem...too many lawmakers.

* * *

A pause. Before I get into more heavy duty stuff, here's something else I've been thinking about. Our relationship. I'm an Apprentice, and that term triggered a memory of something I had to read in an English Literature class. It's a poem written by Johann Wolfgang Von Goethe in 1797 called The Sorcerer's Apprentice, which in turn is supposedly based on an even older story by the Greek writer Lucian, a Priest of the Egyptian God Isis. So, if I'm the Apprentice, does that make you the Sorcerer?

Anyway, because the apprentice screwed up and tried to do something he shouldn't and couldn't do, which was to have a broom do his bidding, the message the poet conveys is that only the Master decides what to do and can direct the broom to do it. In the poem the Master invoked powerful spirits that the Apprentice could not.

So, Danny, you have my pledge of faith to you that despite my tendency to have and express strong opinions on a lot of subjects, I recognize I'm the Apprentice and you're the Master. You decide. If we need to have powerful spirits on our side, only you have the right and power to invoke them...and then employ them to activate a broom to help execute your decisions.

Now I need a bathroom break. Be right back. More coming.

A text response is already on Julie's iPhone when she returns.

Thanks Julie. Rest assured I intend to make good decisions and execute them without resorting to help from the spirit world to transform a broom. Your help is about all I can handle. DP

Julie smiles and then gently pets a dozing Shane. "For good luck," she murmurs as she begins a new e-mail.

Back to DPS programming subject suggestions 2 and 3. How about a two-term limit for all of Congress? Let's get rid of career politicians in the Legislative Branch. Make them go back home and get real jobs. And while we're at it, extend Representatives' terms to four years. So Americans don't have to go through the unrelenting year-round daily overdoses of politicized rhetoric from the media and their politicized guests. How about also capping the number of staff members a Congressperson can have? Include in the restriction both staff on the Government payroll and staff off the Government payroll and bankrolled by others. With new laws now exceeding 2,000 pages, it's obvious that drafting new legislation is not done by members of Congress. I also suspect that very few Congresspersons actually read the full texts of what they pass into law. So, let's attack ERZ at its source.

An effective restriction might be to limit all new laws to no longer than the US Constitution...so, like 25-30 pages max. If employed in the past 20 years, that restriction alone would probably have eliminated more than 95% of new law text added during that period. Put thousands of redundant news commentators concentrating on politics, redundant Congressional staffers, redundant lawyers, and redundant lobbyists out of work. Make America a better place.

On to #4, THE GODAWFUL GOVERNMENT DESCENT INTO THE MAELSTROM OF FUNDING HIGHER EDUCATION FOR ALL.

42.9 million Americans now owe $1.4 trillion on Government-backed student loans. Beginning with Federal legislation in 1965 and through 2010 (I don't have subsequent data), **72 onerous laws** were passed to create and nourish this nightmare of unnecessary and excessive Federal Government intervention into the lives of its citizens.

I guess the prevailing sentiment now is: Government created the problem, they bloody-well should solve it. So it's no longer what "you can do for your country" but what "your country can do for you" for millions of Americans who look to opportunistic politicians willing to use the Federal treasury (and eagerly buy votes at a horrific per-vote price tag) to improperly erase debts for which most borrowers should remain responsible.

Debt erasure (after ten years of payments) is also available to many borrowers who work for Government or for certain not-for-profits. The irony here is that many who could and should repay their entire debt can walk away from it after ten years.

There's also a rational, well-established, and functioning safe harbor for those who really can't repay their student debt, an alternative that doesn't involve more

Government subsidy. It's called **Bankruptcy**. A bankruptcy filing to erase student debt is a burdensome, time-consuming, and complicated process, but it at least filters out the undeserving. I don't consider erasing debt by clever legal assertions of misleading lender or education institution actions to be legitimate grounds for erasure.

Now on to #5 **DODD FRANK ACT** (**DFA**) and other ill-advised bank regulatory practices.

According to Alan Greenspan, the former long-time and universally respected Chairman of the Federal Reserve, the DFA is "the worst law ever passed by Congress." He did approve of the portion of the bill that enlarged bank capitalization requirements. But, look out depositors in the high-flying Signature Bank. Guess who's on that bank's Board of Directors? None other than Barney Frank. Wouldn't it be ironic if that were one of the first big regional banks to fail under the rabidly expanded regulatory system! Sometimes, too much regulation also breeds an absence of proper focus on what's most important.

This original bureaucratic nightmare was a whopping 2,300 pages long. Did anyone read all of it? I didn't read it. I tried but soon gave up. I do have some observations on its impact.

i. There's tragedy in the making. Politicians have intervened to establish accounting and financial reporting rules for banks. A disgusting and dangerous precedent. America's ten largest banks now have to **recognize** all unrealized losses on their bond portfolios. That's good. Regional and smaller banks do not. That's terrible, although they at least have to **disclose** unrecognized losses. Here are foreseeable consequences. When interest rates rise, which is bound to occur when (not if) America enters an inflationary cycle, all banks will experience value declines in their bond portfolios, particularly hazardous for banks with longer term bond holdings. Some declines may impair larger bank capitalization requirements at a time when sources of new capital might not be available. Regional banks may suffer the same capitalization impairment but ironically won't have to recognize it because they are exempt from recording the mark-to-market decline.

Already vulnerable is the high flying Silicon Valley Bank in California. It's a regional bank with a huge long-term bond portfolio. A capitalization impairment could become imminent, but ironically they won't have to record it. Of its holding company's five-member Board of Directors, only one has banking experience. Oh-oh. SVB is a great prospect for massive short-selling of their stock by investor speculators. Also, savvy SVB bank customers with big money deposited in the bank, particularly in Certificates of Deposit are gonna take their money out when they see...or their financial advisors see...that the bank is quickly running out of enough asset value to cover their obligations to depositors. SVB is a big regional bank failure already destined to happen.

Smaller banks will experience similar declines and similar jeopardy but they also won't have to bookkeep their capitalization deficits.

ii. Some banks report that they have more regulatory compliance employees than they have in their commercial loan departments. So, a single administrative function that has zero revenue benefit costs more than an entire department that generates a huge portion of bank revenues. America's fifth largest bank reported it had to hire 4,500 new employees to enable it to comply with DFA. That's $500 million-plus in additional annual administrative costs for just one bank. Extrapolate that to the entire banking industry and that's gotta be a bunch of billion $ in extra nonproductive costs. Those costs filter down to bank customers. My assessments of some specific DFA excessive adverse impacts on bank customers:

iii. Savings (including CDs) at all banks no longer produce any income of consequence to savers. Lower interest rates are mostly the cause, but DFA compliance costs are also a significant piece of the direct income reduction to bank customers. At least American banks don't follow some European bank practices and charge their customers for keeping their savings safe. Yet.

iv. A larger impact has an indirect but significant adverse impact on retired bank customers who don't have a sturdy pension and who rely on banks for providing retirement income from savings and for investment advice and management. Too much of the management fees paid to banks for managing customer money now has to be diverted to cover surging and staggering costs of regulatory compliance. The consequences either significantly increase costs to customers or significantly reduce important services (such as industry research and study of corporate activities and financial results) for customers. Probably both have occurred.

v. The impositions on banks of ever-expanding requirements for Federal income tax reporting has also had adverse impacts on Americans and on the US Treasury. I'll cite examples.

vi. Banks now do basic (a) income tax records-keeping and (b) related reporting to the IRS (on IRS Form 1099) for investment accounts maintained for customers at investor expense...through management fees. Both functions produce enormous data deluges to the IRS and to the taxpayer. For example. The 1099 reporting for a retired couple living on Social Security and a few $100,000 total invested in three bank-managed investment accounts could run to 70 pages. That's 20,000 to 25,000 total words and numbers that have to be accumulated and transcribed by the bank, reviewed by the taxpayer and the taxpayer's return preparer, reported a second time to...and then logged in ...by the IRS. Expanding on the regulatory absurdities imposed on banks that filter down to their clients and customers, here's another example. Just the opening of a new investment account with a major bank's investment services will require that the bank produce a disclosure document of over 100 pages and present it to the investor. That's 25,000 to 30,000 words of regulatory excess per new investment account. Thank goodness there's no regulatory requirement that the investor actually read the bloody document...yet! How much time is wasted on all this defies an answer. The examples are real. Comes from our retired neighbors here in our modest older neighborhood in Boulder. They have $200,000 of life savings in investment accounts with their bank.

vii. Here's an example of a significant adverse US Treasury impact. It gets a bit technical. This was an example used in my advanced college course on Federal Income Taxes and may be too convoluted for TV news commentary. It occurs because of Government's insistence that banks keep investment tax basis records for their customers and report that information on shares sold directly to the IRS as well as to the customer. That works for conventional stock and bonds investments. It doesn't work for what have become significant investment vehicles held in many investment accounts. They're called MLPs...for Master Limited Partnerships. The problem is banks don't have all the information they need for tax basis accounting for MLPs. Won't go into all the details. My perception is that during this early period, many taxpayers filed returns based on **MLP cost** data provided by banks, which was grossly **inflated**, resulting in underreporting of gains on sale. I estimate the unintentional underpayment of Federal income taxes during this period was several hundred million $. Banks have finally discontinued reporting

MLP cost of sales.

Now #6. SARBANES OXLEY (SARBOX) AND SIMILAR LEGISLATIVE BLUNDERS.

Danny, I'm again referencing back to my college days. This time from my first auditing course, where the professor was very concerned...outraged might be a better characterization...about what he considered an excessive, unnecessary, and inappropriate intervention into a profession by our Federal Government. Strong words, even for a college professor.

Here's a quote I saved from his classroom lecture:

> "SARBOX was primarily a response to the implosion of Enron, driven by delusional lawmaker perceptions that having outside auditors examine and report on internal controls would detect corporate collusive fraud and prevent improper financial reporting. Collusive fraud isn't detectable by an auditor, unless one of the colluders discloses his (or her) collusion... and whoever heard of a colluder doing that? There's a false sense of security imbedded in this naive legislation. Co-sponsor Mike Oxley is on-the-record as believing this enormous increase in the workload of outside auditors could be accomplished at no additional cost to shareholders. How naive can a legislator be! Apparently his delusion was shared by others in Congress. Several-hundred million dollars are wasted by companies complying with the law. Stated simply, Congress's medicine doesn't work, won't cure the condition...and which isn't widespread, despite relentless efforts of activists and the media to make it appear so."

MY conclusion. SARBOX is an ineffective and ill-conceived administrative cost burden to corporate America.

And here are some more professorial quotes from my college auditing class:

> "Creation of the Public Company Accounting Oversight Board (PCAOB) was a Congressional overreach, and legal scholars have suggested it's (arguably) an illegally constituted body. The PCAOB now promulgates and overseas auditing standards and practices. Long ago the Securities and Exchange Commission (SEC) was empowered to establish accounting principles. So we now have a once proud profession...Certified Public Accounting...emasculated by Government. There's still some professional non-Government authority remaining in how to account. It's vested in the Financial Accounting Standards Board (FASB). So, at least half-a-testicle remains within the profession."

Back to my conclusions. CPAs no longer express opinions on fairness. No longer are they permitted to or expected to exercise professional judgment in the circumstances. They provide opinions on compliance and are required to follow Government direction on how to account and how to audit.

And, finally #7. COULD THE WORST BE YET TO COME? Now we have a US Senator stumping for President who wants the Government to prepare tax returns for all Americans, thereby forcing tens of thousands of practicing CPAs to quit, retire, or go to work for the IRS; wants Congress to appoint all the Directors who serve on the Boards of all our larger corporations, then have them report to Congress rather than to shareholders; and wants to forgive all student debt. This Senator should be impeached and removed from office on three counts: absurdity, stupidity, and acute fiscal irresponsibility. Preempt this legislator from converting atrocities of the mind and mouth to society-destroying legislation.

Among many others, obviously including his daughter, my father is also bereft of patience with this disgusting brand of career politicians who've lost touch with reality and common sense.

Now, before I sign off for the day, there's something else that's bothered me and many others for a very long time. It's perhaps an insidious example of excessive and offensive Government intervention into the lives of its citizens. You might be interested in pursuing this. And I don't know who might be best to come on the DPS to discuss it. Again, what follows comes from lectures and discussions in my PolySciFi graduate study course. Professor Angel Bright did not shy away from controversial issues. "Government at all levels should stay the hell out of the abortion issue," she lectured us. "Plain and simple, that decision should be left exclusively in the hands of the pregnant woman, her family, and the family physician. Yes, a non-spousal prospective father could have some input, input only. Perhaps also a priest."

Similarly, in a later class session, she also lectured that "Government should stay the hell out of all issues dealing with the sexuality of its citizens, including transgender issues and particularly the issues of marital rights of gay couples." She contended that there's a simple solution to the dilemma of gay-couple rights that would follow what's been done efficiently and effectively in both England and Canada. It pre-empts overly-politicized preoccupations with the issue and also avoids Religion issues associated with gay-marriage...because there is no "marriage." As England and Canada have done, let's grant gay couples the same rights married couples have, but preserve the religious sanctity of marriage and permit the gay couple to formalize their combination and their rights in a civil ceremony. Maybe it's too late for this. What a shame.

The more I think about her, the more I think Angel

Bright should retire from teaching Political Science, run for the US House of Representatives, and give the citizens of Colorado an opportunity to send a superb voice of reason to Washington. I think she'd be a brilliant legislator. Don't know her party affiliation. That was never revealed. No student ever inquired. She totally avoided shit-shaming along party lines. She's for sure radical. So, maybe she's a Socialist. I don't know. Never even thought about that until this very moment.

Okay, enough already. Thanks for listening. I'm outta here. JA

ps. MRABC should invite Angel Bright to come on your show!

WHEN JULIE RETURNS to her work station before dinner, Danny's text response is waiting for her.

> Great suggestion. Sometimes I read your e-mails starting with the last page first. As in move straight to the punch lines. I'd love to have an Angel on my show. It needs that. NB would never allow it. Not now, but someday I'll tell you more about that deranged couple I work for. DP
>
> ps I'll get to the rest of your e-mail blast later. Probably Monday.

MONDAY, JULIE PRACTICES NOT BEING IMPATIENT, and Danny's first text message dings-in late at night, just as she's about to slip between the covers of her new bed in her new bedroom and invite Shane to jump up. "Damn," she exclaims. "he's caught me in my pajamas again. Oh well. What the hell. Serves me bloody right for having the bloody iPhone here with me."

> Sorry to be late with this. Couldn't get to your ERZ stuff today. The Queen commandeered my show this evening, as you may already know if you watched. Not upset if you didn't watch. It wasn't a great show. Too much BS. ERZ is first on my agenda for tomorrow. Sleep well. DP

An e-mail message is waiting for her after breakfast on Tuesday. *That's late for Danny*, Julie thinks. *Nice to have breakfast with Dad again.*

> May not need you much this week. The Queen has taken over most programming. However, for sure, in my opening monologue, I'll condemn the Legislative branch obsession with overloading the Executive branch, the Judicial branch, and hundreds of millions of citizens with regular forced-feedings of indigestible compulsory words. That's fun stuff, also mind-blowing...literally. As you acknowledged, streamlining Government structure to finally exit the Horse and Buggy Era is too radical, even for the NB. What your professor envisioned is also too rational to be practical. Yes, there's an absence of reason in our excess information age. Although some prospective guest candidates were interested, eager even, to come on the show to discuss a looming Student Loan bailout travesty, I Couldn't ID a qualified guest acceptable to the NB. Same with bad-ass Congressional Acts already on the books that you discussed. Felt like I might be going after Goliath with a slingshot. And, oh yes, I hate to accept this but it's reality. It's too late to rescue abortion and gay couple rights from Government insanity at both Legislative and Executive levels. Your cornucopia of idiocies description of an obviously incapable Presidential candidate's platform was spot on. However, that candidate is too transparently idiotic to waste giving her or her agenda any

exposure on prime time TV. Please don't be too disappointed. DP

ps Any suggestions about programming for next week?

She texts out an immediate response.

Danny. Well, you asked for it. I do have a programming suggestion for next week. I'll e-mail it to you. Right now. JA

CHAPTER 15

TAX FRAUD BY NEWS MEDIA AND NOT-FOR-PROFITS

NOV 2, 2019

OKAY, DANNY. HERE 'TIS. During this modern era of PTTT (prime time talk television) and its preoccupation with the Queen, maybe you can squeeze a sort of related but universally neglected subject into your opening monologue. This is another dollar denominated issue. It's income tax fraud on a grand scale. The issue was introduced to me by academia, specifically by two professors I admire and whose judgments and integrity I respect. It involves big dollars, huge dollars, siphoned away from the US Treasury.

In the professors' opinions it's also a systemic and imbedded fraud. Two segments of American enterprise are involved. The Media in general. Also some high-profile not-for-profit organizations who have improperly received 501(c)(3) designations from the IRS that permit contributors to claim (fraudulently) an income tax deduction for their cash donations to rabidly partisan political activism.

The underlying principle is long established in law and in practice. Political contributions are not deductible for income tax purposes.

I acknowledge I'm still very impressed with some of

my college professors. Maybe overly so? Are some in academia too scholarly-driven, too lacking in practical realities? I don't think so. Anyway, back to the tax fraud. Yes, it was included in Angel Bright's baker's dozen listing of important contemporary issues. She featured it in one of her lectures. She said she'd never seen it addressed in PTTT. It was also addressed in my advanced income tax class, where the professor scoffed, "Of course the media won't talk about it. Strikes too close to home. Steps on too many protected toes." Both professors prefaced their media fraud remarks with essentially the same PTTT observation: that Americans are besieged nightly, relentlessly, and obnoxiously by politicized media competing with each other in their clamoring for viewers' attention and vigorously attempting to manipulate the way Americans think about candidates for public office and their agendas.

And the current primary cause for escalating divisiveness in America? No question in my mind. Now in its fifth year of saturating Americans with wholesale and retail mind poisoning, it's the collaborative efforts by high-profile members of Congress (some of whom are woefully unqualified to legislate) and their biased media supporters to defame, discredit, demonize, disenfranchise, displace and ultimately destroy a sitting President. That these efforts provide huge income tax deductions for big corporations and for wealthy individual donors is outrageous. Although more defensive than offensive, Congressional rebuttals and retaliations from the other side of the aisle and their biased media supporters are similarly offensive. Angie Bright called this repugnant stuff "rabidly partisan political pornography." Like it's a word contest between the reds and the blues to see which side can be more obnoxious.

Here are two of the political mischiefs by media

organizations that were addressed in my college classes.

First. After the 2016 election, a **Google** whistleblower estimated that Google's political activism persuaded over two million undecided American voters not to vote for our current President. Google's bias is not subtle. For over four years, the Google news-aggregating website, which I visit regularly, was carefully constructed to refer site visitors to a preponderance of red-negative news features from blue outlets. Yes, they occasionally referred site visitors to a few red outlets, but never to perhaps the reddest two outlets, the National Review and Breitbart News. Most of Google's blue referrals to red sites were cleverly selected to showcase headlines that were red negative. Conversely, the two reddest websites occasionally did present some genuine red-negative stuff.

Interestingly and unfortunately, the Supreme Court has indirectly provided motivation and some protection for corporations and individuals to do end-runs around restrictions on political contributions and their deductibility. Political **party cash** contributions by Corporations and individuals are limited to nominal amounts and are not deductible for income tax purposes. However, in 2010 the Supreme Court allowed Corporations to make **independent expenditures**, ie **spend $$$, not give** $$$, for political purposes and unleashed a growing tidal wave of rabidly partisan media activity.

Rather than contributing cash directly, biased corporations (mostly media) now incur huge payroll costs (all improperly deducted for tax purposes) to deliver frenzied political support to the party of their choice. They do it visually, verbally, and in writing. Indirectly through their employee efforts, they accomplish what they can't do directly with money. Labeling these efforts as news is a flagrant masquerade. This end-run around keeping corporations out of politics is a National disgrace. The ill-advised Supreme Court decision now enables a toxic and never-ending civil war of uncivil and purposefully deceptive words and images to infect our daily lives. There's also lots of disgusting character assassinations going on. The assassins are protected from accountability and legal recourse by the target's status as a public figure or by exorbitant costs of litigation.

Costs of these partisan political efforts should not be allowed as a tax deduction. Unfortunately, separating media political effort costs from nonpolitical effort costs is impracticable. As advocated in classes by both Angel Bright and my income tax professor, there is an alternative. The IRS could levy a communications tax on all media enterprises. A flat 5% of gross revenues. Call it a value added tax (VAT). (Sidebar: someday, maybe America will adopt the VAT concept, eliminate the complexities of taxing business "taxable net income" that has no resemblance to profits publicly reported.) I'm sure media companies would insist that their political activism provides a value added service to Americans. Permit media companies that aren't immersed in politics to justify their exclusion from the tax.

Second example, as outlined for those of us in the advanced income tax class. Pseudo 501(c)(3) shell entities have been established that funnel improperly tax-deducted contributions to political activist groups. Here's one high-profile 501(c)(3) income tax fraud that was featured in the class. To refer to the underlying movement in general, I'll use its generic term, Black Lives Matter (BLM). To be more specific, Black Lives Matter Global Network Foundation (BLMGNF) is basically a shell 501(c)(3) company providing a major source of money to fund Black Lives Matter Global Network (BLMGN...not a 501(c)(3)) political activism. Here are some pertinent facts. In an interview on CNN, a co-founder of BLM said, "What we are going to push for is get the sitting President (sorry, I've vowed not to use his name...ever) **out**." She re-emphasized the BLM purpose a second time in the same interview with, "our goal is to get him out."

BLMGN has 16 chapters, and BLMGNF holds $6.5 million restricted for use by BLMGN for "grassroots organizing," whatever that is. Thousand Currents (TC), which is also a 501(c)(3), holds $3.35 million restricted for use by BLMGN. So, we have very visible tax frauds going on in two 501(c)(3)s collecting tax deducted contributions and using them to fund a non-501(c)(3) organization that has avowed political purposes. Here are the information sources used by the professor. Yes, I kept my notes:

1. The CNN interview transcript.
2. Internet websites for the two 501(c)(3)s and BLMGN.
3. Restricted funds data from financial statements of the two 501(c)(3)s who are holding money restricted for BLMGN, as provided by ***Politifact***.

I may be using her too much, but I do value Professor Bright's opinions highly. She believes that BLM efforts are failing because they've become too political and also too dependent on staging public protests, which involve excessive grandstanding for the press and occasional violence. Oh, I don't remember if I've mentioned it before, and it really shouldn't matter. Angie Bright is black.

Danny, I understand that you're trying to stage a show that avoids taking sides on political issues but is still controlled by left wing owners. A horrible conflict for you. Don't know how you avoid it driving you crazy. Anyway, the NB might not like your attacking their tax deductions. So...don't seek their approval for an "expert" to come on your show. Don't go for an expert. Do it yourself. Go after the improper tax deductions taken by media and political activist groups masquerading as charitable organizations in your opening monologue. What's the NB gonna do? Fire you? OMG, they just might do that. But, I bet your ratings will go up. If so, your NB won't dare fire you. Hell, Danny, go for broke...or as they do at the poker tables, just say, "I'm all in."

So, what do you think? Should I do more research on this subject...go for the jugulars? I haven't researched it yet, but there's also talk out there of tens of millions of improperly tax deducted dollars...real cash money...supporting political activism and being sent to BLM (through their shell 501(c)(3)s organizations) by high-profile non-media corporations like that high-flying Silicon Valley Bank in California.

His e-mail response arrives as she's gathering her work equipment for a weekday trip to Denver to support some upcoming daytime shows.

No more research Julie. And no point in my going for certain jugulars. They're connected to brains too impervious to reason. I get what you're saying about the tax frauds, and I'm gonna go "all in" and use your incendiary comments in an opening monologue. But probably not until week after next. Prime time news commentary is still focused on the Queen. You realize that BLM is a sacred cow to many in the media and probably to many viewers. NB may not like my suggesting BLM is also a tax fraud. For sure NB won't like my challenging media tax deduction for many program hosts' compensation. If viewer response doesn't push DPS ratings way up, we both may be looking for new jobs.

And, oh yes, you're right. Some days I feel like program content conflicts with my NB are indeed driving me crazy. DP

CHAPTER 16

WHAT HAPPENS NEXT?

NOV 16 - 18, 2019

JULIE WAKES UP ON SATURDAY REPLAYING in her head Danny's presentation of her income tax fraud material for his Friday night monologue. Also worrying about the absence of his usual Saturday morning text message. *Have Danny and I gone too far? Gotta wait for viewer reaction. Always about the ratings. Also gotta wait for Network Brass reaction. No text from Danny this morning. Looks like we're both not working this Saturday. Wonder if we'll still be employed next week. Enuf agonizing about work. Time to think about something else. Do something else.*

Busily reorganizing her winter clothing only recently transported upstairs, she stumbles on a manila folder in a bottom dresser drawer she hadn't noticed before. Curious, she reads its contents, two hand-written pages of lined yellow notepad paper, time-stained and stapled together.

WHO am I?
A riddle in small words

Who am I?
I sense your moods
and when you need me I am there
I hold you close
stroke your hair

help dry your tears
and say all the right things you want me to say
The words I speak
and the words I don't have to speak
drive away your pain and say
I am here
with you
You need not fear
No more tears
Your hurt will pass
and soon you will be gay
as the gloom of all old nights must give way
to the bright of each new day
See I even make you laugh
when you think you are so sad
I take you with me
and we climb high peaks
where air is still fresh and clean
to watch the sun rise
then we sail far seas
where winds blow fierce and free
to watch the sun set
By dawn's half light we run to fields wet with dew
to hear the first lark sing
then hand in hand we seek green woods
to hide and wait
'til young deer come out to play
We lay in warm grass by a cool brook
and peek over its bank
to see if a trout is there
there by the old mill race
We go to town
to feel the round and smooth of man's work in stone
then on to a bed of roses

to breathe soft sweet scents
from blooms all hued in pink and red
I take from you those things which cause you pain
and give back those things which bring you joy and peace
I know what you need
with no need for you to ask
and bring that to you too
I keep you safe from harm
free from want
dry in bleak rains of spring
cool in harsh hot days when spring is no more
and warm when fall's last days are gone
And on some gray day
when age
as it must
taunts you with the threat of life's end
I will ask God to take me
and let you live on
Who am I?
I am the man a young bride once thought she saw in me
the man I wish I could have been
had I not been such a fool to let time get in the way
the man I hope my sons will be
the man I pray my girls one day will wed
as in their dream of dreams
All of these I am
yet none of these am I
Who am I then?
I am
of course
the man no man can be

IT'S AN UNUSUALLY MILD autumnal morning. Julie and her father lounge post-breakfast on the front porch and enjoy watching the morning sun emblazon Boulder's Flatirons in a golden glow.

"So Father, can you tell me about this poem I found this morning at the bottom of what I think is Mom's old dresser drawer? It's unsigned, but it looks like your handwriting." She hands him the yellow pages

Tears form in Jules' eyes, and he presses a hand to his head and shakes it. "So long ago. I'd forgotten. Yes, I wrote that for your mom when she was in the hospital and just diagnosed. She was depressed, and we were both trying so hard to remain confident she would recover. We were also talking about having more children. Back home that evening, the words just came pouring out of me. Almost kept up with the tears running down my cheeks. Like I was revisiting our classroom exercise to create something...in monosyllabic prose I think they called it...that would take your mom back to that one CU class we shared together. It's where we first met. Your mom never had a chance to read my composition. Overnight she took a turn for the worse and died in her sleep."

"Father...your composition's compelling. Heartbreaking actually. And it doesn't look like something written by a young man. I've never thought of you as poetic."

A smile returns when he answers, "Julie, I wasn't feeling young at the time, and many scientists are also poetic, or at least appreciative of poetry. We have to be. To survive precision's exhausting demands and failures' frequent despairs, we need some counter-balance of creativity in our lives. You might say we just need to bounce back and forth occasionally between both sides of the brain, so one side doesn't shrivel while the other side threatens to explode from overuse."

"This is a side of you...actually two sides, so a duality I've not been aware of before. Any other science-balancing creative work you haven't shared with me?"

"Yep, actually," he nods his head. "I think there might be. I'll have to look. And Julie...I don't think I've ever told you about that one classroom experience your mother and I shared. It was a creative writing class I took to explore some kind of creative effort in my academic experience. I occasionally got a B+ on work I turned in. Your mom was straight A's all the way. It's from her you've inherited talent with words as well as numbers. Hope that unusual combination doesn't get you into too much trouble."

Now she's scowling. "I know that combo may have already gotten me into trouble. Sometimes I use too many words and too many overly-harsh words of my own making, certainly not inherited from my mom as you describe her."

"But maybe inherited from me? Something for you to think about. And now I have to return to a Saturday morning collision and collusion with my tedious models on climate change, where the only thing I'm certain of is that the subject is always changing. Just never stays the same. It's research that never provides a reliable or practical answer to fundamentally unanswerable questions...what's going to happen in the future and when? It's all about what might or might not happen, should happen, or could happen. What has already happened and why it did also has its own set of uncertainties and scientific disputes. Yeah, for sure my climate change colleagues and I have signed on to an important mission, which is basically a mission impossible." He sighs as he rises. "So, enough about me. I'll look forward to an update briefing from you this evening about your work. Hell, your work week is longer than mine. Here's something else for you to think about. You may need a work counter balance, a diversion from that relentless and restless intensity of effort by all of us whose professional lives are motivated by principle and driven by a sense of worthwhile cause."

"Good paternal advice, and I will think about it. Thank you. And now I'm back to my work station. Danny missed his early Saturday morning text message to me. That's concerning. And I've been agonizing about the results of his Friday night monologue. Harsh consequences are possible. We both may have sacrificed our careers to expose what appears to be a flagrant, systemic, and existential income tax fraud. It's a highly inflammatory issue. We've antagonized untouchables. And I've exposed both of us to our own existential risk. It's a harsh possibility that stalks all of us in this business like a hungry prey animal. Because I agree with them, my source professors and I might be wrong with the tax fraud opinions and allegations.

"Also, I may have placed both Danny's and my career at risk...even if my professors and I are right. Hopefully I'll have something positive to share with you tonight. Give me a hug, Dad, before you leave. I really need it today."

She rises. As they embrace, he whispers in her ear. "Courage, my darling daughter. Even if others disagree with you, you've done the right thing, and I'm proud of you. Opinions are never right or wrong. They're just fodder for disagreement and debate."

WHEN JULIE RETURNS to her work station Sunday morning, two messages await her: a day-late text from Danny, and the weekly Sunday e-mail from Jason. *Which do I look at first? Business before pleasure? No, not today. Jason goes first. I hope his message is what I think it is.*

It is, and it's brief.

> It's confirmed. Returning home Wednesday as planned, and I have my plane reservations. I'm back to Denver via United Airlines with a plane change in Miami. Still up for a Thanksgiving holiday together? I'll understand if that's a special time for you and your dad to spend together. If that doesn't work and you can get time off,

early December's okay too, maybe better...no crowds. Can't wait to see you. More like I can't wait to wrap my arms around you. Love, Jase.

ps. I shaved off my beard. Made me look weird...too professorial and unkempt. So you don't have to worry about how it will feel to kiss and be kissed by a hairy face.

The text from Danny is even briefer.

Too soon for a reaction to last night's show. More next week. Stay tuned. DP

TUESDAY MORNING, Julie is working at MRABC offices in Denver when the message she's been waiting for finally texts in from Danny.

As expected, it's hit the fan. NB is upset. Good news = DPS ratings went off the charts, so I think we still have jobs. Lots of hate mail coming in, also demands for retraction. Too many loud-mouth loonies after my scalp. NB wants me gone until things cool down. Gotta get out of sight and sound for a while, probably outta USA also. Leaving Th or Fr. Please workup DPS program ideas while I'm gone. Go for the jugular. If you're up for it, I am too. Screw the NB. Also take some time off for yourself. DP

She immediately texts back.

Roger that. New programming ideas in process. Also planning for a holiday with Jason. Stay safe. J

And then forwards the text exchange to her dad, adding:

Dad, need to talk to you again this evening. Job is getting really complicated. Life is getting complicated. Obviously. Jason returns to Colorado tomorrow. That's the good news.
Julie

AFTER DINNER, father and daughter linger at the dinner table. No lounging outside. It's snowing. First blizzard of the season. Table clearing and washing dishes can wait. There's an absence of smiles as Julie begins.

"As you know, Danny and I took a big chance last week. But it looks like we still have jobs. Will there be a guest host for his show while he's gone? I just don't know yet. If there is, will I be involved? Probably, but maybe not. I might be persona non-grata for a while also. Danny's gone silent, but he wants programming suggestions from me for him to consider when he returns. And there are four important issues I've been thinking about. Two involve numbers, so they're in my niche of expertise. Two don't involve numbers, and I'd like to discuss those two with you because I'm undecided about suggesting them to Danny.

"On the first out-of-my-niche issue, I need to resolve a big self-doubt. It's like: because there's so much gasoline being poured on it by so many powerful people on a regular basis, should I really suggest Danny piss on a bonfire that's never gonna go out? I just don't know. Should I go ahead and encourage him? If that effort is tasked with me, it's an undertaking I'm not physically constructed with the ability to perform.

"Of course, issue #1 is political. Danny calls politics the Queen, and she demands relentless, focused attention from network news. She always gets it. In spades. So, about politics. Angie Bright lectured that H.L. Mencken said it best, and I found my lecture notes in the class notebook I brought to the table before we sat down for dinner. Hope what we're gonna talk about doesn't spoil our digestion. Here's the quote. 'The whole aim of practical politics is to keep the populace alarmed, and hence clamorous to be led to safety, by menacing it with an endless series of hobgoblins, all of them imaginary.' Although written early in the 19th century, the characterization also fits modern political activism, both left and right.

"The non-numbers issue I'd like to recommend Danny address first is Congressional Committee Oversight Overreach, which could also be titled Improper Trials By Congress, or, to use only two words, Congressional Rascality. Unless they're buried in an Amendment, I can't find the words 'committee' or 'oversight' in the Constitution." She pauses to emit a long sigh.

Jules sighs also. "Whew, sounds heavy. Outta my ken. But, go ahead anyway."

"Hokay, you asked for it. Legal scholars rationalize that Constitutional justification for Oversight Committees is implied rather than specified. That sounds like lawyer 'weasel-wording' to me. Their rationalization may come from section 8 of Article I of the Constitution, which gives Congress the power to constitute Tribunals inferior to the Supreme Court. I read that as the foundation for establishing the District Federal Court system. Only that, not for Oversight Committees in the Legislative Branch.

"So, I'm gonna read to you most of Professor Bright's Congressional Oversight lecture for her PolySciFi class. I've kept her written script which she provided to all of her students. I have it here with me, and I've been trying to decide if I should present it to Danny. You okay with this?"

"Of course. Maybe I'll learn something. Scientists need to listen as well as they argue. And as well as they observe. Read on."

"Okay. Here goes. Feels like I'm about to lecture a Professor. 'Congressional Oversight is abused politically to create false or exaggerated perceptions of wrongdoing by preying on emotion rather than appealing to reason. Encouraged in our current media environment, Oversight Committees purposely manipulate public opinion as they charge, investigate, indict, prosecute, act as judge and jury, and convict. That's not right. It's an egregious sabotage of basic rights to a fair trial. Oversight Committees should be abolished.

"'Sorry lawyers. A gathering of Legislators is not a tribunal. A Tribunal is, by definition, a Judiciary function. It cannot be comprised of Legislators. I can't imagine our Founding Fathers creating a tribunal mechanism so vulnerable to inappropriate infestation and control by rabidly partisan political members.

"'Oversight also spawns incomprehensible legislation of outrageous length and complexity, whose societal and dollar costs are grossly underestimated, and whose benefits are woefully exaggerated.

"'It's my perception, and I suspect that of many thoughtful Americans, that Congress attempts to GOVERN America through its Oversight functions. That's a blatant overreach and an improper usurpation of the powers of both the Executive and Judicial Branches.

"'Govern by a committee of 535? That's really stupid.

"'It's also my perception that Congressional Oversight committees are: ONE, Often chaired by politicians who are not subject-qualified. They ascend to their positions through seniority rather than expertise. TWO, Mostly staffed by ardent and biased political activists rather than dedicated public servants. And THREE, Formatted and conducted with a primary purpose of grandstanding for an enabling press and their gullible audience.'

"That's it. Thank you, Angie Bright. Not only for the insightful and amazingly brief lecture, but also for providing us with a written transcript. I promise never to submit it to a Congressional Committee that may go after you some day for Un-American activities. You are a true citizen. Thank God

Senator Joseph McCarthy is long dead. So, Dad, what's your reaction?"

"Frankly?"

"Of course."

"Briefly?"

"Even better."

He shakes his head. "Forget this one, Julie. It's a systemic dysfunction too deeply embedded in the legislative structure. Ain't never going to change. You might mention this structural outrage to Danny, but don't push it. Let him decide. As you acknowledged, he's better equipped to piss on a bonfire than you are. What's next?"

"Well, it's so absurd I feel like vomiting every time I talk about it."

"That's okay. I'm confronted with vomit-inducing diatribes on climate change most every day. So, I'm sort of inoculated against being infected by the absurdities of others. I'm also curious. What you got?"

"It's the last non-number highly-politicized issue I may suggest to Danny? It's another subject that never dies. Angel Bright called it simply Russia, Russia, Russia."

"My darling daughter. You are indeed on a roll. And the night is still young. Is there really anything to say about Russia that hasn't been said ad nauseam many times before? If so, please enlighten me."

"Probably not. But have you read any of the indictments resulting from the Mueller investigation?"

"Of course not. A horrible waste of time for any busy person."

"Do you know anyone who has?"

"No. But then I don't circulate with a crowd that tries to digest that kind of politicized garbage dumped on American citizens. Do you know anyone who read the indictments?"

"Yeah, Angel Bright did. They're not very long. And we discussed them in class. She didn't really lecture about them, so I don't have a transcript. Nor was the class required to read them, although I did and I think others in the class did also. I have a few notes, not enough to provide Danny with a solid foundation for an opening monologue. And I'm not sure I have the appetite necessary to devour more research into Russian involvement in the last election. It's a quicksand-like subject. You step into it and keep sinking deeper and deeper until you suffocate on a situation that eventually goes moot, except in the minds of political fanaticists."

"So, how about you give me a summary of what you recall...time limit two minutes? If that's possible. Think about the hundreds of millions of hours wasted on that three-year hoax by thousands in Government, tens of thousands in the media, tens of thousands practicing politicians, and millions of citizens addicted to 'rabidly partisan political pornography.' Isn't that how you said Professor Bright branded the profession she helped qualify you to enter?"

Julie smirks. "Wow, yeah Dad. You quoted Angie Bright perfectly. And I love your numbers. Maybe Danny could use them. So, I'll try to summarize a long and complex proceeding briefly. Then I'll go wash my mouth out with soap and vomit what I just said into the toilet.

"First, as Angel Bright also informed us in class, know that a prominent Judge once proclaimed that 'A clever Prosecutor can get a Grand Jury to indict a ham sandwich.'

"Now, on to the indictments. There were two of them. A key political figure was indicted twice. Once on two counts, tax evasion and lobbying for a foreign government without a license. Then a second time for money laundering. The Justice Department settled for a conviction on tax evasion. Brought in a few dollars...if the convicted criminal had any dollars left. Helped compensate the US Treasury for the millions of dollars wasted on the investigation and litigation proceedings. The third indictment resulted in a bunch of misbehaving Russians being scolded and then kicked out of the USA and sent home to Russia. That's it. BFD. Cases closed."

"Okay, Thanks Julie...I think. I timed you. You took 40 seconds. Now, let's go cleanse our minds with an hour of television comedy...if we can find an hour that doesn't waste a bunch of it on politics. Or maybe better yet, let's do an hour of a British period piece on PBS. Best yet, see if we have any Masterpiece Theater programs saved for later viewing. They're television's best drama productions."

PART FIVE

TURMOIL

NOV/DEC 2019

CHAPTER 17
BIPOLAR DISORDER

DANNY'S TEXT MESSAGE is waiting for her when Julie checks her iPhone after a two-day Anders family Thanksgiving in Denver...no electronic devices permitted.

> Julie, I'm back a week early, and we need to talk. I'll be gone next week as planned, and then I take an extra week off after that. Not back in the saddle until Dec 14. Let's FaceTime tomorrow. That's Sat Nov 30. 8:00 AM your time OK? Yeah, I know, it's still a holiday weekend. DP

Julie immediately responds.

> 8:00 AM tomorrow is good. Missing you. Both professionally and personally. Hope you're OK. JA

DANNY'S ALREADY ONLINE and waiting when Julie checks in. *Oh my God. Something's not right. He's unshaven, pasty faced, with glazed eyes. Also shaky hands.* She preempts his greeting, "Danny, what's wrong? I can tell. You look...uh...well, frankly, you look awful. What's going on?"

"It's recent, but it's nothing new. It's personal, and right now it's nasty. What's going on is I was diagnosed bipolar a year ago. The condition is generally manageable with medication, but drugs aren't working right now. Don't know what's worse, the manic side of me that makes me hyper, drives me crazy, and often makes both my work associates and my show guests really uncomfortable. Or the depressive side, which pushes me into a self-absorbed, self-critical funk and makes me barely functional. Mostly I'm in balance, but not right now. Can't shake the depression. A week in the sun and sea of Cabo San Lucas didn't help. So Monday I check into Damore Healthcare for a week. It's a psychiatric inpatient facility here in LA. One of the best. Maybe they can rebalance me with counseling and different drugs." He manages a half-smile to the screen. "Now, I gotta try to stay positive. Can't let despair dominate my life. Makes me feel concerned that I might be a bit like Ernest Hemingway emotionally, but without his literary genius. Hemingway went to Mayo's for help. But Mayo's couldn't help. Hope I have a better outcome with Damore and don't end up like he did. I certainly haven't experienced the war wounds and other physical injuries he had. I'm probably not even close to his near-record consumption of alcoholic beverages, plus both his mental and physical excesses. No wonder he ran out of cope."

He actually sounds better than he looks. "Danny I'm so sorry. I hope I didn't push too hard for what you presented in that last show when you became persona non grata."

"No, you did the right thing...and so did I. Anyone else pick up the income tax fraud theme and run with it?"

Julie also manages a half smile and shakes her bead. "Don't think so. No other networks and no other news commentators had the guts to similarly program a controversial subject that makes them look complicit in income tax fraud. A rebuttal to your monologue's assertions of tax fraud would make them look transparently over-defensive of an indefensible position. They're trapped. At least it seems like most of your regular viewers liked your monologue, and you for sure attracted a bunch of new viewers. A few early complainers made a lot of noise about what they considered your betrayal of their just and righteous causes. And then the complaints were over."

"That's sort of good news. And, so you know, Network Brass encouraged me to insert this additional week into my leave of absence. You're the only work associate who knows why..." his smile broadens, "...that I'm only half crazy.

"But now, how about you, Julie? Gotta be tough for you to scatter your attention over a guest host for my show and other MRABC programs. I know you have some time off planned also. While I'm in seclusion, I'll need to divert my mind away from too much introspection and professionally assisted self-analysis...try to retain some focus on my show. Before you leave, and so I don't go worse nuts and become preoccupied totally with myself next week, do you have any DPS program suggestions for the future?"

"Yep. I do have some suggestions. I've previewed programming ideas with my dad. He's sort of a sounding board for me, and he also listens to me almost as well as you do. So, I do have some topics for you to think about. I hope you'll find them intriguing. And I suspect you can still handle being mind-challenged big time...even while you're trying to repair and rehabilitate your mental function. Here are two program suggestions that might be candidates for opening monologues when you're over the depression thing and back in the saddle again.

"For starters, I'll e-mail you a Word document, which is Professor Bright's treatise on Federal Government malfeasance at the highest level. She entitled her lecture essay 'Congressional Committee Oversight Overreach.' The condition is a systemic Legislative branch dysfunction she'd never seen addressed in the media. It's probably analogous to an eventually terminal disease for which there is no alleviation or cure. Right down your alley if you're feeling like Don Quixote and want to joust a windmill. Challenge Congressional Committee authority? How dare anyone. David vs Goliath also comes to mind. It's likely a mission impossible."

He's laughing now. "Alright already. Nice word seduction. You now have my undivided attention."

"Okay. Here's one treatment for America's legislative dysfunction. Eliminate news media attendance at Congressional Committee hearings. As in close the damn doors and get down to serious business. But that wouldn't address the systemic problem. It wouldn't cure the dysfunction, just reduce its sabotage of the minds of others. It would be sort of like treating cancer with aspirin. However, it might also abate the nonproductive grandstanding for the press that dominates Congressional public hearings and also avoid the millions of hours wasted in public viewing of the proceedings."

"Okay, so I'm hooked already. Can't wait to read the treatise. What else?"

"I'll also e-mail you some comments on another subject, one that the news scene obsesses about off and on, mostly on. For over 50 years now. Just call it Russia, Russia, Russia. That says it all. Politicians, the media, and too many Americans never seem to get enough of Russia. Included in the e-mail will be some interesting numbers on the Mueller investigation from my father. Nothing scientific. Just Dad's sophisticated wild-ass guess about the hundreds of millions of hours wasted on that unnecessary, ill-conceived, outrageous, obviously politically biased and absurd assault on American minds. I'll include my World's record short summary of the investigation. That summary will only waste 40 seconds of your concentration. Dad timed me. Professor Bright, Dad, and I use lots of condemning adjectives in criticizing that masquerade of due process. You could probably avoid some of them and still get well-reasoned criticisms across."

"Julie, I'll have to think more about Russia, Russia, Russia. How long has network news already been obsessed with dramatizing their delusional perception of Russia's latest obscenity and its alleged interference in an American presidential election? Over two years now? With another election coming soon, shouldn't the last one finally become irrelevant? Isn't that alleged Russian travesty about to become just another sound-bite of unpleasant but insignificant history?"

"That's one of the problems, Danny. That history and the attempts to achieve successful invasions of fear and contempt into the minds of others never ever become irrelevant."

"You're right, and you've given me a lot to think about."

"Danny, if you'd like to explore either of these two topics beyond your opening monologue, I've no great ideas for show guests. Maybe a constitutional law scholar on the first, a former Secretary of State on the second? So, what do you think? Will these two potential show topics help distract you from yourself next week?"

"Definitely. And thanks, Julie, I think. Fascinating stuff as usual. I'll do some research too."

"But, what about the Network Brass Danny? Will that kind of programming rile up the NB again?"

"Well, my commentary on the first topic shouldn't. There's no political bias involved in attacking a systemic Congressional dysfunction. The second topic might rile-up the NB because it condemns and ridicules a Government effort that's generally considered left-wing driven. The Mueller investigation should have been politics neutral but it wasn't. If the NB doesn't like my commentary, assuming I decide to present it, they can go do what we both think they should do to themselves. NB can call the shots on my show guests but not what comes out of my mouth in an opening monologue."

"Bravo, Danny. Sounds like your depression is already on the road to recovery."

"And I'm also feeling better. Thanks to you. Any other program ideas for me?"

"Yep, but I'll save them for when you're back in the saddle again."

"How about a hint."

"Okay," she smiles and suppresses a chuckle. "You asked

for it. After next week, I'll be working on two topics that are numbers based and will probably drive-up your viewer count." Then she laughs openly. "And they're also likely to piss off your NB again." She purses her lips and shakes her head. "That's because my takes on both topics are going to deviate from popular views promoted by many politicians and by most in the media."

Now he's smiling and chuckling. "Goodie. What are the topics?" The glaze is finally gone from his eyes.

"A hint, they're two of the most aggressively over-hyped controversies ever to erupt, then contaminate and divide the national discourse. For many years now they've provided an endless supply of brain fodder for politicians and the media."

"So, you now have my undivided attention again. What are they?"

"Racial Bias of Law Enforcement and Global Warming. I've got lots of numbers to review and then figure out how best to condense and present them. You might be disinclined to digest and then program them into an understandable televised viewing format. That's quite a challenge. Hope they don't give you mental indigestion."

"Whew, you are a glutton for tackling tough controversial issues. You're also addressing two sources for media commentaries that never run dry. Like toxic springs that deliver fresh water in perpetuity...although it's badly contaminated. Can't wait to see what you come up with."

"Danny, you'll have to wait a week. While you're incarcerated in mental health care, I'm off on a holiday with Jason-Jerrold Jennings. Hopefully to elevate the level of my personal healthcare, both physical and mental."

"A-h-h, the conservation-minded boyfriend who also puts his energy and effort where his intellect and sentiments direct him. Like some of the rest of us desperately try to do. A role model for commitment to cause. I understand he's just back from a foreign assignment...in Chile, I think you told me.

You've had quite a long distance romance going."

Certain that her blush is obvious, Julie covers her cheeks with her hands and nods her head. "Yep."

"Then, I hope it's okay to switch our conversation focus from me to you. Can you tell me about it? I haven't asked before. I'll understand if you think I'm prying too deeply into your private life."

"M-m-m-m. Actually, I'm flattered. You've always been a good listener, and I appreciate your interest in the non-professional me. No worries, I won't take you in too deeply.

"So...Jason and I endured a long separation that started only a few days after Memorial Day weekend. That was our first meeting as adults. I think a mutual attraction began when we met briefly as teenagers. I'll tell you about that sometime. Not now. It was quite an experience. With that initial attraction confirmed and sort of consummated back in September, you could probably say our relationship has now exploded into a grand passion. Interesting that the explosion is all a consequence of three months' nurturing by long-distance and with long-content e-mails. Amazing the power of the pen. It can deliver intense and passionate feelings when, except by photographs, there's no show, only tell.

"Now it's total show-time for the two of us. Next week Jason and I are off to Zion National Park. Finally, we can enjoy intense time together. Zion is one of America's few National Parks that offers a great getaway destination into December.

"So, it's my turn to ask, Danny. Anyone special to help you through this troubled time?"

He laughs. "Well...you, of course. Thanks for listening and for providing me with such complex diversions of the mind. I also have a brother and a sister. Unlike me, they're both normal, and we're close, although individually very different. Or, maybe you were thinking about my affairs of the heart. Sort of like, I'll tell you mine if you tell me yours. I know some in the media like to gossip about my womanizing. That's pure baloney. Although I've managed to maintain intimate relationships twice in the mature years out of my relatively limited years on the planet, neither worked out. Probably my fault. Nothing romantic going on now. Don't have the time.

"But now, back to business. When I'm back in the saddle again, as you characterized it, I'd like to do some shows from the MRABC Denver studio, and I'd like for you to be there. Maybe we can even have a lunch date...er business lunch at the Brown Palace?"

She laughs. "Sure Danny. I'll be there for you."

"As you've always been. So, until then. Something to look forward to. Now I gotta sign off and prepare for mind reparations. Assuming it's reparable. Thank you for your time today, Julie."

"Of course. Goodbye Danny. Stay strong."

CHAPTER 18

DELIGHTS OF BODY, MIND, AND SOUL

DEC 9 AND 10

"SO, JASE. ARE YOU GOING TO TELL ME about Zion National Park or ask me to read a short story you wrote about it?"

"No to both questions. Yes to either couldn't do justice to the Park. To appreciate Zion's stunning beauty, you have to see it and be immersed in it. It's a spiritual experience. Unless it's overcrowded. Which it shouldn't be in early December. A light dusting of fresh snow is forecast for tonight and ending tomorrow. That should mysticize our travel experience even more. No tells or reads this trip. All shows."

"And no bears to harass us?"

"No bears, Julie. I promise."

"Kind of romantic remembering we first met as teenagers in America's first National Park. Now, as adults, and for our first real trip together, we're visiting another National treasure."

"It gets even more romantic, Julie. We've done the Devil's Causeway in Colorado. And tomorrow we'll be up early and hike to Angel's Landing on Zion's most iconic and most popular trail. So, it's like we've already been to Hell, and now we're about to be in Heaven together. I think I remember you mentioning that."

"Yep, I did. And now you're implying the Devil threw us out after we dared to cross his bridge to Hell?"

"Absolutely."

"Okay." She shrugs her shoulders. "Hope the Angels let us in. So Jase, can you at least brief me on where we'll be staying? I told Dad I'd let him know."

"Sure. The reservation confirmation from Flanigan's Inn is in the glove compartment. You can text the name and phone number to your Dad at his office. We're staying in the Inn's Villa number one. With incredible views, it's also Flanigan's largest and nicest accommodation for just two people. Might call it their honeymoon suite."

She punches his right shoulder...gently. "Jase, we're not married."

"Not yet."

"Well, you haven't proposed."

"And you haven't either."

"Jase!" She punches him again as he arcs off the Denver metro area's foothills highway onto Interstate 70, heading west to Utah.

DAWN LINGERS LONG on the southern fringes of Zion National Park. December's sun finally crests the phalanx of red-rock behemoths towering above the Virgin River as it serpentines its way through Zion Canyon.

When they waken Tuesday morning, they're greeted by three deer grazing shadowless just beyond their east-facing bedroom window. Seasonally-brown grass stubble pokes through a lingering white crust of leftovers from Tuesday's snow flurries. To the East and 2,700 ft. above the grazers, the first rays of morning sun capture an ever-the-guardian summit of The Watchman. West-facing windows frame an even higher summit, now fully-enveloped in morning sun, where the majestic West Temple ascends 1,250 ft. above The Watchman. Now fully crowned in white, its broad truncated summit is the highest in the Park.

Julie's still in her nightgown. *So glad I abandoned pajamas and treated myself to more alluring sleep-wear for this trip.* She's sitting in a swiveling recliner that enables her to enjoy 180 degrees of outdoor landscapes. She's following all the morning views as they develop on both sides of her. She's also remembering last night. She and Jason celebrated their first night together since Labor-day weekend in September. Both mindscapes... her memories of last night and the morning visions that now surround her...are a natural and luxurious combination of delights. *It's like a simultaneous wedding and honeymoon. Joining indulgences of the body, mind, and soul in a single experience. Better than any conventional wedding celebration I could ever imagine.* She swipes at tears of joy beginning to drain from her eyes. *Wow, never thought of myself as this sentimental.*

Jason emerges from the shower and pauses naked in the hallway as she calls out to him. "Jase, hurry-up. Grab a robe and come join me before these amazing dawn images lose their magic."

He does, and she continues, "So Jase...I'm looking at the snow-encrusted West Temple and also reading about it. Listen to what Frederick Dellenbaugh wrote in 1903. It's one of the first nationally published articles about Zion Canyon. 'Niagara has the beauty of energy; the Grand Canyon, of immensity; the Yellowstone, of singularity; the Yosemite, of altitude; the ocean, of power; and this Great Temple, of eternity.'"

AS SUNLIGHT DESCENDS into the Canyon, it filters its way through groves of leafless cottonwood trees and dances along the river's edge. Wild turkeys graze in swaths of browned-out vegetation between road and trees.

Leaving the car parked at the Grotto picnic area, they zip-up matching blue down jackets by Patagonia, shoulder-up LL Bean daypacks, also matching, don their matching Airflo Hats by Tilley, then pause, pose and take a selfie; and then move on to study a large trail-side poster which maps the way to their destination.

After crossing the bridge spanning the Virgin River, they turn right at a T junction and pause again, elevating their right hands to execute a ritual high-five and officially begin an arduous hike that will take them to Angel's Landing 1,500 ft. above the Canyon floor. A five-mile round trip.

Minimal early morning traffic on the wide and pinkish-cemented trail enables them to mostly walk side-by-side, holding hands. They angle and switch-back up sloping, vegetated hillsides that separate the river's riparian corridor from sheer cliff faces. They pause again when they reach a broad cliff face. Brutalized in place by workmen in the 1920s, the trail now enables human traffic to walk where only wild birds of prey flew before.

Literally entering into the cliff face, they continue the hike on wide, dynamite-assisted switchbacks...half-tunnels blasted out of the cliff that have the weird appearance of natural tunnels sheared in half vertically. Hedgerows of stacked and cemented rocks two feet high gird the trail and guard its open periphery. Full-on morning sun heats the semi-enclosed space and compels them to pause and shed their jackets.

Switchbacks soon end. When it exits the cliff face, the trail narrows, becomes more natural again, and abruptly junctions left into a narrow and sunless slot canyon. There, un-melted snow lingers, and patches of glaze ice demand that vision concentrates on the trail, not its surroundings. Air temperature drops, and they re-don down jackets as they enter Refrigerator Canyon, as it's appropriately named. Sunshine rarely dares to enter here.

Elevation gain for the next half mile is modest. That abruptly changes when a 180-degree switchback delivers them onto one of the Park's most impressive manmade wonders, exceeded only by the Zion Mt. Carmel highway tunnel, a man-blasted mile through the flank of Bridge Mountain.

They pause and gaze at stack after stack of pink blocks anchoring another switchback trail cemented into a cliff face. Rising like a corkscrew, this back-and-forth goes almost pure vertical rather than horizontal. "Okay," he says, "I've been up here once before, but you're the numbers guru, and I know you always do your homework. What are we looking at?"

She gasps. "So THAT'S Walter's Wiggles. Photos don't do it justice. Here, let me see what the guide says." She doffs her day-pack, extracts a small brochure, and flips a few pages. "Okay. 'Originally constructed in 1926, there are 21 stubby switchbacks snaking their way up over 200 vertical feet. In 1985 the dirt and rock path the Wiggles used to contain was replaced with concrete. It took 258 helicopter loads carrying 88 cubic yards of cement to complete the job.' Yeah, right. Here I go again with my perpetual numbers obsession. Can't shake it. Not even on holiday. So, let's go wiggle up the famous Wiggles. See who huffs and puffs the least."

"Okay Julie, you're on. Time to shed down jackets again. Lots of sunshine ahead. But watch for lingering ice patches on some of the Wiggles. We'll pause and catch our breath at Scout Lookout."

The Steepness of the Wiggles discourages conversation. Their general fitness enables them to pass several slower hikers, and soon they reach a saddle with open views steeply downward into Zion Canyon far below. Views on either side feature continuation trails. Up and right to Angel's Landing, up and left to the West Rim. Both are steep. Scout Lookout is appropriately named. Views along all points of the compass are compelling. They pause for a few moments to engage the landscapes and admire the collation barrages of morning sun and ever-changing shadows. Their heavy breathing slows. "You know," he says. "I'm not even going to try and photograph any of this. The majesty of all the views defies the ability of any camera to capture. That attempt would be a futile effort to replicate the majesty of this natural surrounding."

Ahead right, post-to-post chain linkings advance steeply. They provide hand-hold assistance on the more popular and more challenging trail to Angel's landing. The hike now becomes a climb. Both briefly shed their backpacks and drain the remaining contents of one of their two water bottles. "Need a rest break?" he asks. "Or an energy bar?"

"No and no," she responds. "Let's keep going. You know the way. You lead. And...now...how about a hug, Jase? I want to keep saying thank you, thank you, thank you for bringing me to such an extraordinary place."

They embrace, and she again feels tears well in her eyes. *I'm giddy. From the views? The elevation gain? The company of the man I love? Probably all of the above.*

TWENTY MINUTES LATER they crest the trail's only significant undulation, a moderate dip before the steep rise resumes up to the long summit ridge and its final plateau. Now they must scramble. Feet alone aren't enough. They look up a long and very narrow trail. Also very steep. Sheer drop-offs on both sides challenge them. Chain-links to stakes again provide hand-held assistance. It's not a climb for those who experience serious mind and balance issues when challenged by extreme exposure.

And it's now a genuine huff and puff ascent. Pausing to catch their breath, they decide to diverge 90 degrees left from the trail. Scrambling over a jumble of rocks, they seek another cliff edge for a more exclusive side-view of Zion Canyon below. There they pause and slow their breathing for a few moments... away from foot traffic that's now becoming congested. A shallow ridge depression encircled with boulders and a few small wind-twisted trees greets them. Just what they are seeking...a tiny haven out of sight and sound of other climbers. Where they can enjoy a bit of privacy on what's rapidly becoming a heavily populated and near-vertical public ascent.

But, they're not alone. "Jase, look," she exclaims. "What is that?"

In the midst of a cluster of Utah Junipers, a lone and patriarchal Ponderosa Pine leans out from the cliff edge at a precarious 45-degree angle over Zion Canyon. Six feet out on its largest branch perches the weirdest looking bird she's ever seen. Also the largest. Also the ugliest.

Jason laughs. "Should have told you about this local guardian of the Canyon. This is his home territory. He's America's largest winged creature, a male California Condor, and he's indeed a rarity. He's probably connected to a massive nest that's imbedded in a large crevice of the sheer rock face below. That nest delivered the very first Condor born and fledged in Zion. Wild-hatched in April of this year, it just flew off the nest on the first day of October. Unlike his Andean Condor cousins I spent some time with in Chile, this bird, if you could call him that, is not a raptor. He's a New World Vulture. So he's a carrion-eater, a scavenger that does not kill other living things. About 100 Condors regularly travel a corridor between Southern Utah and Northern Arizona...mostly the Grand Canyon region. Stand quiet a minute. He may tolerate us for a while, even with an enlarging and noisy cluster of climbers just a dozen yards away.

TWENTY MINUTES LATER they crest Angel's Landing and join a crowded tourist scene at a small summit plateau. Climbers dance and celebrate, hug and congratulate. Busy cameras commemorate. In the depths of Zion Canyon far below, miniature visitors and their miniature automobiles congregate.

Full on noonday sun chases away the remaining chill of a winter day. No snow remains. "Time for another selfie?" he asks. "Didn't do it with that Condor peering at us. Might have scared him away."

"Yep. Time for a selfie."

Linking arms around shoulders, they goofy-smile stare into the face of Jason's iPhone, and he records their joint summit success for posterity.

Then he turns toward her, leans forward so they can be cheek-to-cheek and whispers into her ear. "I know it's crowded here, and we have no privacy. But what better time and place to say what I need and want to say with a few words and absolutely all of my heart? For you and all of eternity to hear, I love you, Julie. Beyond reason. Will you marry me?"

She returns the whisper, "Of course, Jason. I think I've loved you from the second day we spent together." Then she collapses into his open arms.

CHAPTER 19

DESPAIR

DEC 11 AND 12

AS IN THEIR FIRST MORNING TOGETHER, she's first to waken. She slips from bedroom to bathroom and then back again. Snuggling back into bed beside Jason, she starts to advance an arm-hug around his shoulders. But something's not right. She pauses the hug, levers herself into a half-sitting position above him, and whispers, "Jase? Jase...you okay?"

No answer, and he's belly-down in bed with his face turned away from her. *He doesn't sleep that way.* Rising again, she circles the bed and kneels beside him. With her left hand on the floor bracing her, she uses her right hand to deliver a shoulder shake. No response. His face is gray, ashen even, his eyes half-open, his mouth fully-open, his tongue extended, lolling to the side with drool pooled below on the bed sheet.

"JASON," she screams. She settles back on her haunches and frantically searches with her fingers for a pulse in his wrist, then in his neck. There is none. No movement in his chest or abdomen either. *Oh my God, no heartbeat, and he's not breathing. He's dead. What happened? We had a beautiful night. What should I do? I don't know what to do. Why did it happen? How did it happen?* She's shivering now. Her thoughts are muddy and ranging, almost impossible to focus. Her body movements and her racing mind are erratic and uncontrollable. Her heart pounds in her chest. *Focus, Julie, focus. Gotta turn on some heat, warm up, and get dressed before I get too chilled to do anything. No. I'll call 911 first, then turn up the heat, then get dressed, then call Dad. A first responder should be here soon.*

"...AND D-D-DADDY," she sobs. "He j-j-just never woke up. We had a beautiful day yesterday. He proposed in the most extraordinary place imaginable. And I accepted. I don't know what happened overnight. Why d-d-did he die? I have no idea. Help me, D-d-d-daddy. I've never been so scared. I feel like I've gone totally brain-dead. Last night my heart was near bursting with joy. Now it's totally broken. I can't think. And I can't cry. Why am I not crying? And I d-d-don't know what to do. Should I just wait for the paramedics?"

"Julie, you're not crying because you're still in shock. The shock will wear off, and then you may be overcome with uncontrollable grief and tears. So, no, don't just wait. Stay busy with something. Get your mind off of what happened. You were right to call 911 immediately. Now go into autopilot. Occupy your thoughts with what you need to do for yourself. You must care for yourself now. Nothing more you can do for Jason. So, prepare to leave. Pack. Nourish your body, mind, and emotions. Fix yourself a wholesome breakfast. And eat it. Stick to the mundane. Let the paramedics decide what to do about Jason.

"And, Julie, Jason's Dad needs to be called. I'll call him. It's Mark, isn't it? Go get his phone numbers. Both business and home phone. They're probably on Jason's iPhone. Find them now, before the paramedics arrive and require most of your time and attention. I'll stay on the line."

She returns with the numbers, and her father continues. "Okay, first I'll call Mark. Then I'm coming down today to pick you up and bring you back home tomorrow. Trying to fly down commercially would get complicated and take too long. I'll drive. Thank God the weather's decent. It's still before sunrise here. With luck I should be there by nightfall. And, yes, I do know where you're staying. I think Mark Jensen lives close to a small private airport. He's got the bucks and may charter a flight down. If he can add anything to his son's mysterious death, I'll call you back from the car."

"OKAY JULIE, I'M JUST LEAVING. I've talked to Mark Jensen, and he is chartering a plane. He may get there earlier than I can, and he's already booked you and me into a separate room at Flanigan's Inn for tonight. Very thoughtful of Mark to understand a father and daughter's need to be alone together this evening and not in the same space where you've just experienced such a personal tragedy.

"So his workplace also knows of Jason's death, Mark will also call The Nature Conservancy. Mark plans to bring down a close friend with him who will drive Jason's car back to Colorado.

"Now, and this is really important for your own peace of mind. You need to know Jason's death is likely from a genetic inherited condition he never knew about. His mother died of it when Jason was only ten years old. Mark never told his son the underlying cause of her death. All Jason ever knew was that his mother died of an aneurism. Because the underlying condition dramatically shortens life expectancy, Mark wanted Jason to live a normal life without fear of a premature death. The genetic condition is called Ehlers-Danlos Syndrome, and it's rare. Jason was born with very fragile blood vessels, Julie, and it's likely an aortic aneurism that killed him, as it did his mother. And no, it's not the same condition your mom had. Hers was a brain aneurism, a freak condition not genetic."

"Oh, Daddy," she's sobbing again. "What we did yesterday. It was such an aggressive hike physically...and mentally."

"Julie, listen to me. Don't think that way. You and Jason have enjoyed two beautiful times together, both of them in the embrace of natural surroundings that enriched your lives as nothing created by man could ever provide. First, that weekend of self-discovery here in Colorado, then yesterday in one of America's most compelling landscapes. Even if he knew of his condition, both those times together were experiences Jason would have insisted on sharing with you. Together you two made intense memories that will stay with you forever. Indelible. Cherish them. Many people live long lives with scrambled memories not nearly so grand or self-fulfilling.

"Now, back to the present. Are the paramedics there yet?"

"Just. They're in with Jason. I couldn't bear going back into the bedroom."

"Good. Don't go back. They may have already explained some of this to you, but here's what you can expect. The paramedics can't pronounce death. For a patient who is pulse-less when they arrive on the scene, they can only conclude that 'death is already present.' A Doctor has to pronounce death. And Flanigan's has offered to help in any way they can. They told Mark that the local medical clinic is just around the corner and down a side street, with a Doctor on the scene when they open. That's where the paramedics will probably take Jason. So you have as few memories of him in death as possible, I suggest you not accompany them.

"Sometime between here and there, I'll contact Dan Panders and let him know what's happened. I'm sure he'll encourage you to take as much time off as you need. My advice to you is to go back to work as soon as possible. Get your mind back to focus on normal daily life. Don't linger long in mourning. These things I know because I've been there too. The premature death of a loved one brings aches to the mind and soul that never go away.

"Now, I need to sign off and call in my absence from work. So...stay strong, my beloved daughter. Bundle up, go sit quietly in the field behind you, fully engage your mind and your senses in natural surroundings, and wait for the deer to come out to feed at sunrise. Then watch them for a while. I'm sure they'll tolerate your presence, and the peaceful scene will help ease your pain and combat your mental numbness. No, your mind is not dead. Just traumatized. Feed it some soothing visual tranquility. Soon, I will be there with you, and you will have a shoulder to cry on, two of them if you need them. Bye now Julie. Know that I will always love and cherish you."

"Bye, Dad. You've already helped me through this. A lot. And know that I will always love and cherish you."

DRIVING HOME THE NEXT DAY, Julie mostly dozes semi-comatose in the back seat of the car. She wakens as they ease through Boulder's main intersection of Broadway and Pearl Street. Her eyes stray west along the Pearl Street Mall. And then her tears finally flow. "S-o-o little time w-e-e had together, Dad," she sobs. "First, a chance encounter there in front of the Patagonia store. Then a holiday weekend at the Triple J family ranch. Then Jason is three months gone on a special assignment in Chile. We finally enjoy a soul-saving day in a hallowed place, and then our dreams of a future together are destroyed in the silence of the night. How do I get over this?"

"You'll never get over it, Julie. Although it was so...so brief, know always that in your short time together, what you two created for yourselves was beautiful. It will live in your memories forever, untouched by aging or changes in circumstance. That's a good thing. And it's okay to cry. Tears are what you mix with laughter to nourish your soul."

STOP

PART SIX

FRESH BEGINNINGS?

JAN 2020

CHAPTER 20
GOOD INTENTIONS
JAN 6 - 10

"JULIE, THANKS SO MUCH for coming to Denver this morning. Can't believe it's almost three months since we first met here. This is also the last place we met face-to-face without using modern electronic communication devices. It's refreshing to be person-to-person in the heart of metro Denver. When I come to LoDo, I feel a healthy human pulse of normal life here. It's always genuine, never facile. LoDo enjoys a physical setting that presents a fascinating visual blend of the old and the new. Here, dwellers and visitors alike enjoy a concentration of activity that's still relatively uncontaminated by urban dysfunction. Not like our major coastal cities of California. They're all infested with tangles of damaged and degenerated streets that seem to be ruled by the dregs of humanity. So full of civil unrest, crime, and homeless human despair. LoDo feels intensely normal, unsullied, and still vital. Hope it never changes."

"Danny, it's also great to see you again without two screens between us. You're also looking intensely normal, unsullied, and returned to vitality. And you're right about LODO. LODO also hosts one of the most iconic businesses in Denver...The Tattered Cover bookstore. Probably sold more books than any bookstore between the Mississippi River and the Pacific Ocean. Since I was a child, Dad has taken me there. Most of the books in his stuffed personal library...and in mine...came from Tattered Cover showcase bookshelves. Except college textbooks of course!"

"So, Julie, on to DPS 2020 business. You ready to tackle programming for the new year?"

"Absolutely. The ending weeks of year 2019 were tough for both of us. So much happened in our lives as that year wound down, both professionally and personally. I really appreciated the flowers and the personal note you sent after Jason's death. I think I did the right thing to return to work right away. Dad encouraged it. To get my mind off tragedy and back to normalcy as soon as possible. Yeah, fathers do know best...most of the time. So, before we get to the new business of Dan Pander's Show circa 2020, let's keep it personal for a bit longer. How about we celebrate the new year with a big hug, Danny? I suspect we both need it."

Both smiling, they embrace, then part, and then sit down.

"Okay, back to show business," he says. "Subject is programming DPS for this first month of the new year. As the Queen of commentary, politics will always command a big chunk of my program space. But I want to pursue some of the things we talked about just before I checked myself into therapy. And I'd like to start with that subject that never goes away and never grows obsolete. It supports a full-time equivalent of thousands of persons employed in the media. For decades it's dominated modern journalism of all flavors: television, radio, newspaper, magazine. All wasted in a politically spawned and media supported cause that seems devoid of rhyme, reason, or resolution. Your three words define it totally: Russia, Russia, Russia. The hoaxers' delight. For decades Russia has been portrayed mostly by irrational politicians and the media as America's most dangerous and potentially lethal enemy. I've decided to start the new year with an opening monologue on the Mueller investigation, that misguided travesty that seems to have no end in sight. After 674 days in process, his investigation technically concluded about nine months ago, but many in the media just won't leave it alone to rest in peace... or in infamy."

"Do it Danny. Bravo. But, didn't the Network Brass also buy into that politicized Government hoax?"

"Yep. In spades."

"So, aren't you asking for trouble from them again?

"Maybe. But, when the dust settled on the response to my show's allegations of income tax fraud by not-for-profits and news organizations, the NB finally realized that my program that night had more supporters than critics. It's just that critics made more noise. A lot more noise. As usual. So, with your permission I'd like to quote you directly, using your summary of the Mueller investigation, and I'll credit you as the source. By name if you like, or without exploding your name into prime-time television if you'd prefer. I'll limit that opening monologue to exactly two minutes. That's an 80 second intro and 40 seconds to deliver the quote. Then I'll claim the record for the shortest opening monologue ever in the history of network news. Don't think I'm likely to get laid off again for devoting only two minutes to a continuation of the triple R waste of time and its excessive media attention."

"I hope not, Danny. And you for sure have my permission to quote me. But I'd appreciate it if you don't finger me as the source. I'm uncomfortable with widespread name recognition at this stage of my career. Maybe I'll feel differently later."

"Okay, I understand. Then, the other issue you mentioned in December is also something I'd like to pursue in an opening monologue, maybe even expand it into a separate show segment with guests. It's a topic Professor Bright addressed in a lecture. I think you said she called it 'Congressional Oversight Committee Overreach. Very provocative. Unlike Russia, Russia, Russia which is external and goes on and on, infecting network news on ad-nauseam. Great new subject. Let's call it COCO for short, although KOOKOO might be more appropriate. COCO is a sinister and imbedded internal legislative excess. But I've never seen it addressed in any network news programming. Do you think you could get Professor Bright's permission for me to quote her?"

"I still have her e-mail address. I'll try."

"Or, better yet, maybe I should bring her on the show? She could come here to the Denver studio. I'll send the network limousine to Boulder to pick her up."

"Didn't you already tell me the Network Brass would likely say no to her?"

"Yep, I think I remember that. But COCO really intrigues me. Mostly because of its apparent absence from any network coverage. And the Network Brass might actually go along with Professor Bright as a guest, even though COCO seems to be a sacred cow, a news commentary untouchable. To me as well as you and Professor Bright, it seems obvious that Congressional committees and sub-committees flagrantly and regularly exceed their authority. It's gotta be obvious to a great many Americans, maybe even most Americans other than the relatively few who are addicted to following COCO televised proceedings. Surprising that so few of those obsessed with politics don't see their addiction as a waste of time. COCO is an imbedded condition in Federal Government, like a contagious, politically motivated incurable infection. It's a mental pandemic in perpetuity. I have no idea why its excesses go on for decades unchallenged by most prominent persons and avoided...maybe purposely...by so many in the media.

"So Julie, a final philosophical question. How could Professor Bright's malfeasance assertions be credible if oversight committees have such an attentive media and viewer following and acceptance?"

Julie laughs. "That's the problem. There's been no challenge to the oversight overreach. Malfeasance assertions should be granted credibility because COCO breeches constitutional authority. As Angie Bright summarizes so well in few words, COCO originates charges, then investigates, indicts, acts as judge and jury, and finally convicts. COCO excesses have become commonplace. Only actions missing are sentencing and incarceration. It's a modern political reality that denies and defies reason. Pretentious theatrics replace due process. A hopeless paradox."

"But, does it really have a political side to it?" he continues. "Don't answer. Let me take a shot at an answer. Criticizing Congressional oversight shouldn't have a political side. Both parties seem to embrace the notion of unlimited Congressional power, and legislators from both parties love to wallow in the foul-smelling sludge-pile of allegations and investigations that power creates and nurtures. Seems like most every Congressperson, regardless of whether they are emblazoned red or blue, will likely be offended by any challenge to Congressional committee authority, no matter how rational."

"So, Danny, you're saying your show, in its isolated attempt to be rational, will dare to be not only audacious but also offensive to everyone?"

"Absolutely. Time to play some offense."

"Great. Danny Do-right is back. And he's got his dander up. Deal me in."

JAN 11 - 16

AFTER BREAKFAST JULIE OPENS their regular Saturday morning interchange with a brief text message. Still an imbedded family custom, Shane is resting beside her, and she reaches down to give him a comforting pat on the head. *For both of us. Wish me luck faithful one. If Danny accepts my ideas for some special DPS programming over the next several weeks, there may be fireworks consequences that will disturb my life. Hopefully not yours.* Shane licks her fingers in response reassurance. *At least you and Dad will be on my side...I hope. Wonder if Danny will have the guts to present my ideas. Or if his Network Brass will even allow him.*

So, how was your Russia, Russia, Russia monologue received last week? Dad and I watched. He had a short sneezing spell and missed most of it. JA

Danny's response is immediate, ebullient, and not so brief.

Terrific. Responses to R tripled were mostly positive. Most of the public is tired of naughty Russia narratives. Sadly, our own NB is not. NB still wants to perpetuate the myth of American Red collaboration with Russian Reds in the 2016 election. From other network shows, blabbery talking head commentaries on the subject continue. Because of the brevity of my comments and so many supportive viewer responses, I got off with just an NB scolding…this time. DP

Julie texts back.

So, what happens next week with COCO? That still on? COCO will absorb a lot more time than the quicky shot at R Tripled. Professor Bright says have at it and wishes you good luck. I didn't mention you might invite her to be a show guest. JA

Danny responds.

Thanks, Julie. As expected, the NB said absolutely no to Professor Bright. I'm disappointed but not surprised. Monday evening I'll take a shot at COCO in an opening monologue without attribution. DP

Julie signs off with.

And may The Force be with you. Be careful. Sacred cows might have lethal bites. JA

ON TUESDAY MORNING Julie texts Danny.

Nice rendition of Angie Bright's COCO lecture last night. So, how were the reactions? JA

HIS RESPONSE doesn't come until Thursday.

Sorrry, been really busy. Most viewer reactions to COCO were positive. But now I'm the target of politicized talk show hosts and their guests from both sides of the aisle. As expected, they're offended by challenges to Congressional authority. Great stimulus to increase DPS viewer base. Controversy breeds attention. Goody. NB are in a quandary. They disapproved but acknowledge the reality of an enlarging viewer base. DP

Julie responds.

Angie Bright called yesterday. She's thrilled. "Time the public was properly informed about Congressional malfeasance," she said. So, what's next? Lots of numbers dancing in my head that I'm committing to simple charts. Might be too complex for some? Hope not. Can I help program? JA

He answers.

Dunno what's next. You tell me. Liberate your dancing numbers. What topics you got in mind? Let's talk or text about them. On Sat. Early. I'll initiate. DP

CHAPTER 21
RACIAL BIAS IN LAW ENFORCEMENT
JAN 18 - 23

SATURDAY MORNING'S briefing begins with Danny's pre-breakfast text.

> OK. Both R tripled and COCO are behind us. Let's move on. I'm ready for your suggestions. You ready? DP

Just risen and now back to sleeping in pajamas, Julie responds.

> Yep, I'm ready. First I need to feed the dog and let him out to do his business, then get dressed and help Dad fix and eat our breakfast. Then I'll get back to you. I'll switch to e-mail. It's gonna get numbery again. Gotta show as well as tell. JA

NOW FULLY DRESSED and fully fueled mentally, Julie opens their e-mail exchange.

> Danny. Here we go. I appreciate your confidence in me, and I'm juiced about the opportunity to make a difference in commentary on important issues. I've done

my own research on the credibility of another popular belief that has been litigated in the media ad-nauseam: that there's an egregious racial bias against blacks in America's law enforcement ranks of mostly whites.

However, based on actual data, the only credible assertion of racial bias by law enforcement is that it exists against whites, not blacks. Now that I have your undivided attention to my heresy, details with numbers will follow. But first, an example of the impact of biased media reporting of this difficult subject on a hyper-rational mind from which I inherited a hyper-rational mind. My father's.

Dad's not only excluding network news from his television viewing, he's now also banished NPR from his sources as well. He does follow some written news analyses about Government and politics, mostly from Andrew McCarthy, an experienced attorney and litigator. He'll also scan some news headlines but rarely reads the details. But no more NPR news. "It's also too committed to deceit and thought manipulation," he says. I tend to agree with him. On our way back from a father/daughter snowshoe outing into our nearby foothills, we were listening to NPR news on the car radio. Two back-to-back programs reported on the same incident: the death of a criminal suspect at the hands of five arresting law enforcement officers. Both commentators emphasized the skin color of the suspect. Black, of course. Then both commentators carefully avoided mentioning the skin color of the arresting officers. At home I hit the research trail. It was a difficult search, but I finally located a news source that disclosed the skin color of the arresting officers. All five were black.

Both NPR commentators obviously wanted to create the impression that the harsh treatment of the suspect was racially motivated and the arresting officers were white. So sad to see NPR join the practitioner ranks of media deceit.

Okay. My analysis follows. Yeah, it's in chart form, using data from last year: 14 percentages derived from only 12 numbers. Hope that's not too much for a viewing audience to digest.

RECENT BLACK AND WHITE CRIME DATA, compared to BLACK AND WHITE KILLED BY POLICE DATA
(excludes other race/ethnicity stats)

	BLACK	WHITE
% of US:		
Population of these two races only	**15.0%**	**85.0%**
Total murders committed by	**52%**	**48%**
Murders of blacks committed by	82.0%	8.7%
Murders of whites committed by	18.0%	91.3%
Serious, not-fatal violent crimes by	**48%**	**52%**
Shot and killed by police		
Total	**39%**	**61%**
Ratio of "police kills" to murders committed by	**75%**	**127%**

No data on "killed by police" by other than being shot (like kneeling on neck).

No data on the race of police who killed.

SOME RAW DATA:	BLACK	WHITE	Total
Total Murdered	3,140	2,840	5,980
Murders of blacks committed by	2,574	246	2,820
Murders of whites committed by	566	2,594	3,160
Shot and killed by police	235	370	605

Now...my comments. The chart presents last year's data. Key numbers and key percentages in the chart are highlighted. With only 15% of the combined black and white population base (BWPB), blacks committed 52% of the murders and 48% of the non-fatal violent crimes. With 85% of the BWPB, whites committed only 48% of the murders and 52% of the non-fatal violent crimes. Obviously,

America's black population is more inclined to violence than its white population. How much of this big disparity might be attributed to circumstance differentials...like the color dominance in densely populated and relatively poor neighborhoods of cities...I have no idea.

Of the total criminals (or criminal suspects) shot and killed by police, only 39% were black and 61% were white. You'll see I've added another revealing calculation to the data: the ratio of police kills to murders committed by. The ratio is only 75% for black criminals and escalates to 127% for white criminals. If there's a skin color bias in the lethality of law enforcement crime responses, it's obviously against color white. Are cops intentionally more restrained when dealing with color black? The numbers suggest that.

Danny, now I have to acknowledge my latent insecurities are showing. Am I missing anything? Despite its only logical conclusions, I know my data analysis goes against what seems to be the prevailing belief. Also against what is regularly featured in much of America's news commentary. Should your show bring in some genuine guest experts... like those who actually manage law enforcement on a daily basis? Add some honest and incisive commentary to the news scene. Showcase the reality of normal and routine situations. Avoid sensationalizing the abnormal and isolated events. Aberration seems to dominate too many news scenes. Perspective is too frequently absent.

I'm adding some interesting data below on a related hot topic: incidence of gun violence in America...and elsewhere in the World. Note that the USA homicide rates may be creeping up again but not escalating as dramatically as a lot of news commentary seems inclined to imply and promote.

HOMICIDE RATES

Per 100,000 population

IN USA

Year	Number	
1700	30	
1800	Under 20	
1900	Under 10	
2000	5.53	
2014	4.44	
2018	5.01	

USA expected to increase in 2019 and 2020

Compare 2018 with other countries:

So. Africa	36.4	
Mexico	29.0	
Brazil	26.7	
Costa Rica	11.7	
Russia	6.0	Was above 30 in early 2000s
Chile	4.4	
India	3.0	
Canada	1.8	
France	1.2	
UK	1.1	
Sweden	1.1	
Australia	0.9	
China	0.5	
Japan	0.3	

Note: Over 50% of total annual firearm-related deaths in America are suicides. Pew Research Center reports per capita homicides and suicides since 1950 reached a peak of 7.2 and 7.7 per 100,000 in the 1970s, declined gradually after that into the mid-twenty teens, and are now increasing again but still below the 1970s peaks.

That's it for now. Any questions?

DANNY RESPONDS that afternoon with a phone call.

"Nice analyses, Julie. I like your let real numbers do the talking approaches. Don't let your insecurities hamper your search for truth in numbers, even if they seem to go against popular beliefs. More intellectual honesty is needed in news commentary coverage of emotional issues like racial bias in law enforcement and gun violence in America. There's too much emphasis on unfortunate law enforcement outcomes, which are aberrations, not systemic, and not representative of most law enforcement. Irrational extrapolations are common in America today, too often encouraged and promoted by too many in the media. Sensationalization is the name of the game. Sad.

"I'll have a techie look at the formatting, and I'll open with your numbers on Monday. That's also Martin Luther King Day. So, that might not be the best day to give viewers a dose of what might be considered unpopular reality. I'm also looking for a prominent police chief who might be willing to come on the show and discuss the dominance of routine policing not involving violence. Routine, even mundane, policing comprises what, maybe 95 to 98% of policing activities in America. Boring, I guess. Wonder what percentage of news commentary about policing is devoted to police violence. Gotta be a high number. Someone ought to do the research."

"Probably no data out there, Danny. Want me to look?"

"Don't bother. Those aren't stats you'll find. No one's gonna accumulate data on routine police work. Not sure I want to go public with my own percentage speculations. That may be too presumptuous even for me."

"Hokay. Good luck Monday."

"Thanks. I'll need it. And now, let's look further ahead. We've talked about another subject I know you're interested in. Hell, everyone's interested in it. Seems most everyone is affected by it in their daily lives. Never favorably. It makes multiple news headlines on a daily basis. It's considered a

Worldwide threat of immeasurable dimension...worse than Russia. Network Brass is planning a feature series starting next Tuesday, Jan 28, and not wrapping up until the following Monday. NB wants to give our audience a weekend to react before hitting them with a whopper grand finale to start the following week. I'm sure you've already guessed the subject. Global Warming of course. You ready?"

Julie chuckles to herself before replying. "Yep, I'm mostly ready, except for getting input from Dad. I'll do that this week, and you'll have my comments next Saturday. I'm also finishing up some intense research and visual presentations. It's been a fascinating subject for me, and I've tried to be thorough and objective without making a Master's Thesis out of it."

"Okay. Global Warming it is. We both should block out a bunch of time on Saturday to discuss."

"May take two blocks Danny. What I have to present is lengthy. You may want some time to review it before we discuss it. Better set aside some Sunday time also."

"You got it. All day Sunday if necessary. This subject is one of the most important my DPS show is likely to address this year. So, a Global Warming weekend in the dead cold of winter it is for both of us. Climate change deserves a lot of our joint attention before your data deluges again graduate to prime-time wide-screen television next week. Hope viewer TV sets are big enough. Hope their visions are clear, their minds un-befuddled by too much rhetoric from climate change alarmists, and their reasoning still functional. Yeah, right. Good luck with all that."

TUESDAY AFTERNOON THERE'S a terse text message waiting from Danny when Julie returns from a morning in the MRABC Denver studio.

> We need to talk. Let's do a FaceTime tomorrow morning. I'll initiate. Say 9:00 AM your time. DP

"DANNY, YOU LOOK DESPONDENT," Julie says as she signs in. "Let me guess why. Negative response to your Monday night monologue?"

He forces a wry smile. "Yeah, there was a bad response. Two bad responses actually. Maybe I should have expected them. Feedback from viewers was mixed, as usual. Squawking the loudest were activists pushing agendas of white police bias against blacks and excessive gun violence. Hell, from an idealistic point of view all gun violence is excessive. But, from a pragmatic point of view, gun violence can't be eliminated without eliminating guns, and eliminating guns from citizen ownership is an unrealistic expectation. Anyway, DPS viewer numbers were down. Probably a lot of people are just fed up with gun subjects.

"Also, the Network Brass is all over me again. Another scolding. NB said the basic chart on police versus blacks and whites was too complex for viewers. Not very complimentary of our viewing audience. Too contemptuous. NB said no one would be able to make any sense out of the percentage calculations, also said the calculations delivered a wrong message. My cynical conclusion: there's just too much raw emotion involved in public reactions to fatal gun scenarios. Opportunistic news commentators understand this natural condition and fully exploit it."

Julie squirms in her chair. *Am I too naive not to accept NB's open contempt of the MRABC audience base? Most of our viewers must have more intelligence and receptiveness than our NB credits them with.* "Danny," she says, "if it's any consolation, I thought you handled the numbers and the percents appropriately."

"Thanks Julie. That helps some. Maybe we both should just relax, pat ourselves on our backs, tell each other that we tried to do the right thing. H-m-m-m, back patting. That sounds like fun. So, over and out until Saturday and the next controversial issue?"

"Roger that, Danny. Until Saturday. Be kind to yourself."

"I'll try. Bye."

CHAPTER 22

GLOBAL WARMING MANIA

JAN 22 - 25

ANTICIPATING HER SATURDAY MORNING briefing with Danny, Julie collars her father for some serious conversation Wednesday evening...on a subject she acknowledges he's a genuine expert.

"Dad, I'm venturing into your area of expertise, and I'd like you to look over my material...a lot of numbers and analytical comments. Hopefully using most of my work, Danny and his Network Brass are planning an extensive Global Warming focus in daily programming for his show starting Tuesday next week."

"Sure, Julie. Let me read and study what you have so far. You'll have my comments after work tomorrow."

THURSDAY EVENING, father and daughter reconvene. Shane occupies his usual space at Julie's feet. His tail is wagging, likely induced by a pleasant dream, certainly not by expectation of the discussion of a difficult subject to come. Julie softly strokes his head. *Always relaxes me.*

"Nice work, Julie," her father smiles and nods his head.

Good. If he was displeased, he'd begin with criticism. Or follow his first comment with the word but. "Thanks, Dad, any suggestions?"

"Just one," he continues. "Are you familiar with the name Dr. Roy Spencer?"

"Hmmm, I think so. I caught part of an interview with him a couple of years ago...on CNN I think. I was impressed."

"As you should be. To improve the credibility of what you've put together, I think you need references to a recognized Global Warming expert."

"So, how about you?"

"Better leave me out of it, Julie. NOAA might not approve."

"I understand. Does Spencer have a website?"

"Yep, a very active one, with followers and also critics. He's controversial, Julie. Probably the destiny of most climate change experts who have a public profile. Take a close look at his charts of actual Global Warming trends. They compare the reports of dozens of scientific models to his model and also to ours here at NOAA. You'll be amazed by what you see."

"I'm on it. Lots of time before Danny and I convene for our Saturday briefing."

"A few final words of caution, Julie. Be realistic about your presentations. If Danny uses them, he and his show...and implicitly your work...are going to take a lot of heat from a lot of places. Pun intended."

"Thanks for that. I appreciate your help and your concern. Global Warming is too important a subject to soft-play what I'm spending so much time researching. Negative reactions are a harsh reality when actual data is used to confront biased commentary that's polluted public perceptions over so many years. Near-term catastrophic Global Warming may be too deeply imbedded in the minds of too many people to be effectively challenged. If Danny follows my data, he'll present two conclusions to his viewers. First, although Global Warming is a fact, it's not as severe as you've been misled into believing. And second, throwing megabucks and megaregulations at reducing America's CO2 emissions only compounds the problem. That approach fuels the fires rather than quenching them. Gets discouraging. Anyway, I'm at least trying to make the World of network news a better place. Wish me luck. I'm gonna need it."

"Julie, you may need more than luck. I'll also wish that Divine Providence be on your side."

HER SATURDAY iPHONE DING from Danny is right on schedule.

> Let's get going on next week's show. I have NB clearance to dive into Global Warming. Hope we don't get burned. DP

Already dressed and breakfasted, she responds.

> Lots of data to share. Researching the subject kept me busy during that difficult time in my life just after that difficult time in your life. Give me a few hours to finish GW e-mail # 1. I have an inside GW expert connection who's already been helpful. JA

As does he.

> Inside connection? That got my attention. Standing by for your first GW e-mail data deluge. Call me first. Need to talk about prospective show guests. DP

IT'S MID-AFTERNOON WHEN SHE PLACES THE CALL. "Danny, I have lots of numbers and related comments to send you. But you wanted to talk first?"

"Yep. But before we talk about show guests, tell me about your inside connection. Who is it?"

"Jules Anders."

"Your dad!"

She chuckles. "Of course. He also provides me with affordable housing in Boulder, a very expensive town to live in.... bless him."

"What's he do?"

"Just happens to be a career climate scientist. So, he's a genuine expert on Global Warming. Over twenty years now he's been at NOAA here."

"WOW! Is he prominent?"

More chuckles from Julie. "Hardly. Nor does he want to be. Why?"

"Well, here's who the Network Brass has already lined-up for next week. I'm excited about our prospective guests. At least for our ratings. But I'm also concerned that we may be over-populating the guest deck with hard-core alarmists who have prominent names. Our main studio location in Hollywood gives us a great opportunity to attract big-time film celebrities. Already we've got some Hollywood Global Warming activists joining us. Leonardo Di Caprio leads off on Monday evening. Then we follow with Jane Fonda on Tuesday and Matt Damon on Wednesday. For Thursday, the Network Brass is still angling for Al Gore. With our 6:00 evening time slot here on the west coast, we're gonna decimate major networks' viewing audiences and steal a bunch of their regular viewers. Like our network ratings should blow way ahead of the competition next week. However, I don't like stacking the deck on my show with celebrities all on the same side of an issue. It was a Network Brass call, not mine.

"My turn to say WOW. How'd they pull off all the celebrity appearances?"

With a huge laugh, he responds, "Maybe celebrities just love my style. No, sorry about that...just my ego showing off. Thought I lost my ego undergoing psychiatric counseling. But maybe I need some ego to help preserve what sanity I have left.

"So, here's the key to our network's success in attracting

Hollywood celebrities. Please keep this to yourself. MRABC is owned by a very wealthy majority stockholder and her husband. She has big-time dollars to spend and big-time connections. It's rumored she's the unacknowledged daughter of a liaison between Marilyn Monroe and John F. Kennedy. It's also rumored that conception occurred backstage on a very special evening after Marilyn sang a nationally televised happy birthday to JFK. It was a personal thank you gift from the President of the United States to his admirer...or maybe vice versa. Marilyn's daughter has maintained behind-the-scenes Hollywood connections and prefaced this network with MR, first letter in honor of her mother, second letter to honor her Uncle Robert, who established a monster trust fund for her after her father's assassination and before his. Both letters together also provide a presumed gender counterpart to MSNBC."

Julie can't control her laughter. "Danny, that's way too big a secret. I can't keep it to myself. But I promise only to tell one person. Then we'll see how fast it spreads around this college town where small rumors grow into huge fonts for gossip mongers. So, where were we? I guess back to next week. What's on for Friday?"

"Don't know yet. I thought we'd try to finish our Global Warming week with a scientist, a genuine expert who's credentialed but not necessarily name recognizable. I'd like to bring in someone who might even challenge some of the more popular beliefs my other guests will likely dump on my viewers. Would your father consider joining us?"

Julie's response is another outburst of laughter. "Hardly. He'd probably offend your owners and many viewers. He'd likely start-off with his opinion about the fallibility of stupid decisions by World politicians...mostly American...to throw away billions of dollars on proposed solutions to halt and maybe reverse climate change. He says if human activities are the basic causes of Global Warming, then it's the height of human arrogance to contend warming can be halted or reversed without vast reductions in population. He also says there's not enough money on the planet to halt Global Warming, let alone reverse it. And he believes only a Worldwide catastrophe, another international war, or the uncontrollable spread of a lethal contagious new disease can accomplish any significant population reductions.

"Also, he's not into public appearances. Says they're too superficial. He's a behind-the-scenes expert. Kind of like his daughter, except I'm not reluctant to put my big mouth out there in support of where my small but hyperactive brain has gone.

"Plus, Dad can't stand Al Gore. Says the guy's a poorly informed, overly applauded, has-been career politician still seeking attention with misleading information on a hot topic that never cools off. Here are four examples." Julie shuffles through some notebook pages and then continues.

"One. In 2006, Gore predicted a sea level rise of 20 ft. in the near future. Scientists say in the last 18 years sea levels have risen 3.8 inches. At that rate it will take 1,136 years to rise 20ft.

"Two. In 2007 Gore warned if CO2 in the atmosphere doubles, World temperatures will increase by many degrees. Scientists expect atmosphere CO2 will double by 2100 and World temperatures will increase by one degree centigrade.

"Three. Also, in 2007 Gore maintained that stronger storms continue to threaten entire cities. In the last 30 years, the accumulated cyclonic energy index, which measures tropical storm intensities, shows a slight downward trend.

"Four. In 2009 Gore said there's a 75% chance the polar ice cap will be gone in five to seven years...so by 2014-2016. We're into the 2020s, and there's still polar ice. Dad says scientists think ice may no longer form in the Arctic Ocean by the 2040s.

"So much for Gore's credibility."

"Sure Julie. But, when it comes to future climate change, there's no reliable crystal ball out there, even from the scientific community. All crystal balls are clouded. Too many variables, too many eons of time are involved. In a single word... climate change is an incomprehensible."

"Well said, Danny. My father always makes sure his private listeners like me know that only a few decades ago global temps went cooler rather than hotter. Fear mongers went nuts then also, but that period of Global cooling was short-lived. Thankfully. So what's gonna happen when the Earth cycles into another sustained natural cooling cycle? Some scientists think that's inevitable, regardless of human activity. Who knows how far off. Hundreds, thousands, hundreds of thousands, millions of years? Maybe too far into the future to have any idea how far Global Warming might take the planet without an intervening Global disaster. So, enough already. It becomes imponderable. I do have an alternative scientist suggestion for Friday."

"Yeah, who?"

"Dr. Roy Spencer."

"Who's he?"

"A well-credentialed climate scientist. A meteorologist by trade. Has his own web-site with a huge following, some of whom openly disagree with him. Check it out."

"I will. But first, can you brief me a bit about him? Not now. I'm too busy. E-mail me so I can study the info."

"Roger that. I'm on it."

AN ALL-DAY WORK DAY COMMITMENT binds Julie to summarizing her research and designing tables to present her numbers. Saturday evening she composes another long info e-mail to Danny. *As long as we need a record of what Danny and I consider, I guess long phone conversations are out. Unless we record them. Sure don't want to do that. This will be the longest e-mail deluge yet.*

Can't do numbers properly without visuals, and I need to have my data inputs documented somewhere. Can't just wing them verbally into a conversation. Hope Danny's willing to read what I send him...and then program it for his show. Anyway, it's my first extensive info e-mail blast since he returned to his intensely public hot seat. He needs the mind challenge to help bolster his self-confidence. It'll be a sizable polemic. But also timely and informative. Not for anyone only interested in sound-bite briefing. It's time Global Warming had some fully nuanced, objective, in-depth, and non-biased media attention. Hope Danny can deliver it.

DANNY, FIRST ABOUT DR. ROY SPENCER. I've studied his work in some depth. I also saw Spencer on television a few years ago when he appeared on a CNN evening news commentary devoted to climate change. My initial reaction? A thoughtful and formidable scientific mind devoted to his profession. He was imposing. Had his books and research materials stacked on a table behind him. Seemed a consummate professional both in appearance and presentation. I trust my father's confidence in the importance and reliability of what he has to say and write.

I also acknowledge that Spencer's been branded a climate change denier by some, even though he acknowledges that the planet is warming, just not to the extent others contend. He also acknowledges humans have to accept some responsibility for Global Warming, just not to the extent others contend.

Wikipedia also takes a shot at him, claiming that his views on climate change "are rejected by the scientific community." Often criticized for having biased content and making agenda-driven comments, Wikipedia apparently whipped out a quick-draw, overly simplistic, and misleading characterization for Spencer. That kind of derogation also seems to be popular with many in the media these days. Hell, Dad says scientists disagree all the time, and he thinks Spencer has as much support from other climate scientists, including himself, as he has rejection.

Anyway, I'm inclined to rely on an endorsement from the family expert. I think Spencer would be a good addition to next week's program. Isn't that what we're supposed to do? Provide a venue for ventilating both sides of controversial issues?

Frowning, she pauses her flying fingers. *In his striving for high ratings, is Danny also agenda driven? Says he's not. Says he wants to be independent, and I believe him. He's already gone against the flow of popular opinion...and his own Network Brass.* Then she shrugs her shoulders and continues.

Here are some of Spencer's credentials. He's published several books (see below) and articles on climate change. His awards include the NASA Exceptional Scientific Achievement Medal and an AMS Special Award.

Spencer's books are likely repugnant to Gore worshippers. They include **Climate Confusion: How Global Warming Hysteria Leads to Bad Science; Pandering Politicians and Misguided Policies that Hurt the Poor;** and **The Great Global Warming Blunder: How Mother Nature Fooled the World's Top Climate Scientists.** A favorite is **An Inconvenient Deception**, published in 2017 and subtitled **How Al Gore Distorts Climate Science and Energy Policy**, which is a scathing indictment of Gore's second slide show/movie, **An Inconvenient Sequel: Truth to Power**. I won't get into Spencer's criticisms in detail, but he contends that movie "is bursting with bad science, bad policy, and some outright falsehoods."

So-o-o, for sure you don't want to have Gore and Spencer on the Dan Panders Show the same night. They might get into a fist fight. But then, wait. Wouldn't that be an unusual and compelling show for viewers to see?

If you do your own checking, please look at another Global Warming issue Spencer has addressed with data rather than diatribe. On his website, Spencer presents a simple chart that debunks assertions that GW has caused a huge increase in the number of class 4 and 5 Florida hurricanes. Because of massive increases in coastal settlement development by humans, there's been an enormous increase in the $$$ cost of hurricane storm damage. Probably an increase in human deaths also. But no well-established trend of huge increases in big storms. Listed below are Class 4 and 5 hurricanes coming into Florida in the last 100 years by decade. Note that there were seven in the first five decades and six in the following five decades.

1920s	1
1930s	1
1940s	3
1950s	0
1960s	2
1970s	0
1980s	0
1990s	2
2000s	3
2010s	1

Dad has his own strong opinions about Global Warming, and he rails at our Governments' throwing away huge taxpayer $$$ to subsidize alternate clean energy sources both at the supplier and consumer levels. Calls them futile. He contends there's not enough subsidy money in the World for governments to reverse Global Warming without a reduction in population. He calls the subsidies fools' missions.

Danny, I realize celebrity views and comments will dominate your show next week. However, here are four Global Warming program topics that could bring important information to our viewers, information that is routinely denied in-depth coverage by other networks.

ONE, AND MOST IMPORTANT...MONSTER MISSES IN MOST MODELS OF *ACTUAL USA* WARMING TRENDS.

For the USA, Spencer provides a chart that shows us that 36 widely used **climate forecasting models** were used to promote changes in America's energy policies. The models report **historic** summer surface air temperature increases measured over a 50-year period (ending in 2019) ranging from .28 to .71 degrees centigrade per decade. The official NOAA observations report an increase of .26 degrees centigrade per decade. Spencer's independent calculations also arrived at .26 degrees centigrade per decade increase. Look at those numbers closely. They reveal that 36 other scientific models report actual USA warming increases that are 108% to 273% of NOAAs (official) and Spencer's.

Similarly, and narrowing the focus a bit to just America's 12-state corn-belt summers over the same 50-year period, those 36 models report historic surface air temperature increases ranging from .20 to .91 degrees centigrade per decade. The official NOAA observations report an actual increase of .13 degrees centigrade per decade. So, the 36 other scientific experts report actual USA summer warming increases in America's corn belt at **150% to 700% of the official record**!

So much for scientific consensus. Consensus doesn't exist. Scientists can't even come close to agreeing on what's already happened over a 50-year period. As my resident expert constantly reminds me, scientists disagree all the time, not only on what might happen but also on what has already happened. He also emphasizes that all these increase models, including NOAA's and Spencer's, could be overstating actual warming trends if increasing urban heat-island effects have spuriously inflated the trends.

Most television network coverages feature the higher warming models. Dad got so pissed-off he now turns off the TV whenever it goes to Global Warming. And he flat refuses to watch MSNBC, CNN, or FOX NEWS commentary on any subject.

I haven't delved yet into the never-never world of Global Warming FORECASTS. If scientists are in such extraordinary disagreement on what's already happened, imagine how disparate and unreliable their forecasts are of what might happen in the future.

Dad's concerned that too much US energy policy and other Government actions are unduly influenced by excessive warming forecasts from so many flawed models. Because of his work and the work of his NOAA colleagues, he may have a predisposition to be hypercritical of the other models. Unfortunately, it's the flawed model exaggerations that seem to be routinely promoted by environmental groups, anti-oil activists, and many in the media. And probably most politicians. I wonder if there is such a thing as good science in a venue where the range of disagreement is so huge.

TWO...AMERICA'S ENERGY POLICY CHANGES ARE PROMOTED BASED ON FLAWED MODEL SIMULATIONS WHICH HAVE PRODUCED GLOBAL WARMING RATE **FORECASTS** AT LEAST DOUBLE THOSE **ACTUALLY OBSERVED** IN THE PAST 40+ YEARS.

Switching from land to sea, Spencer shows us that actual global ocean temperatures are warming at less than 50% the rate of 68 simulations from 13 climate models. Over the last 40 years, the observation record indicates an **actual** ocean surface warming trend of about .12 deg. c/decade. Most **model simulations** ranged from .27 to .32 deg. c/decade. So models forecasting the future are over-estimating ocean warming by 125-166%. Conclusions about the future drawn from the models produce over-reactions.

Spencer acknowledges warming is at least partly due to human greenhouse gas emissions. However, he also concludes, "there is no Climate Crisis." At least not quite yet. Dad goes even further than that. He and his colleagues at NOAA have studied the actual Global Warming data and concluded the rate of Global Warming peaked in 2016. No, that's not saying Global Warming has stopped, just that its rate of increase is declining and expected to continue to decline. That's important information you never see in network news coverage.

"Here are the actual numbers that support the 2016 warming rate peaking conclusion. Using a 29 year average of annual actual globing ending in 2019, the deviations from this average were as follows:

DEVIATIONS (ie INCREASES) IN GLOBAL TEMPERATURES FROM 29 YEAR AVERAGE

	IN DEGREES CENTIGRADE			
	2016	2017	2018	2019
Largest monthly increase	0.7	0.6	0.5	0.4
Average monthly for year increase	0.4	0.35	0.25	0.3

Maybe this declining trend won't continue. It might even begin to increase again as the Earth's human population continues to grow. Dad cautions that it's likely the declining trend will reverse.

THREE...CO2 EMISSIONS BY PLANET EARTH.

I've condensed a bunch of data into the four charts that follow. They present CO2 emissions data from fossil fuels and industry: Worldwide and for the three largest emitters: China, USA, and India. The data source for all charts is the Oxford Martin School at Oxford University.

Here are my comments highlighting the information:

- Since 2000, World CO2 emissions have increased 46%. However, the rate of increase has slowed somewhat since 2015.
- Now by far the biggest emitter at 29% of the World, China has more than twice our USA emissions. At just 14.3% of the World in YK2000, their emissions then were only 60% of the USA.
- USA emissions have actually decreased by 13.2% since YK2000 and are now only 14.2% of the World, compared to 23.8% in YK2000. Despite significant population increases, USA per capita emissions have also declined significantly, by 28% since 2000. Hurrah for team USA.
- An up-and-comer, India's emissions have risen to third place at 3.8% of the World, with a 169% increase in emissions since YK2000.

WORLD CO2 EMISSIONS

In Metric Tons (000 omitted)

		From 2000
Year	Amount	% Increase
2019	37,080	**46%**
2015	35,520	40%
2010	31,560	24%
2000	25,450	

Source: Oxford Martin School at Oxford University

CHINA CO2 EMISSIONS

In Metric Tons (000 omitted)

Year	Amount	From 2000 % Increase	% of World
2019	10,740	**195%**	29.0%
2015	9,870	171%	27.8%
2010	8,620	137%	27.3%
2000	3,640		14.3%

Source: Oxford Martin School at Oxford University.

USA CO2 EMISSIONS

In Metric Tons (000 omitted)

Year	Amount	From 2000 % Decrease	% of World
2019	5,260	**-13.2%**	14.2%
2015	5,380	-11.2%	15.1%
2010	5,680	-6.3%	18.0%
2000	6,060		23.8%

Source: Oxford Martin School at Oxford University.

NOTE:

From a peak in 2000, America's Per Capita CO2 emissions have steadily declined. By 28% through 2019, with a 5% further decline expected in 2020.The decline is largely attributable to the replacement of coal with natural gas a an electrical power generation source.

INDIA CO2 EMISSIONS

In Metric Tons (000 omitted)

Year	Amount	From 2000 % Increase	% of World
2019	2,630	**169%**	7.1%
2015	2,270	132%	6.4%
2010	1,680	72%	5.3%
2000	978		3.8%

Source: Oxford Martin School at Oxford University.

Here's a grotesque irony, and one that's reflected dramatically in the data charts. As America struggles valiantly to reduce its CO2 emissions, China's emissions are soaring. A primary cause? Critics of America's unilateral efforts to combat Global Warming connect China's soaring CO2 emissions to China's power needs to maintain

World dominance in manufacturing the equipment needed to (1) develop renewable energy sources and (2) enable consumer use of renewable sources. There's a credible contention that our and other countries' CO2 emission reduction efforts are futile without a similar effort by China. The irony here is that the more America and other nations push for renewable energy sources, the more likely China's response to supply equipment for that push will thwart those efforts.

FOUR...AMERICA'S ENERGY CONSUMPTION BY SOURCES.

Again, I've condensed a bunch of data into the chart that follows. It presents our total energy consumption by sources in 2019 compared to 2006. This is important information also generally omitted from news networks' coverage of Global Warming and America's contribution to it. Here are my comments:

- In 2006, America's coal production supplied only 22% of our energy needs. By 2019 energy consumption supplied by coal had dropped a whopping 50% of total to only 11% of our needs.
- Natural gas supplied 22% of our needs in 2006. That source increased to 32% of our energy needs in 2019. Natural gas CO2 emissions are half that of coal.
- Petroleum supplied 40% of our energy needs in 2006, only slightly declining to 37% in 2019.
- Energy needs supplied by renewables increased from 7% in 2006 to 11% in 2019, fueled by massive Government subsidies during much of that period.
- Needs supplied by nuclear sources remained constant at 8% during this period.

USA ENERGY CONSUMPTION BY SOURCE

in percent	2019	2006
PETROLEUM	37%	40%
NATURAL GAS	32%	22%
COAL	11%	22%
RENEWABLE	11%	7%
NUCLEAR	8%	8%
ALL OTHER	1%	1%
TOTAL	**100%**	**100%**

FIVE...AMERICA'S PRODUCTION OF COAL AND NATURAL GAS.

- My final chart compares America's YK2000 coal production and 2008 natural gas production to that expected in 2020. My comments follow.
- Our natural gas production has increased 79.7% since YK2000.
- Our coal production has declined 51.7% since its peak in 2008.

USA PRODUCTION OF COAL AND NATURAL GAS

		COAL PRODUCTION in 000 short tons		NATURAL GAS PRODUCTION in bcf	
	Year	Amount	% Decrease From 2008 Peak	Amount	% Increase From 2000
Expected	2021	570,000	**-51.7%**	34.5	**79.7%**
Expected	2020	535,000	-54.7%	33.5	74.5%
	2019	706,000	-40.2%	33.9	76.6%
	2016	728,000	-38.3%	26.6	38.5%
	2010	1,080,000	-8.5%	21.3	10.9%
	2008	1,180,000			
	2000			19.2	

Here's an important CO2 emission issue you might find an expert to address next week. It's another subject we discussed at length in the PolySci post-graduate level course I was required to take for my Master's Degree. It's also a topic Angel Bright was particularly interested in. It relates to the interplay between alternate renewable energy sources and clean coal-fired electrical power generation.

Technology to eliminate CO2 emissions from coal-fired power plants is available. Japan is doing it. It's expensive, and it's not widely used in America, possibly because of excessive government interventions. The point here is that Federal, state and local governments are providing billions of taxpayer dollars for renewable subsidies, which might not be necessary if natural economic forces were relied upon to motivate America's consumers to convert to renewables on their own $$$. Costs of cleaning up coal-fired plants could push the cost of power from those sources above the cost of unsubsidized renewables, thereby removing the need for subsidies.

Professor Bright also said too many in the media underestimate the capability of Americans to understand the complexities of Global Warming. Or maybe most in the media purposely don't cover this situation because of their commitments to hyper-inflating American perceptions of the seriousness of the Global Warming condition.

To summarize. Here are the **60-year** (1960 to 2020) increases in three important data sets that surround and capture the magnitude of climate change in relation to CO2.

- Global temperatures have increased 7%. Land temperatures (only) maybe 10.5%.
- CO2 in the atmosphere has increased 31% (1).
- Global CO2 emissions from human activity have increased 276%.

(1) Up to 414 parts per one million particulates in the atmosphere or up to slightly over .04% of total atmosphere particulates. That's four 100ths of one percent. CO_2 comprises a tiny part of our atmosphere.

Now to what I believe is the worst deception by most presenters of this data. They purposely manipulate visual structures of CO_2 emissions compared to global temperatures. Charts and graphs are cleverly drawn that present parallel increases between Global temperature increases and CO_2 emission increases. Hard to make a 7% increase and a 276% increase look the same? Not at all. The visuals simply use two different vertical measures of increase, one on the left side of the chart for Global temps at a .13 degree increase per decade, the other on the right side for CO_2 emissions at a 40 billion tons increase per decade. And voila, the two lines run nearly identical left to right. It's a not-so-clever manipulation designed to mislead readers into believing there's a directly proportionate correlation when there isn't. That's a fact overlooked (purposely?) by all fear-mongers. Al Gore also used this deception in his initial slide show presentation of An Inconvenient Truth. A chart done properly would show a left-to-right line for World CO_2 emissions over a 60 year period exploding in elevation upwards from bottom left of the chart to upper right...from 9.4 to 35.3 billion tons. Whereas global temps would creep along elevating from about 14 to about 15 degrees Celsius. Land only temps would show a slightly higher trend.

You might have a techie chart both these measures properly...for a visual look by television viewers at the obvious deception.

Maybe my summary would make a great beginning for a DPS-opening monologue?

Okay, enough for tonight. Whew. Let me know if you have questions or need to discuss any of this with me before you roll-out next week's programming. I'm tired, and I have a pet Golden Retriever needing some attention.

Onward, Julie

JULES ANDERS CONCLUDES their Sunday morning breakfast discussion with, "Bravo Julie, I'm proud of you. Thanks so much for letting me read your final info e-mail to Dan Panders and for discussing it with me this morning. It's long. But it's right on. Do you think he'll accept some of your suggestions?"

"Dunno, Dad. I hope so. And some final questions for you. Is it feasible...and affordable...for the World to try to reduce CO2 emissions back to where they were in 1960? If so, is it likely Global temps will then drop one degree centigrade or more? If so, will that bring back glaciers and lower ocean levels in the World's vulnerable coastal areas? Is there a World CO2 emission level at which Global temps should stabilize and not continue to increase?

"Well, thanks, I think, for four difficult questions no one can answer. Not even an expert on climate change...like me. Even scientists can't speculate into the future with any expectation of producing reliable answers. To start with, I'm not convinced the planet's big increase in human-generated CO2 emissions is the primary cause of Global Warming. Obviously there's no direct correlation. I also believe returning to 1960 CO2 emission levels is impossible. Reducing them to a level that might slow the increases in global temps might be possible. However, if humans are mostly responsible for increasing World temperatures, then the only rational way Global Warming can be arrested is through huge reductions in World population. And how's that going to happen? World wars with unprecedented deaths and devastation? Catastrophic natural disasters unlike any seen by the World in modern times? New terminally contagious infectious diseases that escape spread control or cure? Under any scenario it will be impossible for World CO2 emissions to stabilize without extreme measures in China and India to halt their rapid expansion of activities that generate CO2. How's that going to happen? Maybe America should provide one trillion dollars to each country as an incentive to curtail expansion.

"Then...and finally, my final comment. If you haven't already done it, you should review NOAA's official climate information site at climate.gov. One of the most important conclusions our website presents is that compared to most of the Earth's history, today is unusually cold. We're living in what geologists call an interglacial. That's a period between glaciations of an ice age. For most of the last two million years Global temperatures have been mostly below the 1850-1900 average, with fluctuations varying from only two degrees above to four degrees below the average."

Julie raises her hand. "Two last questions?"

He laughs. "Persistent aren't you. For sure you're already adapting to an interviewer's role. Go for it."

She's chuckling. "Thank you. So, do you think it's impossible for human efforts to slice one degree centigrade off present Global temperatures? And also highly unlikely that a continuing trend of increasing CO2 levels can similarly be halted?"

"Leading questions. Answers are yes and yes. Depressing, isn't it, Julie? And now we need to get off this diabolical subject."

"Right. So, end of interview. And now it's my turn to thank you for doing breakfast. You're much better at meal preparation than I am."

He's still laughing, "That's only because I have so many more years of experience. And isn't breakfast also expected to be provided by me to my favorite bed and breakfast tenant?"

She's still chuckling. "For sure...I'm your only tenant. And to show my appreciation for your landlord services, is it okay if I do the breakfast dishes?"

"Of course."

"And this is for providing all these services and charging your tenant absolutely nothing." She rises from the table and circles it to give her father a big hug and look deeply into his eyes. "And for encouraging me to pursue my dream and being my incredible rock of support in my agony of despair at Zion, here's my pledge to you...my eternal love and respect. Thanks, Dad." Breaking away, she swabs at tears beginning to form in her eyes, and says, "Now I need to check to see if I have a response from Danny. Last night I sent him a huge deluge of information. If you'll excuse me..."

"Sure." His expression sobers, and he adds, "But first some final words of caution. I hope you get an encouraging response, and your work certainly deserves that, but don't be surprised if it's suppressed. MRABC is obviously more interested in gaining advantage over its competition than providing a broad spectrum of coverage. Worse part of that scenario is the NB is trying to compete with other major networks by pursuing a similar bias. Unfortunately, biases always seem to have a political side, and there seems to be a partisan differential as to the primary cause of Global Warming, its severity, and what to do about it. If MRABC really wants to make a difference and attract viewing audiences away from the competition, it should present more factual Global Warming information. It should also acknowledge the enormous range of expert opinions and the absence of consensus. For guest appearances the network should avoid overloading the stage with drama Kings and Queens. I applaud Danny's desire to follow the path of reason rather than emotion. But he's likely to find himself at loggerheads with his network decision-makers. He cannot prevail in that conflict. Be reconciled to the possibility that Dan Panders is going nowhere with all your hard work and rational analyses. Sobering situation, disgusting even, but an unfortunate reality of modern times."

A glum expression accompanies her response. "Yeah. I get it. Hard to take, but I appreciate your thoughtful evaluation of the situation. I still hope Danny can prevail. After all he's the one who built the show's following. However, from what he's already told me about his Network Brass involvement in next week's programming, I'm not optimistic. If he's denied screen time for all I've put into next week's programming, I'll have to decide if I'm at the right place...or even in the right profession. It's hard for me to accept that the profession has become so driven by bias and sensationalism that it's abandoned independent and rational thought and voice."

THAT EVENING Julie continues to obsess about the week ahead. *Dad sure figured that out. Will MRABC reject my work? Will Danny use it and risk his own career for the sake of balanced programming? Hope he doesn't lose this opportunity to anchor Global Warming week in reality. Does objectivity still have a place in the ipso-facto-nutso race for ratings? Not taking any bets.*

Will the NB judge my Global Warming analyses too complex for a viewing audience to understand? How insulting to viewers! Or, will the NB reject them because my charts and comments don't conform to the owners' agenda and are too contrary to currently popular beliefs? That's network news pandering at its worst. The ultimate censorship. Angel Bright warned me about this. She called it the emasculation of thoughtful work by agenda-driven programming.

If they reject my work, will MRABC continue to decline rational presentations and analyses of complicated and important issues?

How do I respond to this situation?

Hm-m-m, slowdown Julie. Don't rush to judgment. Don't respond now. Wait and see what happens next. See if Danny has the guts to go against a tidal wave of doom and gloom and his Network Brass. His present show, maybe even his career, may be in jeopardy. What a dilemma.

CHAPTER 23

IRRECONCILABLE DIFFERENCES

JAN 26 AND 27

SEATED AT HER WORK DESK on Sunday morning with faithful Shane dozing on the carpet beside her, Julie opens her iPhone. Finally, there's a text from Danny.

> Thanks Julie for your hard work. I need today to study it and finalize plans for next week. Big meeting with NB tomorrow AM. Never seen them so involved in programming details. I'll get back to you after. DP

WITH MONDAYS now regularly scheduled for Julie to be in the Denver studio and offices, she arrives early as usual. Transmitted while she was in transit, a text message from Danny awaits her. It's brief and blunt.

> Finished your treatise late last night. It's perfect opening monologue material.
>
> NB says no to Spencer. Too controversial. Too many scientists disagree with him. Still looking for a suitable, non-celebrity expert for Friday. NB lined up John Kerry for the grand finale next Monday. An idealist, he's a decent man

still trying to accomplish something. A modern day Don Quixote.

Unfortunately there's more bad news. We need to talk. Let's do a FaceTime. Please initiate it ASAP. I'm standing by. DP

She does, and they connect immediately. "Danny, your facial expression always gives you away, and today it's really glum. What's up...or more appropriately, what's got you down?"

"Obviously I'm not good at masking my feelings, and you've probably guessed already. What's down is your work. All of it. Your charts and your comments. I think they're appropriate, also important, timely, and needed. But the Network Brass says no to them. Actually they say absolutely no. Also, I'm ordered to confine program guests to those who promote public fears for the harshest case of Global Warming consequences and to those who endorse extreme and irrational abatement actions. I'm also ordered not to deliver any contrarian comments in an opening monologue. And if I don't like the restrictions imposed on me I can resign. It's the ultimate censure."

Julie gasps. "Can they actually mandate restrictions like that?"

"I guess so. They own the network. I suppose I could ignore their intervention, still do and say what I want. Then they can fire me. Some days I'd really like to change my last name. Too deceptive. I don't pander to anyone or to any cause. Never have. I don't even know where my last name emigrated from."

"And if they fire you, is that stigma so great you become unemployable elsewhere?"

"Dunno. That's a good question. Maybe I'd be considered too tainted with network disloyalty to be seriously considered elsewhere. At least I wouldn't be fired for inappropriate sexual advances, which seems to be the way so many male news commentators are tossed out of work and become unemployable these days. But now, back to you. I'd hate for you to fall innocent victim to any decision I make."

"Danny, forget about me for right now. I don't really care what your Network Brass might think of me. If you decide to reject censure and do your monologue saying what you want to say...like, is there some way the Network Brass can intervene and cut you off while your show is in process?"

"Dunno for sure. Probably not."

"And...like if you ignore the Network Brass intervention, then do, say, and present what you want, you'll be fired?"

"For sure."

"And will that...like brand you unemployable elsewhere?"

"Maybe. Hell, I don't know. Fuck it. Not sure I care."

"Careful, Danny. That sounds like depression kicking in again. And you're starting to look as well as sound depressed."

"Well, hell. Fuck the depression. I'm entitled to be depressed. At least if I decide to present your hard work results, I could tell myself I did the right thing."

"And if you cave to your Network Brass, what then?"

"I'll feel like shit. Like my show has become a farcical facade for parading owner bias. Like I'm a dancing puppet on a string, totally controlled by owners I don't respect."

"More like owners you haven't respected for some time now?"

"For sure."

"So, back to where we started with this dilemma. How about do the show your way and then quit before you get fired?"

"I'll likely be blacklisted, unemployable for sure."

"But you'd at least preserve your dignity and your integrity?"

"That's true."

"Here's just a spontaneous, crazy thought. Your Network Brass doesn't have a mob connection do they?"

"So, like they might have me killed if I refuse to comply with their censure?"

"Yeah. But I'm just kidding. Showing you that despite all my precision with presenting factual information, I still possess a wild imagination. Maybe we're both taking this Network Brass censure too seriously. Maybe my stuff isn't all that important, and if you present it, maybe it'll only fall on mostly deaf ears already programmed for contrary belief. Maybe I have to be pragmatic and accept that I...and you, if you sponsor my work...are pissing against a hurricane of contrary views. Danny, on a personal basis, please know I appreciate and value your endorsement of my work. But I also think you should comply with the Network Brass censure. Hang around with your popular show for a while longer. Demonstrate that you can indeed offer programming that might make a difference. You can still be a bright light of hope in a dangerous, dark dungeon of deception. So, go ahead then...flush my stuff. Stay in the game."

"But what about you? Where does our Network Brass denial of your work leave you if I can't program it?"

"Frustrated obviously. But, no worries about me, Danny. Please. I'm quitting MRABC effective the end of next week. So, please also convey these, my parting words, to your network's owner and her husband. From me to them...individually, 'Go fuck yourself.'"

PART SEVEN

REPORTING THE VIRUS

In the beginning
there was chaos.

CHAPTER 24

COVID ONE

MON APR 13, 2020

COVID-19 CASES AND DEATHS ON 4/10/2020

Reported by "Worldometers" Sat 4/11/2020

	Population In Millions	Total Cases	New Deaths	Total Deaths	Deaths Per Million
USA	**331**	**503,000**	**2,030**	**18,800**	**56.8**
Italy	61	147,600	550	18,790	308.0
Spain	47	158,300	600	16,100	342.6
France	67	124,900	1,000	13,200	197.0
UK	67	73,800	960	8,960	133.7
Germany	84	122,200	170	2,770	33.0
Euro-5 total	**326**	**626,800**	**3,280**	**59,820**	**183.5**

FROM HIS DENVER OFFICE as Station Manager of Rocky Mountain PBS affiliate KRMA-TV Channel 6, Alan Knight sits in his swivel chair, drums his fingers on his desk-top, and talks at his old-fashioned speaker-phone.

"Julie, get your Friday's COVID data and come on up. It's important."

"Sure chief. Just printed it. I'll be right there." Julie grabs a single sheet of paper, dons a protective mask, jogs upstairs, and heads for the corner office.

Located at 1089 Bannock Street, Channel 6 operates from a studio and offices in a nondescript, two-story cement building, block-house styled and squatting on a shabby side street in the shabby western fringe of downtown Denver. Here, streets run in conventional square blocks, without the confusing cross-hatched diagonal streets that complicate the city's main business district.

Commanding premier corner-office space, Alan Knight enjoys modest mountain views from a window facing north and another facing west. He swivels in his chair to smile at morning sunlight creeping down snowfields that parade down from the summit of Mount Evans. Then, fitting his mask into place, he swivels back to face Julie as she enters.

"First," he says. "you should know PBS has changed its evening format effective this evening." His mask conceals a broad smile as he pauses and then continues. "Now...here's how this change affects you. Congratulations are in order, and I'm delighted to deliver the news. You go on camera here in our studio at 4:00 this afternoon, with a hookup to PBS Headquarters. You'll be on the screen nationwide at 6:10 Eastern time."

"WOW, Alan," Julie gasps. "That's Judy Woodruff's News Hour." *Not sure I'm ready for this.*

"Sure is. Better sit down." He gestures to the chair in front of his desk.

She shakes her head in disbelief as she sits on the edge of the chair and crosses her legs. "B-b-but...why me? I'm a behind-the-scenes, off-camera support staffer. Basically, I'm a numbers cruncher and analyzer, with almost no on-camera experience. Expert with details, not necessarily clever with their presentation."

"That's why I recommended you and why Judy wants you. She's impressed with your undergraduate studies as well as your Masters in Broadcast Journalism. Quite an education combination. And you've already demonstrated your ability to transform your education and limited work experience into news commentary. You're especially gifted at understanding, summarizing, and explaining data that might be otherwise considered too complex for many in a television viewing audience. In short, you're a genuine numbers expert. Judy also likes that you'll bring convincing, research-based topical expertise to her show. Also youthful enthusiasm. Yours is a combination of talents sorely needed in today's media environment. Your sensible objectivity, driven by reason rather than emotion, is a breath of fresh air. We've worked together long enough that I know you're not agenda-driven except by your commitment not to be agenda-driven.

"So...you're on solo with Judy for a scheduled five to ten minutes. She wants fresh new faces on her show. She believes too many activists, politicians, and similarly biased colleagues dominate prime-time television. And they're too agenda driven. She wants to showcase non-biased professionals from around the country, not just prominent big mouths mostly from Washington D.C. or New York City. Is that refreshing... or what!"

"Well yeah-h-h, Alan. But, aren't you uh-h...over-selling me a bit?

"Of course," he chuckles. "And on purpose. I'm a really big fan of yours as well as your Station Chief."

"Do you realize who I'll be going against in that time slot?"

"Of course...Dan Panders. Dan the Showman, as many of his colleagues still call him. I'm also aware of your history as a data backup for his Dan Panders' Show on MRABC, and..."

He hesitates, and Julie also hesitates, *but, maybe not aware of all my history with that show, the MRABC owners, and with Danny Panders himself, an extraordinarily complex man.*

"...and," he continues, "I need to know. Will that be a problem for you in going coast-to-coast with Judy?"

"No, actually," she says. "At least I hope not. But...when I left MRABC I was not on good terms with Danny's Network Brass. That's putting it mildly. It's like I just couldn't help being in perpetual disagreement with the network owner and her husband." She frowns behind her mask. *Do I still have resentments against that network? Am I gonna feel conflicted about participating in a show for another network in the same DPS timeslot? Hell yes. But so what? This is the chance of a lifetime. I have to accept the assignment.* Her mask conceals a broad smile of determination that spreads across her face. Her eyes are visible and blaze with excitement as she casts a fisted palm above her head to emphasize her response. "But I won't let my history with Danny, his show, and his network interfere with my new gig here. What an opportunity! Alan, I really appreciate your confidence in me. I won't disappoint."

"Great, Julie. Love your enthusiasm. And, hey, I know this is short notice. But I also know how well you do your homework. Do you have time now...for me to rehearse you before you go nationwide tonight?"

"Absolutely. You be Judy and pose the questions. I'll give the answers my best straight-shot. No BS added. No obfuscations. No omissions of important information that might contradict popular narratives. So...here's the COVID data you wanted to see." Julie passes the single sheet across the long oblong table that serves as Alan's desk, well-cluttered as usual. "Keep it, Alan, and e-mail it to Judy. I have a copy. Take your time. Study it carefully...and please tell me if it gives you any mental indigestion. Beware, my favorite graduate-school professor, Angie Bright, loved to tell her students that most viewers of television news commentary have limited capacity for absorbing numbers, for fully understanding their significance, and for perceiving the deceptions embedded in the way they are often presented by the media. And, yeah, Angie could also be harshly judgmental of viewing audiences as well as the media.

"She also complained that most viewer number-absorption capacity is limited to about 25 numbers. And, as she emphasized in a comment that's burned into my college classroom recollections, 'It's one of the reasons our modern TV news analyses are so poverty-stricken when it comes to relevance. Too often,' she said, 'commentator dialogs intentionally restrict number presentations and irresponsibly interpret them.'

"She expressed similar disappointment about media coverage of many events. 'Dominating our contemporary news scene,' Angie said, 'is too much concentration on isolated events, irrationally magnified extrapolations of their significance, and highly speculative attributions of causes for their occurrence. These events indeed and sadly stand on their own as terrible and newsworthy incidents, without flawed and biased interpretive media commentary.'"

Julie shakes her head. "Whew. Enuf of my favorite memorized quotes from an often controversial college professor. Sorry, Chief. So...back to current COVID numbers. Although my data sheet has 35 numbers, I've reduced demands on viewers' mental digestion systems by highlighting the 10 most significant numbers. Enjoy."

Alan grimaces behind his mask and studies the data before him. Waiting patiently, Julie drags her facing chair around Alan's table-desk so she can sit beside him. Then she leans forward, elbow on the desk, her left hand cradling her chin. It's her favorite let's get down to serious business pose, from which a pointing right forefinger can emphasize what she wants her chief to see.

"Wow...," he exclaims, blowing air through his lips and mask. He asks, "How did the networks present this stuff over the weekend?"

She grimaces behind her mask. "In a word...poorly," she responds. "They reported it fragmented, then headlined it in a misleading fashion, as usual. I first saw it Saturday on Fox News, where a senior program host reported...here, let me find my notes..." She shuffles through pages in a notebook. "... and I quote the story headline: 'USA Overtakes Italy to Have the Highest Death Toll in the World...After 2,000 Deaths in a Day.'"

He chuckles, "So, what's wrong with that? It's factual isn't it?"

"Well, sort of. But it's deceptive, blatantly deceptive. The headline uses raw numbers in a way that's misleading. As you can see, the country with the highest death rate is not the USA at 56.6 deaths per million of population, and also not even Italy at 309.0 deaths per million, but Spain at 342.6 deaths per million, six times the USA rate. Both France and the UK also have much higher death rates than the USA. With such a wide differential in population, it's inappropriate to compare raw data between countries. For proper comparisons, the reputable on-line data accumulators present per capita data...that's per million or per 100,000 population results.

"Also easily determinable by networks, but so far ignored by them, is a five-country Europe population total equivalent to ours that could have been used for proper USA comparisons...as I've shown."

As Alan studies the data, she leans back in her chair and crosses her arms. "Plus," she adds, "as the virus spreads, and if news commentators really want to present meaningful data comparisons between countries...or between our states...they should use tabulations based not on calendar days but based on days from the virus' first significance appearance. This is really important, Alan. This virus has had a couple of weeks head-start in Europe over the USA, which naturally causes their calendar date per capita numbers to be higher than the USA. This virus onset timing differential hasn't been factored into any news reporting I've seen. None. Zero. I'm developing my own analysis on the proper basis, and I'm hopeful others with a non-biased agenda will do the same. My approach will permit the only relevant between-country or between-our-states comparisons of the virus spread, of its lethality, of different systems' effectiveness in dealing with the spread, and...."

Noticing a vacant stare developing in Alan's eyes, Julie pauses again and shakes her head. "And...yeah, I get it. I won't discuss this better approach tonight. Save Judy's audience... and you...some brain damage until later. This stuff is a tough 'tell.' No, that's wrong. It's not a tough tell. And it should be the only acceptable show and tell unless the purpose is to mislead. Although it's still not the best approach, I'll use that simple chart you're looking at this afternoon. It really isn't rocket science."

"Whew...thanks Julie. But I really did get it...what you just said as well as the chart. Boiled down, the COVID comparison approaches that dominate current network shows are seriously flawed?"

"Yeah, big time...and you wanna bet if any of our major media networks will also get it and start presenting COVID data properly and with appropriate commentary?"

"No bet," Alan says. Then he scratches his head and asks, "You think both the misleading headliners and improper commentaries were intentional?"

"Of course."

"Why?"

"There's not enough A-S-S...that's short for Awe, Shock, and Scare...in informative proper comparisons. The headline and the story that followed hyped negative narratives popular with so many in the media. Danny tried unsuccessfully to keep that approach out of his program. 'ASSing the viewers' he cynically called it. 'Jaded journalists' way of mooning their audience.'"

"And the negative narratives in Covid's case are?"

"That America has been late with a proper response to Covid; that the virus is out of control; that material and supply problems are crippling; that our healthcare facilities are overwhelmed; that our healthcare delivery has not been effective; and that our national leadership is tragically flawed."

"Yeah, I've noticed those criticisms are widespread. It's disgusting." Alan shakes his head and continues questioning, "Did Fox go on to disclose USA and Italy population numbers?"

"No."

"Did Fox report the death rates as well as death totals?"

"No."

"Did Fox present death data for the rest of the EURO 5, as you call them?"

"No."

"Did Fox even mention the huge population difference between Italy and the USA?

"No."

"How about other media coverage?"

"Later in the day both CNN and Rachel Maddow at MSNBC hyped the same improper comparison. So did other prime-time networks. It's like they all have the same conspiracies of purposeful deceit going."

"Julie, you're obviously agitated. And justifiably angry. But you'll need to calm your responses when you're on camera. Try to avoid inflammatory accusations or other emotional button-pushers."

"Got it, chief. I'll simmer."

Alan pauses for a moment. "Sorry for this question, Julie, but I've got to ask it. Judy probably won't. Do you have any personal media issues involved here?"

She squints her eyes in thought. "Well...I don't think so. When I interviewed at Fox, I met and was impressed with some of their editors and program hosts, but not impressed with others. I didn't meet the author of this piece. It's quite possible he's just incompetent. No network has an exclusive on incompetence. I turned down the Fox offer mostly because I decided not to associate with another bias-branded network. Too distasteful for me. I'm an independent voter with no affiliation with any party. I need to remain independent in thought and action. Plus...I really wanted to stay in Colorado, keep breathing clean air, and treat myself every day to uplifting mountain views. For which, by the way, I'm forever grateful to you. You took a big chance with me."

A sparkle in his eyes accompanies his hidden smile. "And we're all delighted you're here. Now, what about MRABC and the Dan Panders Show? Any axes to grind there?"

Should I tell him all of it? "Possibly," she says, nodding her head. "I've already told you about MRABC's denial of my Global Warming material. That triggered my decision to resign so abruptly. Although Danny's shows that week were popular and attracted a big viewing audience, that was only because of widespread audience recognition of Danny's prominent show guests, not because of the quality of what they said. His Global Warming shows were a huge professional disappointment for me during that last week of my employment. So sad that Danny's boss is so devoted to trying to develop a large following by promoting what she and her husband perceive as public demand for news commentary dedicated to fear and loathing. Danny's show my last week was overloaded with climate change shock and scare alarmists and lots of finger-pointing at overly-hyped human causes of Global Warming.

"Angie Bright, my PolySci Professor, attributed the origin of this media shock and scare commitment to prominent pundits from the past. She liked to quote the 20th century writer and journalist, H.L. Mencken. Mencken claimed that the whole purpose of contemporary journalism by mouth is...u-h-h-h, here let me find Mencken's exact words." Pausing, she flips more pages in her notebook, finds what she's looking for, then continues. "According to Mencken, journalistic purpose is 'to keep the populace alarmed, and hence clamorous to be led to safety, by menacing it with an endless series of hobgoblins, all of them imaginary.' Big time disrespect for Americans' intelligence and perceptiveness is imbedded in that contemptuous quote. I've used it a lot. Maybe too often. I believe that quote improperly defines network news audiences, and that's why I'm so committed to a more positive approach.

"Danny did acknowledge love as mankind's strongest emotion, but his boss believed fear and loathing could combine to trump both love and other emotions. Honesty was not a concept she understood or even acknowledged. In that last week, when he was most upset with network owner dictation of his show content, Danny told me she argued that respect and decency were obsolete considerations not applicable to modern news commentary. For her and her husband, reality was a myth, sound reasoning couldn't compete or prevail in our excess information age, the truth didn't exist, and creating perceptions was a journalist's or commentator's moral imperative. Her network, as with so many other contemporary networks, desperately wanted to manipulate the thoughts of their viewers.

"Danny also told me about the comments of another prominent news commentator who claimed the nobility of the cause justified the brain-buggery of the means. Danny wouldn't name him but said the guy called his evening gig a 'glorious nightly mind-fuck.' When Danny argued that trying to force-feed socio-politico word pornography to the masses would eventually backfire on him, his colleague argued the masses needed and deserved it. His colleague's show was a thinly-veiled cynical tease bound eventually to fail. And it did.

"Unfortunately, Danny also became an addicted ratings junkie. He checked his show's ratings every morning. They began to decline persistently about a month after I decided to leave his network. I suspect his ratings decline either put him in a seething rage or a sullen-faced depression. And, yes, although it's not widely known, Danny has been diagnosed with and treated for bipolar disorder."

Her fingers begin tapping the table in front of her, and she pauses before continuing. "You'll notice I'm using past tense. That's because I'm convinced Danny's show is done. H.L. Mencken was wrong. Danny's Network Brass is wrong. And his show is faltering... predictably. For years now, his show has competed with Rachel Maddow's show on MSNBC for high ratings in TV evening shows...and lost. Rachel is a brilliant commentator whose star will never fade.

"Although I'm still not confident I could follow as successfully in their footsteps, my TV news and commentary role models as a teenager were some of television's pioneer women headliners. Trailblazers like Christiane Amanpour, Lisa Ling, Ann Curry, Katy Couric...and of course Judy Woodruff. More recently I've also followed Megyn Kelly, Meghan McCain, and Abby Huntsman. But, yes, until I did the research for Danny's commentaries on the Department of Justice indictments related to Russian involvement in the 2016 election, Rachel Maddow was my personal heroine. Also my inspiration for seeking a graduate degree in broadcast journalism. I even met her when she was in Boulder as a guest speaker at a CU event.

"Now," she shakes her head, "sadly, I think Rachel's become delusional and obsessed with Russia, but I also acknowledge she's still sincere, eloquent, confident, and assertive...a commanding presence. Her rabidly partisan political commentary is passionate and convincing. She's also blessed with a loyal viewing audience. Danny's catering to the purposeful deceit of his Network Brass is transparent. And he's now stumbling with words. His audience was never loyal and is dwindling. I'm sure his ego now suffers big time...and I feel sorry for him. He's just another falling star that burned brightly for a moment but may be destined to slowly extinguish into the deep, dark abyss of irrelevance. I worry that he may again fall victim to depression. I discussed this concern with you when I hired on here, and I only mention it again because Danny still seems unable to overcome his Network Brass programming bias."

She pauses and sighs, "So...now Danny and I are both on the screen at the same time. How ironic. No worries, Alan. No axes will be grinding tonight. I can't be influenced by or comment on what Danny hasn't said yet. He'll have the same restraint."

Alan hand-claps three times. "Good answers, Julie." His laugh is muffled as he grimaces. "Long, but good. Anything else I should know that might brand you with a conflict."

"Well...yes. My Aunt Winnie. She's a Physician's Assistant. Works the emergency rooms at Denver General Hospital. She and many of her healthcare colleagues are outraged about media coverage that purposely ignores America's treatment success stories that are embedded in reality but denied balanced attention by media focusing mostly on raw COVID fatality numbers."

"Can you explain?"

"Sure. Look at those death rates again. The EURO-5, with a combined population base roughly equivalent to the USA, has a death rate more than three times ours. And that's from a case load only 25% higher than ours. Here, our healthcare workers risk their health...maybe their lives...every day to save lives. They're mostly producing remarkable results under extraordinarily difficult circumstances. Then they get slapped in the face and punched in the gut with deceitful media commentary that makes their efforts appear unsuccessful."

"Julie, maybe it's time they had a voice...a spokesperson."

"Past time, actually, but I'll try. And...Alan, I'll also try to avoid the usual hype, use all the relevant data, and apply my 'sensible objectivity,' as you so graciously put it. Mostly, I'll try to let the numbers do the talking. With Judy's help, I'll try to bring a needed contrast to Danny's show...challenge his show and other rabidly parasitic media dialogs that abandon reason, prey on emotions, and spread mind infections among us faster than COVID infiltrates our bodies."

He extends a hand to grasp her arm. "Again...be careful, Julie. Beware the pontifications. You'll be accused of parroting the style of those you criticize."

She squints her eyes and nods her head. "Whew, you're right, chief. I'll try to tone it down."

"And...Julie, know I'll be rooting for you. Okay if I and the rest of our staff watch the show from the viewing room?"

"Sure, I'd be honored."

"And...," he grins behind his mask, "...we'll also tape the

Dan Panders Show. You can join us later, and we can all endure his show's 'mind-buggery' before we call it a day."

"Thanks, Alan." Her laugh is muffled, "But I don't think I'll join you for that. I don't want to close my work-day with another dose of what I left behind three months ago. And... just so you know. I don't do political. Never will. I'm issue oriented, and I've resolved never to name a political party or use the names of our current President or his challenger. I'll maintain that resolve on Judy's show. Those four words are too inflammatory.

"I get that Julie. I don't do political either. And as long as I'm a PBS station manager, there will be no partisan political bias in our programming. Not on my watch."

CHAPTER 25

COVID TWO

MON MAY 25, 2020

AS JULIE ENTERS his office, Alan swivels back from his usual morning window-gaze, rises from his desk, strides around it, and out-stretches his hands. With a huge, hidden grin, he mimics a hug with open encircling arms and says, "I'd love to come around the desk and give you a well-deserved bear-hug, but..." he shrugs his shoulders... "we're still under restraints. Maybe soon...." His eyes announce an ebullient mood as he continues in an excited voice, "Julie, some really good news. Judy just called. Ordinarily she doesn't follow ratings. 'Ratings are not my show's purpose,' she's often told me. 'But you should know,' she said to me, 'last week our ratings went off the charts.'"

Julie mimics a return hug and takes her customary seat. "Thanks, Alan," she says. "You know I'm not in this for ratings either. A high profile has never been my ambition, nor do I want it part of my persona on or off screen." She laughs. "And for sure I'm not interested in competing with Monday Night Football...if," she grimaces behind her mask, "if there is an NFL season."

Alan steps back to his desk, sits down, joins his hands to support his chin as he leans forward, eyes still intent, and continues, "Judy said her audience loves your weekly no-nonsense, straight-to-the-point, data-supported commentary. Word-of-mouth is spreading about a refreshing new voice on Monday night television. Congratulations. You've earned the recognition. So-o-o, what are you planning to talk about tonight?"

"If it's okay with Judy, I think it's time to present some rational perspectives on our current pandemic situation...how it is now compared to how awful it might have been and also compared to prior pandemics or epidemics. There's still too much media fear-mongering, too many attempts to over-convince Americans about what we already know. For example," Julie frowns and continues, "Congress brought in epidemiology experts to tell Americans that...if we moderate restrictions too early, virus cases and deaths will go back up dramatically. That's like hiring expert swimmers to tell people if they dive off the deep end of a swimming pool before it's filled they're gonna hurt themselves. After the Congressional circus side-show, many in the media couldn't resist redundant use of the if-word. Hell yes...if we open up too soon, it's plain and simple logic there'll be dire consequences.

"And, when is too soon? Doesn't that vary significantly in different locations throughout the country? One size doesn't fit all. And who are we? Who are the openers? Congress? The Federal Executive Branch? Governors? County administrators? Mayors? How about we the people? In any reality scenario, it's the behavior of individual citizens that counts, his and her willingness to accept responsibility for themselves, be considerate of others, and use some judgment about what's appropriate in the circumstances. Not depend entirely on Government to mandate what to do and not to do. Have most citizens become so conditioned to believing that Americans are entitled to and can live in a riskless society and that the Government should, can, and will provide that kind of Utopia...that they've lost their own sense of personal responsibility? I don't think so.

"To promote a 'worst is yet to come' narrative, many in the media still feature the most dramatic negative examples of what's currently happening. A lot of it is statistically irrelevant and inappropriately extrapolated to a larger population. Lots of screen time is wasted on continuing a useless blame game, and..."

He interrupts with a raised hand and an outstretched palm. "Whoa, Julie. No rants. You'll lose your audience."

"Yeah," she laughs, "I know. It's like you're my own personal and private mind ventilator. You drain my peachiness and anger at media colleagues, salve my hurt feelings, calm me down, and refocus me before I go on camera. Thank you, Alan. I really appreciate these pre-appearance briefing sessions. But, you need to know how frustrated I am. Like there's an absolute absence of wisdom in this excess information age, and there's nothing I or any other rational news analyst can do about it. I feel like sprinting to that window behind you, throwing it open, and screaming out, 'I'm mad as hell, and I'm not going to take it anymore.'"

"Julie," Alan laughs, "you're not original. I also watched the Turner Classic Movies rerun of ***Network*** on Saturday night. Great movie. Also timely."

"Ho-o-o-oh kay," she sighs. "You caught me. Yeah, so I just plagiarized Paddy Chayefsky. Seemed a great way to express my feelings." She sighs again. "So-o-o, back to tonight. I've already sent Judy an outline of what I'd like to talk about, and here's a copy for you." She passes a single sheet to Alan. "I'll present it to you just as I plan to do for Judy tonight. Please ask me any questions you think are appropriate and Judy may ask. And...oh hell, you're my boss. I'll even try to answer any questions you have that I think are inappropriate, just like so many polite responders do for talk show hosts whose questions demonstrate the host's shallow thinking, negative bias, or lack of preparation. Whoops, I apologize Alan. I don't mean to imply either you or Judy are that kind of host stereotype. Just fire away as I go on with my usual focus on letting the numbers do the talking."

They both laugh as Julie begins. "For numbers," she says, "there's always a bottom line, and for COVID the final answer seems to be...death, of course. I don't know why so many in the media don't also focus on the numbers of survivors. Being positive is difficult for them, I guess. Their next most important number seems to be cases.

"So...here are the more prominent and published expert death expectations.

"First appearing on the national news scene a couple of months ago, the Center for Disease Control (the CDC) said America should expect 200,000 to 1,700,000 COVID deaths from 160 to 214 million infections. That got everyone's attention."

Alan holds up his hand. "A question please."

Julie laughs. "Already, Alan? Okay, shoot."

"So...the CDC's projection is over what period of time?"

"Congratulations, Alan. You asked the perfect first question. The answer is I don't know. For only 2020? For the duration of the pandemic? The CDC didn't say, or maybe the media just chose not to report the time period in order to maximize the shock effect. And when does the pandemic period end? Again, the CDC didn't say. So, all the CDC has to do is call the pandemic still in place, and the actual numbers may eventually catch up with their estimate."

"So, Julie, let's assume the CDC used a time-period convention similar to that used for our annual flu seasons. Or maybe, in COVID's case just used the calendar year until a seasonal pattern is established. What's your take on the CDC projections?"

"Well, I haven't tried to develop my own forecast, but the CDC infection numbers look high to me even if their forecast period extends beyond a year. Their deaths forecast covers an absurdly wide range of outcomes...200,000 to 1.7 million deaths. Really? Their death numbers are useless. Guess you could say these numbers reflect two extremes, neither likely of occurrence. The high number equals no spread prevention efforts of consequence; let the bug run its course. The low number equals prevention efforts to the max: warp speed on new vaccine development, production, and distribution; high levels of new vaccine efficacy; reasonable willingness of citizens to get vaccinated; and perhaps even an extraordinary shutdown of normal human interactions that, together with monumental Government-funded citizen subsidies, might well jeopardize America's economy and propel us into a recession."

A long "whew" escapes from Alan as he holds up a palmed hand. "Okay, stop already. So much for the CDC hedging their bet by not being period or response specific. Is there anyone out there with a supposedly credible forecast?"

"Well, also about two months ago, a well-crafted, mathematical model from Tomas Pueyo forecasted 480,000 American deaths from 96 million infections in just this year 2020. His study and internet forecast went viral and received tens of millions of hits. Although his infection rate at 30% of the USA population in the virus' inaugural year looked high to me, his death rate at 1/2 of one percent of infections looked low."

"So, any other forecasts of national or international prominence to highlight for Judy?"

"You bet, and this one was a game-changer. Also two months ago, a credible epidemiologist from the Imperial College in Britain predicted 2,200,000 COVID deaths in America in just 2020. It's reported that his predictions influenced the draconian shutdown measures imposed by both countries.

"Wow. Any critiques of this guy's forecast?"

"Not that I've seen. But, again, his death numbers look high to me. That may be my natural skepticism about numbers that don't look rational. Call it not passing the smell test. I've not seen any details of his forecast methodology in any news report. So I can't comment on how he developed his forecast."

"Okay, Julie, you're doing great so far. What you got next?"

"Some current numbers. Let's suspend forecast scenarios and take a look at what's going on right now."

"Go for it."

"Okay. Six days ago the IHME model forecasted 137,000 to 223,000 USA deaths by Aug 4. Through yesterday, and..."

"Hold on, Julie," Alan interrupts. "What's the IHME?"

"I expected the question. You're right on cue. Although the IHME isn't well known generally, it's highly respected. It's the Institute for Health Metrics and Evaluation funded by Bill and Melinda Gates for the University of Washington in Seattle. The folks there are genuine health numbers experts."

"Okay, got it. So they're credible. Go on."

"Anyway, through yesterday, May 17, with about 80 days to go on the IHME forecast, COVID has taken 91,000 American lives. Our daily deaths are now below 1,000, and our daily infections have dropped below 20,000. So, the IHME model expectations sure look reasonable to me. Now, in terms of how we're doing compared to Europe. Team EURO...that's Germany, Italy, France, Spain, UK and Germany...is also recording new lows for daily cases and deaths. Team USA still has a lower per million death rate at only 72 % of Team EURO. But I'm not planning to comment in detail on these numbers...at least not yet.

"First, I want to summarize America's prior epidemics adjusted for population differentials to give an idea of where COVID will have to take us this year to match our past history. This is another area where current media focus improperly compares raw data without acknowledging population differentials. Are those broadcast journalists deceitful? Do they purposely mislead? Or are they naive? Or just plain stupid? I don't have answers to those questions.

"Let's start with our 1918 Flu outbreak, which killed 675,000 Americans. That's the media's favorite benchmark. But it's misleading. To match that lethality, this year's 2020 COVID deaths will have to rise from 91,000 now in May to 2,275,000 by year-end. Innagonna happen.

"Then there's the Asian Flu outbreak in 1957. To match that outbreak, COVID deaths this year will have to rise to 223,400. That could sure happen.

"And to match the AIDs outbreak in the 1980s. Our COVID deaths will have to rise to about a million. That's not likely this year but certainly achievable if we expand the surge period to cover more than a year.

"We should also keep in mind that our annual non-COVID flu infections are still significant, running 35 to 50 million reported cases each year. That's right, 10% or more of Americans get sick enough from conventional flues annually to enter the database. Our widespread vaccination programs have kept death rates from flu at about one tenth of 1% of cases for many years."

Allen chuckles. "Good stuff, Julie. Any more comments to add?"

"Yep, I did some more detailed data gathering after sending the perspective summary to Judy."

"And?"

"Bottom line is that, much to the dismay of many networks, graduated approaches to reopening seem to be working...so far. Country-wide infection surges so many in the media wanted Americans to believe were sure to happen haven't happened...yet. Here's the most important revelation from my data studies this morning. At this stage of reopening, there's not a single state in America that's experienced a significant surge in case growth or new hospitalizations. Is that likely to change? Of course...it's inevitable. New virus variants and new virus surges will emerge. They must...eventually. Particularly in heavily populated states where the virus or a variant hasn't really spread to yet. Like California, Texas, and Florida. What happens in those states will likely dominate the data scene in months to come. My data source sticks to facts and doesn't forecast or speculate."

He leans back from his table and nods his head. "Julie, I love your 'let the numbers do the talking' approach. I believe most of your viewers do too, and I'm sure you're well-prepared to answer any questions Judy may have." He reaches up and scratches his head, "But, there are other new developments I want to ask you about. You've been buried in the numbers and may not have heard. Dominating this morning's hot news topics is speculation that Al Gore and Greta Thunberg may combine and go on tour to advocate full-throttle immediate reopening of economies and relaxing of restrictions both here in America and elsewhere in the World. Journalists are speculating that those two are convinced that a resulting explosion in virus deaths will be the Earth's natural way of punishing mankind for causing excessive Global Warming. Journalists are also speculating that Al and Greta have concluded that population reduction is the only rational and affordable way to reverse Global Warming and enable environmental recovery.

"What's really scary is a much more sinister development than this Save the Earth agenda. Some networks are also circulating a story speculating there's a similar and broader 'bring on more deaths' conspiracy among others, particularly China, who have a different vested interest in reducing Global populations. Are you planning to address either of these two new stories?"

She chuckles, and her eyes squint in disbelief. "Chief, I haven't heard those speculations. First a wrath-of-God viral reduction of population as a just consequence of humanity poisoning our environment? Then something even more sinister? Both those sound really weird, and I wouldn't touch them with a ten-foot pole. Let other networks have an open-field to pursue them and further discredit themselves."

He nods his head in agreement and adds, "On another subject, did you know Dan Panders' Show ratings are down again, and last Friday Danny promised his viewers something special for his show tonight? Wanna watch the rerun?"

"Well, I heard about his 'come on,' Alan, but I still won't watch re-runs of his show. Would make me feel too sorry for him. But, I would like to share a text message I received this morning from Danny. Haven't heard from him in weeks, and then this came in. Here, I have it on my iPhone. It's short and enigmatic. I'll read it to you."

She shuffles to retrieve her phone from her purse and then speaks hesitantly. "'Julie, I want you to know. Yes, I've always wanted a top-rated show. But not at the price of my integrity. I'm not the Sorcerer. Never was. Nor were you the opportunistic Apprentice. Our network owner is the Sorcerer. I've become her broom, and I am broken.'

"A bit of explanation. When I was hired on for the apprentice position at MRABC, I mentioned Goethe's famous poem 'The Sorcerer's Apprentice' to Danny and analogized Danny to the Sorcerer."

"Julie, he sounds depressed."

"To me too."

"Have you responded?"

"No, I don't know what to say."

"Probably just as well. Sure you don't want to watch the replay of his show tonight, catch his 'something special'?"

"Yep, I'm sure. I still can't bring myself to watch his show. It's a refusal that also makes me feel like is there something I could have done or can still do to help Danny? Two questions I just can't answer. Or maybe I'm afraid of answering, afraid of trying to help. Plus, Alan, I can't watch any TV tonight. I'll be buried in revising my COVID spreadsheets to convert cases and deaths data to days from onset rather than calendar days. As I've mentioned before, that's the only way to make meaningful country and state comparisons.

"Then, Dad and I are planning a special day off for both of us tomorrow. He has some vacation time he needs to take. We need some father/daughter catch up time. Outside, not inside.

As it's been for everyone, it's been an intense spring for both of us, and we're feeling recreationally deprived."

"Know what," he laughs. "I'm gonna give the Dan Panders Show a pass this evening too. No TV news for me tonight either. We'll both celebrate the absence of that intrusion. Enjoy tomorrow off with your father. See you Wednesday." He pauses, and a broad smile of determination hides behind his mask. "You've also given me an idea. Actually, it's been brewing for a while. How about you and I have a special outing next Tuesday? No masks. I know it's your day off, but there are some things I'd like to talk to you about. They're both professional and personal. I'll bring a picnic lunch for both of us, and if our balmy spring weather accommodates, we'll go up to a special place off Highway 285 on Kenosha Pass. There we'll junction with the Colorado Trail, which bounces back and forth along or in proximity to the Continental Divide. With nothing but natural surroundings on both sides, you can head north and hike all the way to Wyoming or do a much longer stretch south all the way to New Mexico."

"Now you've aroused my curiosity. Sure Alan. I'd be delighted. Promise you're not asking me to elope with you all the way to another state...on foot?"

He laughs, "No...not yet."

CHAPTER 26
THE SHOW IS OVER
7:00 AM, TUESDAY
MORNING MAY 26, 2020

To the lonely Corner broom! Hear your doom.
from *The Sorcerer's Apprentice*

"ALAN...I'M SO SORRY to call you this early...but...but, have you watched the morning news?"

"Hell no Julie. I don't watch television news before breakfast. Bad for the digestion. What's happened?"

Julie breaks down sobbing, "He...he...he..."

"Why Julie, you're crying. What's wrong?"

"It's...it's on all the morning news channels. He...he actually did it. On his own show."

"What are you watching now?"

"Th...th...the morning news on MRABC."

"So, who did what?"

"It's Danny Panders. He's dead. Went out Hemingway style. Gun to the mouth. Blew his brains out. Last night. Did it on his own show. And...and..."

"Go on."

"His show's ratings from last night...they're down again. The network owner and her husband will be disappointed. They'd have been so sure his show ratings would finally go back up."

EPILOGUE

ON THEIR FAVORITE HIKE up to and then along the extended ridge to Mt. Sanitas, Jules senses his daughter's state of mind. To burn off the shock of another untimely death...this one in her professional life...she needs both physical exertion and an absence of conversation. They move fast, soon gain the summit, and then finally stop to rest. Both are breathing heavily. He extends a comforting arm and hand around her shoulders and squeezes. "Hey kid, I hope you know this about yourself. You're a genuine American patriot, and I'm proud of you. Also, I'm so sorry about Danny. I know you suppressed your feelings at breakfast. Are you ready to talk about his death? Do you need to?"

"Yes and yes. Finally. And briefly. I have big-time regrets about Danny's death. Also some guilt feelings. After the shock of Danny's suicide wore off, I've been obsessing about what I said to him when I decided to quit MRABC. He was despondent, and I encouraged him to stay with the network and try to make a difference with balanced programming. I realize now that for him it also continued a huge conflict with his Network Brass. A division he couldn't do anything about. The depressive side of his bipolar disorder must have taken over. It's likely he eventually felt helpless, like a voice in the wilderness. But, I'm really over that chapter in my life. I'll be okay, Dad."

"And this new chapter in your life, now that you have a speaking role?"

"I do need to update you about that. But first let's just sit for a few minutes and enjoy the view. Right now we have the summit to ourselves, and that won't last long. This hike's become too popular."

They're soon seated on a flat rock beside a huge boulder that extends six feet above them. An inscribed bronze plaque commemorates trail builders who enabled easier access to the summit. The trail accommodates runners who seek challenge and hikers from nine to ninety who merely seek...what? Perhaps each is on a different search. There's a broad smile on Jules' face as he leans against his daughter. "Do you know the meaning of the word 'Sanitas'?"

Julie's expression turns dreamy. "No, do I need to know? Now?"

"Yes, it's appropriate."

"So."

Jules exhales a big "Whooow" and nods his head. "Hokay. It's derived from the Latin root word 'sanus,' which means healthy, sound, and sane. Can you think of anything the World needs more of right now?"

"No. Can you Dad?

"Nope, unless it's just love...sweet love. It's what we used to have so plenty of."

ABOUT ATMOSPHERE PRESS

Founded in 2015, Atmosphere Press was built on the principles of Honesty, Transparency, Professionalism, Kindness, and Making Your Book Awesome. As an ethical and author-friendly hybrid press, we stay true to that founding mission today.

If you're a reader, enter our giveaway for a free book here:

SCAN TO ENTER
BOOK GIVEAWAY

If you're a writer, submit your manuscript for consideration here:

SCAN TO SUBMIT
MANUSCRIPT

And always feel free to visit Atmosphere Press and our authors online at atmospherepress.com. See you there soon!

ABOUT THE AUTHOR

All Denver Post bestsellers and recipient of literary accolades, **Graydon Dee Hubbard**'s previous works include *Slim to None*, a poignant narrative from his daughter's perspective chronicling her battle with anorexia; *Charlie's Pride*, an ode to a modern-day *Last Mohican* with deep ties to his Native American heritage and unwavering devotion to a river; and *At the Altars of Money*, a #1 Amazon bestseller that ventures into the intricate world of high finance with a contemporary *Robin Hood.*

Hubbard's life has been dedicated to public service, spanning two years in the military, 32 years as a CPA, eventually managing the largest audit practice in the mountain west, and 20 years serving as Director and Board Designated Financial Expert for two public companies. Additionally, he has held roles as Director or Trustee for twelve educational and civic organizations.

Embracing the allure of high mountains at age 65, Hubbard has conquered 29 of Colorado's 14ers and explored 25 of Scotland's

Munros. On his more grounded days, he enjoys flyfishing with his loyal companion, Cholla, a golden retriever.

Adding to his impressive journey, Hubbard has also been to a podium deep in the heart and soul of Wall Street to help ring the bell that opens the New York Stock Exchange.

Milton Keynes UK
Ingram Content Group UK Ltd.
UKHW010824090624
443692UK00026B/216/J

9 798891 322455